Glynis whirled around, her eyes wide.

A man was slouched against the doorjamb, a Stetson pushed back on his head. It was as though he had appeared out of nowhere.

But Cort McBride was no mirage. His tall, rangy frame filled the doorway and seemed to shrink the room to dollhouse proportions.

He'd changed very little. Light brown hair swirled with gray shadowed a face of strong, masculine lines, with a firm jaw and a mouth that might have seemed sullen if not for the fascinating fullness of the bottom lip.

But it wasn't his mouth that held her rapt attention; it was the way his worn jeans rode low on his flat belly, molding his lean thighs to perfection.

Glynis shivered, forcing her eyes away.

"Well, well," Cort drawled, his blue eyes cold and unyielding. "Will wonders never cease? I heard you were back, but I didn't believe it."

* * *

Special end-of-the-book bonus—
"Made To Measure"
by Joan Elliott Pickart!

MARY LYNN BAXTER

wish giver

BONUS: An original story by JOAN ELLIOTT PICKART

Published by Silhouette Books
America's Publisher of Contemporary Romance

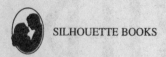

SILHOUETTE BOOKS

Copyright in the collection:
© 2003 by Harlequin Books S.A.

ISBN 0-373-83552-3

The publisher acknowledges the copyright holders
of the individual works as follows:

WISH GIVER
Copyright © 1989 by Mary Lynn Baxter

MADE TO MEASURE
Copyright © 2001 by Harlequin Books S.A.

This edition published by arrangement with Harlequin Books S.A.

® and TM are trademarks of Harlequin Books S.A., used under
license. Trademarks indicated with ® are registered in the United States
Patent and Trademark Office, the Canadian Trade Marks Office and in
other countries.

Visit Silhouette at www.eHarlequin.com

Printed in U.S.A.

CONTENTS

WISH GIVER

Mary Lynn Baxter

* * *

To Freddie Ingersoll—
what can I say, dear friend,
except thanks for everything?

Chapter 1

She would rather be anywhere other than where she was, but then Glynis Hamilton had learned long ago that choices in one's life were luxuries, not God-given rights. That bit of knowledge had reared its ugly head two years before when her son had been diagnosed as having leukemia.

Even now, just thinking about that day brought chills to her skin and made her shiver with the same feeling of rage and fear that she'd experienced then.

"Glynis."

At the soft-spoken use of her name, she blinked and focused her eyes on the tall, gray-haired man with eyes the color of the sky on a clear day. Dr. Eric Johns had a bedside manner to match his voice: gentle. And though he was just one of the many white-coated specialists who had paraded through her and Todd's life of late, he was the one she thought of as

"Todd's doctor," the one who had been instrumental in holding her together through these trying times.

He was watching her intently, with concern etched in his features. "You seem a million miles away, my dear."

Glynis forced a smile. "Sometimes I wish I could pretend this was all a bad dream, and just run away."

They were sitting behind closed doors in Dr. Johns's office at the Texas Children's Hospital in Houston on a lovely spring morning. Glynis had left Todd at the day-care center and driven across town for the appointment. Dr. Johns's receptionist had called and left word that he wanted to talk to her.

Shaking his head, the doctor stood up from behind his massive desk and crossed to the window. He still didn't respond to Glynis's comment for a moment, seemingly content to watch and listen to the traffic below on Fannin Street. Even though his office was on an upper floor, the sounds of the afternoon traffic did not escape them.

After a moment he turned and faced Glynis. "You know you wouldn't run away, but I can understand why you would be driven to say it. Under the circumstances, you've handled Todd's illness with a remarkable strength." His voice was filled with admiration.

Glynis looked skeptical. "I appreciate your saying that, Doctor, but we both know it's not true. I fell apart at the seams."

He smiled in spite of the seriousness of the situation. "But you glued yourself back together, and that's what counts. So many don't." A frown replaced the smile. "The most dreaded or feared word in our society today is cancer."

Glynis leaned back in the cushioned chair and at the same time pushed an unruly strand of strawberry-blond hair behind her ear. "If only it had been me," she whispered, more for her own ears than for his.

"That's a natural reaction, too, my dear, but unfortunately we're not calling the shots. Someone higher up is doing that."

A silence fell over the room, and Glynis took the opportunity to draw a deep breath, to try to get hold of her frayed nerves. She had known what the doctor had wanted to discuss when he'd called, and she'd dreaded this visit. Todd had just recently undergone an updated battery of tests and she had prayed that his leukemia was still in remission.

"Anyway," Dr. Johns was saying, "I didn't call you here to give you bad news, or to let you wallow in self-pity."

"Oh." Glynis felt her pulse leap.

"Quite the opposite, in fact."

Glynis scooted to the edge of her chair and peered up at him. "Then...Todd's still in remission." It wasn't a question, and her voice had a croaking sound to it.

The doctor smiled, a genuine smile this time. "That he is, and—"

"Oh, thank God," Glynis cried, cutting him off in midsentence, her eyes raised toward the ceiling.

"You didn't let me finish," Dr. Johns chided, though with long-standing patience.

"There's more?" Glynis spread her hands. "I don't understand. What could possibly be more exhilarating than to learn that my six-year-old son is cured, that—''

This time it was the doctor who interrupted. ''Not cured, Glynis, in remission. Remember, there's a difference.'' He paused and sat back down at his desk and, after leaning forward on both arms, peered at Glynis, a mixture of emotions playing across his face. ''However, what we're about to discuss could lead to that cure.''

Glynis was only capable of staring at him wide-eyed. Her heart was in her throat. She had prayed that one day she would hear these words, but she had about given up hope. And though she was hearing them now, she couldn't help but wonder if it would turn out to be another false alarm, another in a long line of many.

It had been shortly after her husband, Jay, was killed in a head-on car collision that she had begun to notice that something was wrong with Todd. Her worst fears were realized when the pediatrician, along with a specialist, had diagnosed leukemia. Since then her life had been like a yo-yo, up with hope one day, only to bottom out in despair the next. Dare she hope? Dare she truly hope?

''Please,'' Glynis whispered at last, wetting her lips, ''tell me. Don't keep me in suspense any longer.''

Eric Johns peered at the charts in front of him before transferring his gaze to Glynis. ''After studying Todd's test at length, we feel he's a prime candidate for a bone marrow transplant.'' He held up his hands when Glynis would have interrupted. ''Hear me out, then you can ask all the questions you like.''

Unable to sit still a moment longer, Glynis got up and walked to the window and stood in the same spot that Dr. Johns had recently occupied. She stared outside also, but scarcely noticed the richness of the sun's glare as it bounced off the tall medical buildings across the street.

The doctor's calm voice drew her back around. "If the bone marrow is a success, and we have every reason to believe it will be, Todd should live a normal, healthy life."

A light flashed in Glynis's golden brown eyes, and tears glistened on her long lashes, making her appear suddenly younger than her twenty-seven years and much more vulnerable. "Oh, Dr. Johns, I don't know what to say...or do...." Her voice broke as she rushed toward him. "How to thank you..."

He cleared his throat. "Don't thank me yet, Glynis. While we're extremely fortunate that Todd qualifies for a transplant, there is a problem." For the first time, he seemed to be less than confident.

Fear gripped Glynis. "And what might that be?"

The doctor sighed. "The down side is that you're not a suitable donor. Your HLA, which are you blood antigens, do not match your son's."

"Oh, God," Glynis responded, feeling as if she'd just been kicked in the stomach. With trembling fingers she delved deep into her purse for a Kleenex, then on unsteady legs made her way back to the chair and sat down.

A furrow appeared between the doctor's blue eyes. "Hey, don't fall to pieces on me, especially now that we can see the light at the end of that long, dark tunnel."

Tears clung to Glynis's eyelashes. "I fail to see how you can be so optimistic when…when you just said I wasn't a suitable donor. And I know how hard other donors are to find." Her tone turned bitter as her sense of jubilation turned into utter hopelessness. "It seems like it's every day that the president or some senator is interceding for a family, asking for help in obtaining a suitable donor for a transplant." She knew she was rambling, but she couldn't help it. It just wasn't fair to come so close, only to be turned away.

"True, but it's not impossible. Donors are located all the time, and we'll find the right one for Todd."

"If only he had a brother or sister or…"

"Or father," Dr. Johns added quietly.

Glynis went white. "What…what did you say?"

Eric Johns looked at her oddly. "I said it would be a godsend if Todd's father were still alive." He paused, then went on, still looking at Glynis. "But since he isn't, and since you're not compatible, and since there is no brother or sister, we'll just have to go with what we've got and do the best we can. But I don't want you to worry," he stressed. "Todd will be taken care of."

"Dr. Johns, I…" Again Glynis's voice faded.

"Glynis, for God's sake, what's the matter?" Dr. Johns's voice was rough with concern. "You look like you've just seen a ghost."

Glynis circled her dry lips with her tongue. "Maybe…maybe I have."

The doctor frowned. "You're not making sense."

For another moment Glynis stared straight ahead.

She felt as if she were drowning, drowning in the painful memories of her own past.

Pushing himself upright with his arms, Eric Johns came around the desk and stopped in front of Glynis. Leaning down, he took both of her hands in his. They were cold.

"Glynis," he said, "what's wrong? What did I say that upset you?"

Gently withdrawing her hands, Glynis stood and eased past him. It was only after she reached the center of the room that she turned around, digging her heels deep into the plush carpet for support. The dazed look remained on her face, robbing it of its natural color.

"Glynis." Again that gentle tone.

Suddenly Glynis blinked. "I'm...I'm sorry, Dr. Johns," she said at last, her composure once again intact. "I'm not in the habit of freaking out this way."

"Of course you're not. But still you haven't confided in me."

Glynis took a deep breath. "Todd's father is not dead."

Dr. Johns looked stunned, then confused. "Not dead. But I don't understand. I thought..."

"Jay, my husband, is...wasn't Todd's father."

His eyebrows raised, the doctor exhaled loudly. "Oh, I see."

"No, I doubt you do," Glynis countered softly, twisting her hands together. "It's a long and ugly story, one that I'd just as soon forget."

"While I understand and while I certainly respect

your right to privacy, I have to know if Todd's father is alive.''

''Yes,'' Glynis said dully, twisting her head back around.

The doctor was silent for a moment, as if he were deciding how best to phrase what had to be said. ''You know what you've just told me sheds a whole new light on the situation.''

Glynis nodded.

''Is...is Todd's father available?''

''I'm...not sure. He...he works out of the country a lot, and I have no idea where he is. There's been no contact between us since...since before Todd was born.''

Dr. Johns leaned heavily against his desk and folded his arms across his chest, his forehead wrinkled in concentration. ''I know how difficult this must be for you, Glynis, but I have to have some answers. If Todd's father's antigens match, he could be the donor.''

''I know.''

''So would you be willing to get in touch with him, explain the situation and ask for his help?''

Glynis swallowed against the hot bile that surged up the back of her throat. However, when she spoke, her tone was firm. ''That goes without saying.''

He was solemnly reading her face. ''Even if it's painful for you?''

''I'd do anything short of murder to save my son's life, Doctor.''

He let out another deep sigh. ''Then I'll expect to hear from you soon.''

When Glynis reached the door, she stopped and

turned around. "As soon as I know something, I'll call."

"I don't need to remind you to keep your chin up, do I?"

Though weak, Glynis's smile transformed her face. "Thanks. I'll be in touch." Then, with unsteady hands, she opened the door and let herself out.

Instead of going to the day-care center and picking up Todd, Glynis went instead to her apartment. Her intention was to call her longtime friend in Lufkin, and she wanted to be alone when she did so.

She strode into the living room, tossed her purse on the couch, then switched on the lamp beside the telephone table. But when she sat down in the chair beside it and reached for the receiver, her hand froze. With a groan, she fell back against the cushion and closed her eyes, feeling once again as if her heart would stop beating.

She'd known the minute Dr. Johns had mentioned Todd's father what she would have to do, no matter how much pain it would cause her personally. Her son came first; he always had and he always would. He was the only decent thing that had come out of her life.

But knowing she had no choice did nothing to abate the pain associated with it.

Without wasting another minute, Glynis forced herself upright in the chair and punched out the long-distance number. On the third ring Milly Tatum's high-pitched voice came on the line.

"Milly."

"Well, it's about time I heard from you, Glynis

Hamilton! You were about to get on my bad list, and you know what that means.''

In spite of herself, Glynis laughed. ''Milly, Milly, you wouldn't do that.''

''Maybe not, but still you shouldn't go so long without calling me.''

''In addition to Todd, it's been a tough year in the classroom.''

Milly chuckled. ''Your thirty-two fifth graders never settled down, huh?''

''Oh, they settled down, all right, but still—the sheer number of bodies in the room is enough to drive you crazy. You can imagine what it was like trying to teach them something.''

Laughter sounded through the line. ''Better you than me. I love owning a day-care center and playing with them, but if I had to teach those buggers how to read and write, our country would be in deep trouble.''

''I sometimes wonder if I'm cut out for the job myself.''

''Ha, you were a born teacher, if I ever saw one.''

''Look, Milly,'' Glynis said following a moment of silence, ''as much as I'd love to chat, that's not why I called.''

''I guessed as much. So what's the matter? You sound like you're down. It's not Todd, is it?''

It was uncanny, Glynis thought, how Milly was able to detect her mood without her having to say a word. ''No, at least not directly.''

''What does that mean?''

''I need a favor.''

''Name it.''

"I need to get in touch with Cort."

Milly was silent a moment, then said, "Cort McBride?"

"Milly…"

"All right, honey, I'm sorry. But why on earth would you of all people want to get in touch with *him?*"

Glynis sighed. "Don't ask, Milly. Not right now. It's a long story, and I'll explain when I see you. Do you know where he is?"

"As a matter of fact, I do. He's here, at his ranch."

Glynis felt her mouth fall open. "He is."

Milly laughed. "Yes, he is."

"But why, I mean…"

"Are you ready for this?"

"Milly." Again Glynis's exasperation showed.

"He's recovering from a gunshot wound."

Glynis's lips tightened, though not before a harsh sigh had escaped.

"My sentiments exactly," Milly said sarcastically.

"Well, I can't say I'm surprised, though that doesn't change a thing." When Milly didn't answer, Glynis went on, changing the subject. "Since I don't know how long I'll be staying in town, would you please have the utilities turned on in Dorothy's house. Todd and I will bunk there."

"But…but…" Milly spluttered.

"Just do it, Milly, please. And I won't forget I owe you one."

Once the receiver was back in place, Glynis sank again into the cushions, fear and uncertainty numbing her. She could say it had started building inside her when Todd was diagnosed. But she knew better. It had started with her marriage to Jay. The marriage that had turned into a living hell.

Besides the fact that Jay couldn't hold a job, he had resented Todd, mostly because the boy wasn't his child. As a result he'd found solace in the bottle. If it hadn't been for Glynis's salary, they wouldn't have made it.

But now Jay was gone and so were her funds. Even though she had hospitalization through the school, it paid only eighty percent, which left twenty percent for her to pay. And twenty percent was a staggering amount in light of Todd's expensive medicines and treatments. The small insurance policy she had kept on Jay's life had been spent long ago.

So, as she'd told Dr. Johns, circumstances left her no choice. She felt tears saturate her cheeks as she looked up toward the ceiling. She had to see Cort.

Yet, how was she going to approach a man she hadn't seen in years and tell him that the child he thought was his best friend's was actually his?

Chapter 2

"Mom, are we really going to move to Lufkin and live in Aunt Dorothy's house?"

Glynis stopped what she was doing and faced her son. Suddenly an indulgent smile broke out across her face, softening her intense features. "I'm seriously thinking about it," she said, peering closely at Todd, thinking again how beautiful he was—"too beautiful to be a boy" was the standard comment from those who came in contact with him.

And he was. He was blessed with the best of both his mother and father. He had Glynis's fair coloring and light hair and Cort's bone structure and cornflower-blue eyes.

In spite of the fact that he was not taking chemotherapy and hadn't for the past two months, Glynis thought he was still too pale, too angelic-looking for his own good. And it was only a few more weeks before he would more than likely start another round of the strong toxicant in order to ready him for the transplant.

Every time she looked at him, her heart skipped a beat. If something happened to him, she knew she wouldn't want to live.

Yet, when he was feeling good, he behaved like any typical, rambunctious six-year-old, chattering nonstop about anything and everything.

"I don't know if I wanna move, Mom."

Glynis sighed. "I'm not sure I do either, son. But the house does belong to us, and we can live in Lufkin more cheaply than we can live here in Houston." She hadn't discussed the idea of moving with Todd, purposely saving it until now for fear of his reaction. He had gone through so many changes and upheavals in his young life that even a small one seemed big to him.

"Well, nothing's set in concrete," Glynis added with what she hoped was a reassuring smile. "Why don't we see how we like it and go from there? And you know how you like to play with Milly's two boys. They're anxiously waiting for you to come."

Todd's eyes lit up. "Can I go see them the minute we get there? Can I Mom?"

"We'll see. But for now, you go get your other pair of tennis shoes and put them in the car, while I check the apartment one last time."

Todd twisted his head to one side and frowned. "Do I have to?"

"Yes, you have to," she mimicked him in the same whiny tone, and then lightly smacked his bottom. "Off with you. We're running late as it is."

The moment she was alone, Glynis took a deep breath and scanned the room. She was leaving things neat and orderly. The apartment, as far as apartments went, had a homey atmosphere. And for the most part she and Todd had been satisfied here.

But for some time now, she had been toying with the idea of returning to Lufkin, getting out of the city with its pollution and traffic problems, not only for Todd's sake but for hers as well. However, unhappy memories haunted both places. Here there was guilt associated with the tragic death of her husband. And back home... Back home there were memories that she couldn't even face.

She felt sure she could get a teaching job without any problem. The main drawback was the two hours it would take to drive Todd to and from the medical center. But she wouldn't worry about that at the moment. Aunt Dorothy's house was hers, and even though it was not in the best condition, it was livable. For now that was a blessing in disguise.

"Mom, I'm ready," Todd said, sailing into the room, grinning his endearing toothless grin.

"All right. Get in the car. As soon as I lock up, we'll be off."

As she went to follow Todd out the door, she stopped to grab the sack of fruit on the bar. In doing so, she caught a glimpse of herself in the mirror above the couch. She stared at her reflection, looking for outward signs of her inner turmoil. There were none. Her finely drawn features and creamy, ivory skin were as flawless as ever. On closer observation, however, she noticed her eyes, usually as clear as glass, appeared slightly glazed.

"Mom!"

Shaking her head and smiling, Glynis called, "I'm coming, son."

The drive down Highway 59 toward Lufkin was pleasant, especially during the springtime. Glynis, however, because of the nonstop chatter of her son, barely had a chance to notice the patches of bluebonnets scattered on both sides of the highway or the tall pines and oaks that seemed to reach up to the sky. But that was fine by her, as it kept her from thinking about the awesome task ahead of her. The thought of facing Cort caused her stomach to turn inside out.

What if he refused to help? she asked herself. What if...what if...

"Don't, Glynis!" she spat aloud, then cast a swift glance in Todd's direction. But her fierce reprimand to herself failed to disturb her son. The thick, curly lashes that reminded her so much of his father's remained closed.

It wasn't until she reached the city limits and subsequently pulled up in front of Milly's day-care center, suitably named "House of Tots," that she loosened her death grip on the steering wheel.

After nudging Todd awake and getting out of the car, Glynis shoved her sunglasses closer to the bridge of her nose and peered down at her watch. Three o'clock. They had made good time after all.

The air smelled so clean and fresh, as though it had recently rained. She took a whiff, inhaling it deep into her lungs before turning and following her son up the walk.

Just as they reached the first step, the front door

flew open and a short, slightly overweight woman hurried across the threshold. "Hey, you two, you're a sight for sore eyes."

Even though Milly Tatum had a dark complexion and dark hair, she reminded Glynis of a ray of sunshine bursting through a dark cloud, especially when she smiled. And she was smiling now; her pixy features were alive and her green eyes were sparkling.

Glynis hadn't seen Milly since the day after Glynis had buried her husband, a little more than two years ago. And though they had kept in contact by phone, it wasn't the same as seeing her friend.

Now, as if starving for the sight of her, Glynis took a closer look at Milly. She hadn't changed, Glynis thought, except maybe for her weight. The fact that she'd had twins was beginning to tell on her, but it wasn't enough to detract from her natural beauty.

"Oh, Milly, I've missed you so much," Glynis said after a minute, giving her friend a fierce hug.

"Me, too," Milly responded before stepping away from Glynis and turning to Todd. She reached out and mussed his light-colored hair. "And how's my boy?"

"Okay," Todd mumbled. Then, looking around, he asked, "Where are Adam and Kyle?"

Milly mussed his hair again and grinned. "Out back, waiting for you."

"Can I go see 'em, Mom?" Todd asked anxiously, looking up at Glynis.

Glynis smiled. "Of course, silly, go on. But be careful," she called to his retreating back, her eyes filled with guarded anxiety.

Milly flashed her an understanding look. "It's hard to let him out of your sight, isn't it?"

"Sure is," Glynis admitted honestly. "He's...he's been through so much, been so sick...." Her voice faded, but she knew she didn't have to explain further. Millie understood; she had two boys of her own.

Without another word, Glynis and Milly locked arms and walked inside, where Glynis admired the large room with brightly decorated walls, a table and chairs, and shelves filled with toys and books. Her gaze then traveled to a large window, and through it she could see a yard saturated with children of all ages and sizes.

When Glynis turned her attention back to the room, Milly was talking to a round-faced woman who was sitting at one of the tables reading to a little girl.

Introductions were made, and then Glynis commented, "I always get such a warm feeling when I walk in here, Milly. You've done wonders with this old house. The years seem to make no difference. It's fixed up just precious."

Milly grimaced. "Believe me, it takes every ounce of energy I have to keep it this way. But I'm proud of it and what I've accomplished."

"Well, you should be," Glynis said, following Milly into a small but efficient kitchen and sitting down in one of the padded chairs circling an oak table.

Milly crossed to the cabinet, where a Mr. Coffee set steamed and sputtered, and pulled out two cups. "You still take your coffee black?"

Glynis nodded and waited silently while Milly filled the cups.

"So what's going on?" Milly asked the moment she sat in the chair across from Glynis. "Why the sudden need after all these years to see Cort?'' Her eyes were serious, as was her tone of voice.

Glynis expelled a breath and, pointedly ignoring the question, announced, ''Todd's a candidate for a bone marrow transplant.''

''That's great news, honey.'' Milly reached across, grabbed Glynis's hand and squeezed it. ''That poor child has suffered enough, and so have you.''

''I know,'' Glynis said. ''I'm excited and scared to death at the same time. It's going to be a long, drawn-out process. But if it works, and the doctors have every reason to believe it will, then he'll be cured.'' Her eyes brimmed with hope. ''Just think, no more painful needles stuck in his tender veins and no more toxic medicines poisoning his body.''

''Praise the Lord,'' Milly whispered, her smile overshadowing the tears that had sprung in her eyes. Then the smile suddenly disappeared, and a puzzled frown took its place. ''But what does that have to do with you coming back here and wanting to talk to Cort, of all people?''

Glynis diverted her eyes for a moment, realizing that Milly was not going to let her get by with being evasive.

''Glynis, I'm your friend, remember.''

''I know, and you don't know how much it means to me to have your support, but...'' Glynis broke off and shifted in her chair, still unable to meet Milly's direct gaze.

''But you're not ready to confide in me, right?'' Milly pointed out softly.

Glynis paled. ''It's not that. It's...''

''Never mind,'' Milly said, pausing to take a sip of

her coffee. "I'm just a nosy old busybody anyway. When you get ready to talk, I'm ready to listen." She smiled. "It's just that simple, okay."

"Oh, Milly," Glynis cried, "I don't know what I did to deserve a friend like you."

"Let's not get maudlin, okay?" Then clearing her throat, Milly added, "Why don't you and Todd stay with Buck and me, until you decide what you want to do, that is? You know we have plenty of room at the house."

"You didn't forget to have the utilities turned on in Aunt Dorothy's house, did you?" Glynis sounded distressed.

"No, of course I didn't, but that darn place is so rundown. I hate to think of you and Todd staying there even for one night."

Glynis sipped her coffee, then said, "It's a mess, all right, but I still think it's livable. Anyway, I wouldn't think of imposing on you, not with your hectic schedule. And since it looks like I'm going to be here awhile, I may as well get settled."

"But you're not at all happy about seeing Cort, are you? You're smiling with your lips, but your eyes are telling a different story." Then, before Glynis could respond, Milly held up her hands in mock surrender. "Here I go again, interfering, asking questions that you're not ready to answer."

This time it was Glynis who reached out and squeezed Milly's hand. "Thanks again for everything. But right now I need to get Todd and let you get this place closed up so you can go home." She drained the cup and stood.

It was after they were outside again that Milly

asked, "Why don't you let Todd stay here for a while? I have a mother coming late, so I can't leave. I know you have things to do."

Glynis sighed. "That I do." Without it being said, they both knew that as soon as she stopped by the home place and unloaded, she was going to Cort's ranch. "Sure you don't mind? I mean…"

"Just go. And don't worry, Todd'll be fine."

The moment Glynis pulled up in front of the dilapidated farmhouse nestled among huge oak and pine trees, she felt her heart plummet to her toes. Milly was right; it was in sorry condition. The wooden frame structure had obviously settled, causing it to sag toward the middle. Besides that, the paint seemed to have fallen off in chunks.

But on the bright side there appeared to be no broken windows, at least in the front. And it was blessedly beautiful and peaceful here, she told herself, especially after the grinding hubbub of the city.

Yes, it definitely had possibilities. It could be made into a showplace, if one had the money. And the desire. But at the moment, she had only the latter.

With renewed determination, Glynis opened the car door and got out. Once inside the house, she flipped on the light to her right and paused on the threshold. Her breath caught in her throat. Everything was exactly as she'd left it, furniture and all, just as if her aunt still lived here. However, the carpet was tattered, the linoleum was worn and the wallpaper hung in shreds.

Feeling the tears well up in her eyes, Glynis walked through the rooms, memories both good and bad drifting through her mind. As if in a daze she walked to the kitchen and opened the back door, letting in the fresh, warm air and feeling it caress her skin.

It was while she was standing there watching two squirrels chase each other around a tree that she suddenly found herself remembering the day her aunt brought her to this house for the first time. She had been nine years old, and a doll had been waiting for her in a chair in the living room. She had grabbed it and hugged it close to her lonely little heart and cried until her aunt had pulled her into her arms and held her.

Her mother had deserted her when she was only a year old, and until she turned nine, she had been shuffled from one foster home to another.

Dorothy Bickman, her mother's widowed sister, had learned of her existence and had gone to court to get guardianship of her. She had treated Glynis like the daughter she never had up until her death when Glynis was in college.

And even though they didn't have much in the way of material benefits, the shabby house was filled with love and kindness.

But her mother's rejection had left scars. As a result, the longing for roots and a family to love and cherish was the force that drove her. And she'd thought she'd found those roots in Cort McBride, the only man she'd ever loved.

She'd been wrong, and now, years later, having to approach him and ask for his help was a challenge she hadn't bargained on, and it was proving to be one of the most difficult things she'd ever had to do.

She wasn't sure when the warm breeze turned

chilly. Nor was she certain when she experienced the crazy feeling that she was no longer alone. But she felt it, nonetheless, like a cool breath upon the back of her neck.

Suddenly, she whirled around, her eyes wide.

A man was slouched against the doorjamb, a Stetson pushed back on his head.

''Oh, God,'' were the only words she was able to get through her paralyzed throat.

Chapter 3

It was as though he had appeared out of nowhere, but Cort McBride was no mirage. He was excruciatingly real. His tall, rangy frame filled the doorway to capacity and seemed to shrink the room to doll-like proportions.

For an instant they both stopped dead, standing like tongue-tied statues as they stared at each other.

Six years. Had it really been six long years since this man had walked out of her life, since they had shared the most intimate of secrets? It didn't seem possible, Glynis thought, her eyes greedily taking in his every feature.

He'd changed very little. An overabundance of light brown hair swirled with gray overshadowed a face composed of strong, masculine lines, with a strong jaw and a mouth that might seem sullen if it weren't for the fascinating fullness of his bottom lip.

He'd always had the long, smooth muscles of an accomplished athlete and unfortunately an ego to match. His skin had the same leathery look as before, as if he spent all his time outside in the sun.

Yet on closer observation, he *was* different, and the difference was in his blue eyes. Where once they had been penetrating and alive, they were now cold and unyielding, the lines around them etched more clearly than she remembered. His mouth, too, was different. It was drawn tight as if controlled by physical pain.

However, it wasn't his mouth that held her rapt attention; it was the way his worn jeans rode low on his slender belly, molding his lean thighs to perfection, thighs that she had touched and kissed in moments of wild passion.... Glynis shivered, forcing her eyes away.

Her unexpected movement blessedly proved to be the key that unlocked the ominous silence.

"Well, well," Cort drawled, "wonders never cease. Heard you were back, but didn't believe it."

"I'd forgotten how fast news travels in this town." Glynis's voice sounded foreign even to her own ears.

A smirk touched lips that appeared to have forgotten how to smile. "I guess you figured you could just sneak in and right out again without anyone being the wiser." It wasn't a question, and his tone was clearly meant to be insulting.

Determined to control the situation, Glynis began uneasily, "Look, Cort, couldn't...couldn't we simply start over and say...hello?"

Not only was she trembling, but she was stammering as well. It was uncanny what just being in the same room with him could do to her mind and body, not to mention her equilibrium.

"You're unbelievable, you know that?" Cort laughed, but it wasn't pleasant-sounding. "The way I see it, you and I don't have anything to say to each other, not even so much as a hello."

"Cort...please." She spread her hands. "You're being unreasonable."

He laughed again. "Unreasonable, huh? Well, I'll tell you what's unreasonable and that's to think I'd give you the damned time of day in the first place." He lurched away from the door and strode toward her, stopping just short of touching her. "I'll have to hand it to you. Yeah, you were always a pro at turning men's heads, mine included. And poor Jay—well, he had about as much chance as a snowball in hell. The minute I turned my back, you suckered that poor slob into marrying you...."

Hot, boiling fury drove Glynis into raising her hand as if to strike him. "How dare you!"

"I wouldn't if I were you." It wasn't so much what Cort said but the way he said it that made Glynis lower her hand and step back, turning away.

"That's better," Cort said softly, but with no less power.

Facing forward again, Glynis found it difficult to speak. By letting him goad her into saying things that were better left unsaid, she was jeopardizing her mission. But then Cort had always affected her that way. Finally, she said wearily, "I didn't come back to..."

"What? To see me. Was that what you were going to say?"

''No,'' Glynis said carefully and with extreme patience. ''That wasn't what I was going to say.''

''Just out of curiosity, why the hell *did* you come back?''

In spite of her efforts to curb her tongue, to keep her cool, Glynis felt herself bristle. And before she knew it, she was saying, ''If you'll recall, this also happens to be my home.'' The sarcasm was free-flowing. ''I have as much right to be here as you do.''

Her comeback silenced him for a moment, and they glared at each other, the pain of the past pulling on them like quicksand, threatening to suck them both under.

Again it was Cort who broke the silence. ''But you're just passing through, checking on the old home place, right?''

She swallowed hard. ''No and yes.''

''What the hell kind of answer is that?''

She pulled her slender frame straight. ''Actually, I'm here for a purpose, Cort.''

''Life's full of little surprises, wouldn't you say?''

Ignoring his mocking sarcasm, she said, ''I...I came to see you.''

''Why?'' His tone was without mercy now—flat and icy.

She breathed deeply to keep from panicking, then averted her gaze. The moment had finally come, and still she hesitated. But again she asked herself, *How does one go about breaking the news to a man that he has a six-year-old son?* There was simply no easy way.

She closed her eyes and tried to concentrate. Instead she suddenly found herself remembering what it had been like in high school when Cort McBride and his best friend, Jay Hamilton, had taken her under their wing.

Although Cort was six years older than Glynis and two years older than Jay, they were nevertheless a firm threesome. Glynis adored the ground Cort walked on, saw him as her knight in shining armor, while Jay adored Glynis, saw her as the girl of his dreams.

But she hadn't known how to deal with her feelings for Cort, nor he for her. Each had been afraid to make a move at the risk of offending the other.

Glynis had just graduated from college when Cort returned from the Army. Finally, emotions that had been kept under lock and key for years exploded, and they came together with declarations of love. Glynis was certain Cort would ask her to marry him.

Cort, however, had other plans. He told Glynis an Army buddy had offered him a job in his security company and that he was accepting it and was due to leave on an overseas assignment within the week.

Glynis was stunned and hurt, unable to comprehend how Cort could just walk out of her life and leave her, especially after the heady hours of passion they'd spent in each other's arms since his return.

Cort tried to explain that he was *not* walking out of her life, that he was merely planning for their future. He went on to say that he remembered what it meant to be poor, even if she'd forgotten. He wanted better for them. Eventually they would get married, he added.

Eventually was not what Glynis wanted to hear. Harsh words were exchanged, and in the heat of the moment, both said things they didn't mean, damaging their relationship beyond repair.

A few weeks later Glynis discovered she was pregnant....

"Dammit, Glynis, you've got exactly two seconds to tell me what this is all about, or I'm out of here."

Cort's harshly spoken words drew Glynis back to reality with a start. She twisted her head back around, only to clasp her hands tightly in front of her, noticing with dismay that they were trembling.

He was staring at her through narrowed eyes, his hands stuffed into the pockets of his jeans. He appeared at ease, unperturbed. But Glynis knew better. Underneath that cool exterior, he was seething. Cort McBride didn't take too kindly to being played for a fool, and he believed that Glynis had indeed played him for one long ago. In his book that was unforgivable.

"I...have...there's something I have to tell you," Glynis said at last. "Would you mind if we sat down?" At this point, she wasn't sure her wobbly legs were capable of holding her up much longer. Confronting Cort was becoming more of a nightmare than she'd ever imagined. But she wouldn't fail Todd. Never.

Suddenly the thought of her son gave her the new burst of strength she needed to cross to the old chrome table and chairs in the middle of the kitchen.

"If you don't mind, I'll stand," Cort muttered tautly as she lowered herself into the chair facing him.

A hard glint sparked in Glynis's eyes. "You're not going to make this easy for me, are you?"

"Why should I? You didn't make things easier for

me when you married my best friend behind my back.''

Glynis felt the blood rush to her head and wanted desperately to defend herself. But rather than risk starting another argument, she controlled her overactive tongue and let his question slide.

''I'm waiting,'' Cort said, his arms folded across his chest, holding that same easy stance, which again she knew to be deceptive.

Still she didn't speak. She concentrated on the relatively cool breeze stealing through the screen door. Even so, perspiration broke out over her entire body.

''You...sure you don't want to sit down?'' Glynis asked inanely, continuing to stall for time, while questions with no answers raced through her mind. What would he do when she told him?

''Glynis!''

''I came to ask for your help, Cort,'' she said at last, knowing that she had pushed him as far as she could.

''Help. What kind of help?'' There was a wariness in his tone now.

She lifted her eyes to his. ''Todd is...sick.''

Cort stood a little straighter. ''Sick.''

''Yes. Very sick. He...was diagnosed with leukemia two years ago.''

He looked stricken.

''Actually, he took sick only a few months after...after Jay died.''

Muttering a crude expletive, Cort moved for the first time, striding toward the back door.

With his back to her, Glynis watched the way the

muscles in his shoulders bunched together. She knew he was holding on to his temper by a mere thread.

The hostile silence seemed loud as she listened to the birds' delightful chatter outside.

''He's…in remission right now, but…'' She broke off, pushing her sweaty palms down the sides of her jeans. ''But he won't be if he doesn't get the kind of help he needs.''

''I see.''

I wish to God you did see, but you don't. Glynis forced herself to speak again. ''Because…of his age and other factors that I won't go into right now and that I don't really understand myself, Todd's a good candidate for a bone marrow transplant and…''

Cort swung around, cutting her off in midsentence, his eyes blazing. ''If it's money you need, why the hell don't you just come right out and ask for it? Why the elaborate charade?''

''Please, Cort, let me finish,'' she said on a ragged note, trying her best to ignore the contempt she heard in his voice. But it was there, and it hurt like a hot knife piercing her heart.

He shrugged and kept his eyes pinned to hers. Frustration showed in his face.

''As I was saying, Todd's a candidate for a transplant, but…but we need a donor.''

His eyes were hard. ''So make the hospital find one.''

''They…the hospital, I mean, hasn't tried. You see…''

''You needn't go any further.'' He exhaled loudly. ''I know it takes a helluva lot of money to get a donor and have such an operation. Just tell me how much you need, and I'll deposit it in your account.''

She began shaking her head. ''Cort...''

''Let me finish. But just so there's no confusion, I'm not doing it for you, baby.'' His eyes were as cutting as blades. ''Oh, no. I'm doing it for the kid, for Jay's kid.''

''Todd's not Jay's child.''

Glynis's softly spoken words had the same effect as a rock splashing into a pool of water. After the initial shock of the noise, the ripples thereafter were all-consuming.

Blood vessels stood out at the base of his neck. ''Then whose...''

''Yours.'' Glynis stood, her lips white.

The long silence took its toll on both of them.

''Todd is your child, Cort.''

Another silence, deeper than the one before, fell over the room while Glynis saw a look of naked panic cross his face. Then Cort took a step toward her, his panic now replaced with naked fury.

''That's a damned lie!'' His voice was almost a shout.

Glynis fought off waves of nausea. ''No, no, it isn't.''

Suddenly and without warning, Cort closed the distance between them, knocking one of the chrome chairs over in his haste to reach her. For a second, as he loomed over her, Glynis thought he was going to strike her.

Unconsciously, she swayed out of harm's reach, but she wasn't quick enough. He grabbed her wrist and held firm. ''Tell me that's a lie,'' he said between clenched teeth.

''Please, Cort, you're…hurting me.''

''Believe me, this is nothing to what I will do if you don't call a halt to this little game you're playing and tell me the truth.''

''It's the truth,'' she cried, looking up at him, feeling his harsh breath on her face. ''I swear Todd is yours.''

For another long moment they stared at each other, golden brown eyes clashing with deep blue ones. Then, dropping her arm as though she were contaminated, Cort whirled around, but not before another expletive colored the air.

''Cort, please, hear me out,'' Glynis whispered to his back, stopping just short of begging. But she would beg, if she had to, if that was what it took to save her son's life. She'd even get down on her knees and grovel. ''You have to know it's true. Do you think I'd lie to you about something like this?''

Cort swung around, and her resolve wavered again. His features were a mask of vivid, ugly emotions.

''Yes, damn you, I do!''

Glynis felt another onslaught of nausea hit her, but she rallied. ''Believe me, I don't like this any better than you do. I wouldn't be here if I wasn't desperate. Surely you don't think I'd make this up because I want something from you?''

''Why now? Why the hell now?'' There was fury in his voice, but there was something else as well. Was it pain? Yes, she believed it was, and in that moment she longed to crawl off in a hole and cover herself.

Instead, she whispered through a maze of tears, "Because I'm not a suitable donor for Todd and… and as his…father, you could be. In fact," she rushed on, "you more than likely will be."

His head snapped up, but he didn't say a word, which added to Glynis's already mounting apprehension.

She finally broke the silence, her voice taut and unsteady. "You believe me, don't you, Cort?"

The fight seemed to have gone out of him, yet his eyes had not tempered. They were as cold as ever. "If he…if Todd hadn't gotten sick, you would never have told me, right?"

She didn't have a ready answer, so she didn't say anything.

"Answer me!"

"No," she said in a dull tone, "I wouldn't have told you. I never meant for you to find out."

The silence in the room was like a wall of ice.

"Damn you, Glynis, damn you to hell." His words were sharp, his tone whiplike. "How could you have done it? How could you have married Jay knowing you were carrying my child, knowing I'd be back?"

"That's just it, I didn't know you'd be back. You wanted your freedom, remember?"

"Like hell, I did. I wanted you. You knew as soon as I got set up in the job, I'd be back."

Glynis balled her fingers into fists by her side, trying to remain focused on her son, on the matter at hand, not on the man in front of her and the sea of memories in which she felt herself drowning.

"You knew I'd be back," he repeated bitterly.

Sunlight poured through the window in a blinding slant.

Glynis turned away, not bothering to hide the tears streaming down her cheeks. "No, I didn't, not after the way you stalked out of here, furious because I accused you of putting ambition and money before me. And anyway, I..." Her voice broke.

"You what?"

"Nothing," she replied in that same dull tone, reaching into her pocket for a Kleenex. Then, after wiping the tears from her face, she added, "I can't...won't discuss us anymore."

"That's where you're wrong. You *can* and you *will* answer my questions. You did this to me, Glynis! I have a right to know what happened."

"You did this to yourself, Cort."

"This was your revenge, was it?"

"There was no revenge to it. You wanted to be rid of me, to be freed from your commitment...."

"Dammit, how many times do I have to tell you that I wanted no such thing. Do you think for one instant that if I'd had any inkling you were pregnant I would have let you go?"

Glynis's eyes were lit with fury. "Nothing would have induced me to beg you to marry me."

"Don't be a fool," he said roughly. "I loved you. You had no right to conceal this. The child was as much mine as yours."

"Well, it's too late now. Anyway, I told you I don't want to talk about us."

"I don't care whether you want to or not. It's what I want that counts now, right?"

Recognizing the tone she knew so well, Glynis

nodded, feeling the fight drain out of her like water through a sieve.

"So tell me, when you found out you were pregnant, you went running to old Jay, who was bored to death working for his dad in the logging business, and conned him into marrying you. How am I doing so far?"

"Cort..."

Ignoring her, he went on, "Yeah, I guess old Jay fell for your line like a ton of bricks and waited in the wings just to pick up the pieces."

Glynis flinched, but her gaze was unerring. "Damn you, Cort McBride."

"Sure enough, Jay always did have the hots for you, so when he got the chance, he took it, even though you—"

"Stop it!" Glynis cried, her eyes flashing. "Would you rather I'd ended Todd's life before it had even started?"

This time it was Cort who turned visibly white.

"I could have, you know," she hammered on, knowing for the moment she had the upper hand, "but I didn't. To tell the truth, the thought never crossed my mind." She paused and swiped at the new surge of tears with the back of her hand. "But having a child out of wedlock did. It crossed my mind every waking minute of every day."

Suddenly Glynis realized that Cort had moved and was looming over her, so close that she could smell him. Her heart skipped a beat.

"So tell me," he said softly, "how did it feel to have his hands on you? Did you moan for him the way you did for me?"

"You bastard!" she cried, backing up, knowing if she stayed within reach of him, she'd end up slapping his face. "Stop thinking about yourself for once," she spat, "and think about your son."

The silence was heavy.

"I thought you wanted my help."

She stared at him in disbelief. "Are you saying you'll cooperate, do what needs to be done?"

"Both physically and financially."

Glynis let out her pent-up breath. A semblance of a smile broke across her lips.

"But it's going to cost you."

The smile faded. "What? What's it going to cost me?"

"Your son."

Chapter 4

Inside Glynis froze like an icicle. She touched her throat and kept staring at him. Surely, he wouldn't... No, of course he wouldn't, she quickly assured herself. It was impossible. Todd was *her* son. He wouldn't, couldn't take Todd away from her. Could he?

"What...what are you saying?" she asked finally, trying to curb the rising hysteria inside her.

"You figure it out."

Hysteria overcame her. The fear that had been there all the time, just beneath the surface, emerged like a monster to sink its claws into her heart. "Damn you, Cort McBride! There's no way I'm going to let you take Todd away from me, so don't even try."

"Don't threaten me, Glynis. You're way out of your league." His voice held a dangerous undertone that even Glynis in her highly agitated state could not miss.

She ignored it and went right on, her tone as frosty as her eyes. "No lawyer or court in this land will side with you."

"I wouldn't be too sure of that, either, if I were you."

Glynis's throat went dry. "Don't...don't you dare threaten *me*."

"I want to see my son. Now."

If he so much as tried to take Todd away from her... Oh, Lord, it didn't bear thinking about. "Until you've been tested, Todd and I are...are going to stay here, in Aunt Dorothy's house. Then we'll see..."

"Here? Did you say live here?"

"Yes... What's wrong with that?"

His laugh was short, biting. "What's wrong with that? Have you looked around this firetrap?"

"I resent that," Glynis responded coldly. "Just because it doesn't have all the amenities you're used to doesn't mean it's a firetrap."

"Amenities, hell. It doesn't have even the basics. You're not living here, not with my son, that is."

"Well, it'll have to do because I just might decide to stay here permanently. I've thought about applying for a teaching position in the district and..." Suddenly she stopped in midsentence as it dawned on her what he'd just said. "I beg your pardon?" she asked, blinking.

"You heard me." Irritation darkened his eyes. "No son of mine is going to live in this dilapidated house, now or ever. Hell, Glynis, this thing ought to be bulldozed to the ground, if anything."

"You have no say in what I do or where I live." She was holding her voice steady, but her hands were balled into fists, her fingernails digging into her palms. She wouldn't give in to his demands. To do so would be a grave mistake. She knew him well enough to know that. She'd let him control her life once before, and look where it got her.

When he didn't readily respond, she went on. "Anyway, that's not true." She quickly looked around the premises before turning back to focus her eyes on Cort. "Why, it…it just needs a good cleaning, a paint job and a few other things, and then it'll be just fine."

He snorted. "Just goes to show you how little you know about houses. For crying out loud, the place doesn't even have water. The pipes burst this winter and still haven't been repaired, not to mention the roof. It leaks like a waterfall."

"How do you know?" Her voice was toneless.

"Does it matter?"

"Yes, because you could be lying just to get your way."

It was obvious that Cort's temper was on a short fuse. "Trust me," he said cynically, "I don't have to lie to get my way. Now why don't you just simmer down and listen to what I have to say."

"How dare you talk to me like that?"

Cold fury etched his features. "If it'll make you see reason, I'll talk to you any way I damn well please."

"I won't have you trying to take over Todd's life— our life." She was becoming desperate. "You had your chance years ago and threw it away. You made it quite plain when you walked out where your loyalties lay."

"Damn you, Glynis, how can you talk about loyalty when you, pregnant with my child, married another man? Pardon the old adage, but that's like the pot calling the kettle black."

A cry tore loose from her throat. "What about you? All you could think about was the almighty dollar and a career. And not necessarily in that order." Her tone was filled with scorn. "And nothing's changed. Correct me if I'm wrong, but I bet you have a big deal pending right now, one that's going to make you even richer and more powerful than you already are."

"You're right I do. A government deal that I'm proud of."

"That's why I have Todd and you don't."

His sharp intake of breath was the only sound in the room, and for a moment Glynis feared she had gone too far, pushed him over the edge with her sharp tongue.

Suddenly, feeling as if something had ripped apart inside her, she whispered brokenly, "Why are you doing this, Cort? Why are you making things so difficult for me? If it's to get back at me, you're doing it at the expense of your son. Can't you see that?" She was pleading now, but she didn't care.

"It's my son I'm thinking about. That's why I can't, won't, let him live here." Cort paused and snatched the Stetson off his head. "Anyway, I'm afraid my helping…Todd might not be as simple as you think."

Glynis bit her lip. "Why? I mean what makes you say that?"

"In case you haven't noticed, I'm not exactly in tip-top shape."

She put a hand to one cheek. "Oh, God, I forgot about your wound."

"You know?"

"Milly told me."

"Ah, Milly. I should've known."

His mocking sarcasm was not lost on Glynis, but she ignored it. "You...you think the doctors might not let you...?" She was looking up at him out of seemingly bottomless eyes.

"Don't panic. It's just that right now I have a hole in my side that seems to be taking its time healing. I'm not sure how it'll affect things, that's all. They may want me to be completely healed."

"How did it happen? The wound, I mean?"

Glynis could tell by his hesitation that he'd rather not talk about it, which didn't surprise her at all.

"Do you really care?" Cort asked after a moment, his voice hard and strident.

Glynis's chin rose a notch. "For myself, no. For Todd, yes."

Another smirk crossed his lips. "Well, then for Todd's sake, I'll tell you. I took a bullet meant for a client."

"I'm not surprised. Danger always did turn you on."

"And what turns you on?" he asked silkily.

Color flooded her face, but she wouldn't give him the satisfaction of rising to his bait. Instead she pulled her dignity around her like a shield and steered the subject back to the matter at hand.

"If we have to delay the transplant, I'll have no choice but to accept that," she said stiffly. "But what

I don't have to accept is you telling me where to live.''

He gave her a long, dark look. ''Well, accept it, because that's the way it's going to be.''

Glynis scanned the room again, feeling what energy she had left completely desert her. Cort was right. This place *was* a disaster. Oh, it had possibilities, all right. It could be made livable with a lot of money, money that she obviously didn't have. Yet it galled her that Cort was once again pulling the strings of her life. For Todd's sake, she had no choice but to go along with it—for now.

''All right, Cort.'' She felt drained and tired, but most of all she was angry. ''We'll stay with Milly and Buck until I can make other arrangements.''

''I have a better idea.'' His voice was as smooth as plastic.

She jerked her head up, distrust written clearly on her features. ''Oh, and what is that?''

''The ranch. You and Todd stay at the ranch, with me.''

As before, she should have seen it coming, but she hadn't. For a moment she stared at him, totally stunned, as if she'd just run headlong into a mirrored wall. Glynis's mind was spinning, her breathing erratic. She took a deep breath and tried to calm down.

''I know what you're thinking, and you needn't worry.'' Cort's words were a sneer. ''I have a live-in housekeeper who will serve as a more than adequate chaperon.''

There was no sound in the room except her heartbeat, which Glynis thought was thunderous. She shook her head. ''No, no, that's impossible.''

"Why?"

"You know why." She couldn't look at him. "Be-cause…because…"

"Because you're afraid I'll jump your bones. Is that it?"

Glynis narrowed her eyes. "You're despicable!"

Cort moved then with lightning speed and didn't stop until he had her pinned against the nearest wall, his hands on either side holding her captive.

Silence blazed between them.

"There was a time when you didn't think so. Re-member?" The softly dangerous tone dared her to deny it.

"Please," she protested weakly, her breath coming in shallow gasps.

"Please what!" he whispered, his voice sounding hoarse, almost guttural, while his deep-set eyes shifted from her mouth to her heaving chest.

Glynis tried to ignore the look. But she couldn't, not when she could feel his hard thigh pressing against her leg and her nipples jutting against the fab-ric of her top.

A tide of heat washed through her even as she moved her head frantically from side to side, trying to downplay the effect his nearness was having on her.

"Cat got your tongue?" he taunted, rubbing his palm across one of the distended tips.

She groaned, his hand lighting a fire inside her, a fire she'd thought could never be rekindled. "Please," she whispered again, shrinking from his seductive touch.

Suddenly, mercifully, he stepped back, but his eyes

lingered on her for another heartbeat. "You're not worth it," he spat. Then, muttering a crude expletive, he turned his back and strode once more to the door and looked out.

The still spring air screamed with silence.

When she thought she couldn't stand it another second, he swung back around. What she saw in his eyes again sent her heart rate up a notch higher. "You've had our son for six long years. Can't you at least share him for a while?"

Glynis eased down into a chair and lowered her head. She wanted to cry, to wash away all of the anguish, all the hurt, all the shame. But she couldn't. The tears wouldn't come. They were now locked deep inside her.

"Well?"

Her gaze slid to him. In that moment she knew he had won, in spite of how he had humiliated her. The look on his face, the pain in his voice were the catalyst that completely destroyed her resistance.

"We'll do it your way for now." She ran a hand over her hair. "But when it's all over, you'll let us— Todd go."

"We'll see."

"Cort," she began, fear curling anew in her stomach.

"Not now, Glynis. I want to see Todd. I want to see my son."

"He's…he's at Milly's."

"Get him."

"What then?"

"Meet me at the ranch."

She sighed and rubbed her temples. "It's getting

late, Cort. I think it would be better if we…uh, spent the night with Milly. Then tomorrow…''

''No. I want to see my son today, damn you.''

He was doing it to her again, making her feel guilty, making her the guilty party when he'd been the one who had deserted her. But she had given her word, and even though her heart felt like a piece of lead, she was committed. ''I'll…we'll be there shortly.''

For a long moment Cort continued to look at her, a strange expression on his face. It was an expression she couldn't decipher, yet it made her feel uncomfortable.

Then he pivoted and in long, angry strides made his way toward the door, closing it firmly behind him.

It was not until Glynis heard him crank the engine on his Jeep that she relaxed. Sinking against the cushion, she gave in to the throbbing at her temples while her mind raged.

The thought of living under the same roof with Cort for so much as one day, much less several, made her crazy. My God, she thought, did she still care about him? No, absolutely not. Any feelings she had for Cort were dead.

Suddenly she grabbed her stomach, fearing she was going to be sick. Who was she kidding? She had known the moment he'd touched her, stirring passions both old and new inside her, that she hadn't gotten him out of her system. But then she'd known long before that—she'd known it when she'd turned and saw him standing in the doorway.

Feeling anything for Cort was the last thing she wanted. But she needed him. For her son, she needed him.

"Sure you won't take time to have a cup of coffee before you go?" Milly asked anxiously, following Glynis to the car. Todd was already inside the Honda, his seat belt buckled, looking at a comic book.

Glynis stopped at the edge of the sidewalk, out of hearing distance of Todd, and gave her friend a wan smile. "I'd love to, but I want to get to the ranch before it gets any later." She paused and stared at the point beyond Milly's shoulder, her face pensive. "Cort's...waiting."

Milly sighed, frowning gently. "I assume you know what you're doing?"

"Well, you assume wrong."

"Then why are you doing such a fool thing as going to his place?" Milly shook her head. "Why don't you and Todd stay with Buck and me? I've already told you we have plenty of room, and we'd love having you."

Impulsively Glynis reached out and hugged her friend. "I know that and I'm grateful for the offer, but..."

"For God's sake, Glynis, what kind of hold has Cort McBride got over you? I know how crazy you were about him way back, but when he took off and refused to marry you, I thought you had come to your senses, gotten him out of your system. Now, years later, not only do you ask to see him, but agree to move into his house with him." She rolled her eyes. "Talk about crazy."

Glynis's features were pinched. "I know how it

looks and how you could misconstrue everything. But trust me, I have my reasons, and as my dearest friend, you certainly deserve an explanation. As soon as I get settled, we'll have a long talk. But not now. Cort is waiting and…''

Milly's eyes suddenly widened and lit up, as if a light had just come on inside her head. "Cort is Todd's father, isn't he?''

Glynis flinched, but she didn't turn away. "Yes.''

Milly balled a fist and slapped it into the palm of her other hand. ''I should have guessed it a long time ago, should have known when you married Jay in such a hurry. I never thought…''

''That I'd marry one man, while carrying another's child.''

Although Milly flushed, she recovered quickly. ''Don't get me wrong, I'm not criticizing. It's just that I'm surprised, that's all,'' she finished lamely.

Glynis knew what Milly was thinking and she didn't blame her, didn't blame her in the least. ''It's all right, really it is. I should've told you a long time ago, but I couldn't. I couldn't…couldn't tell anyone. I was so torn up, so mixed up, so vulnerable.…'' She smiled through the sudden tears that had sprung up in her eyes. ''But now I'm glad you know.''

Tears also glistened in Milly's eyes as she answered Glynis's smile with one of her own. But it was a fleeting moment. And when it disappeared, Glynis was once again reminded of the sun dipping behind a cloud.

''Cort didn't know, did he?''

''No, he didn't know.''

''But he does now?''

"Yes, he knows now."

"I won't ask what his reaction was."

"Don't."

"Did...did Jay know?"

Glynis pawed at the concrete with the toe of her shoe. "Yes, but he never accepted it."

"I'm sorry. I know your marriage must've been more of a hell than I ever imagined."

"There were times when I thought I wouldn't make it, but then I'd think of Todd and the world would right itself once again."

"So is...Cort going to do his part?"

"Yes, thank goodness," Glynis said, glancing down at her watch and then toward the car, where she noticed Todd squirming restlessly.

"He's going to be the donor, right?"

"Right. Plus he's going to help me financially. But his help is not without a price." She caught her breath sharply. "He...wants to spend time with Todd, get to know him. And he feels the only way he can do that is for us to stay at the ranch. And, like you, he thinks Aunt Dorothy's house is unlivable. So, as you can see, I have no choice."

"You're right, you don't, but how do you feel? About Cort, I mean? How's being around him going to affect you?"

"Oh, Milly," Glynis said wearily, "I don't know. At this point I think I'm numb."

"Mommy."

At the sound of Todd's plaintive cry, both women turned in the direction of the car. Todd had rolled down the window on the driver's side, and his head was sticking out of it.

"Mom," he said again before Glynis could respond, "I'm ready to go."

"I'm coming, sweetheart." Then, facing Milly, Glynis added, "Look, I'll call you later and we'll get together and talk some more."

"Take care," Milly whispered, squeezing Glynis's hand. "And if you need me…"

"I know, and thanks."

With that, Glynis hurried to the car and, once inside, slammed the door behind her.

Nothing was the same. Yet everything was the same. The land had not changed, Glynis noticed as she brought the Honda to a stop at the beginning of the long road that would eventually take her to the front door of Cort's sprawling ranch-style house.

But of course the house had changed. The small, unsturdy frame structure where Cort and his brother, Barr, had lived with their drunken father had long since disappeared, and in its place was a new, elaborate home on top of the hill, the setting sun reflecting off the windows.

Glynis, feeling her mouth go dry as cotton, gripped the steering wheel until she felt her fingers go numb. How could she do it? How could she share the same space with Cort? See him day after day? No one should have to endure what she was having to endure. But then she'd learned as a young child that life dealt you no special favors, that if you were to survive, you had to be a fighter.

"Mom, what's the matter? You sick or something?"

Glynis loosened her grip on the wheel at the same

time as she smiled down at her son. His eyebrows were drawn together in a frown. "No, I'm not sick or something. I was just thinking, that's all."

"Are we really going to stay here in that big house?" He was pointing toward the hill.

"Yes, we're really going to stay here, for a while, anyway."

"All right!"

"It is beautiful, isn't it?" Glynis said, unaware of the wistful note in her voice.

"It's neat."

The minute Glynis had nosed the car onto Highway 69 toward the small community of Pollock, she had explained to Todd the change of plans. Of course he was delighted they were going to be staying on a ranch.

Todd's nose was pressed against the glass. "Wow! Look, Mom, look at all those cows! They're everywhere."

The sloping hills that graced the front and sides of the house were dotted with cattle contentedly munching on the green grass underfoot. The serene beauty of it almost robbed Glynis of her breath.

Cort had come a long way from the struggling, penniless teenager. She'd have to hand him that. From the looks of this place, he'd more than reached his goal. Suddenly, in an indulgent moment, she wondered what it would be like to share a house such as this with a man. With Cort...

"I bet Mr. McBride's got horses, too."

Glynis shook her head as if to clear it. "Uh, why don't you call him...Uncle Cort."

Todd wrinkled his nose. "Is he my uncle?"

"No, no, not in the true sense. But he's been my...friend for a long time." This was going to be harder than even she had imagined. "And I think he'd like it...if you called him that."

Todd shrugged. "Okay." Then, changing the subject, he asked, "If he's got horses, do you think he'll let me ride one?"

"More than likely," Glynis responded with a smile. Then, yanking the car back in drive, she drove it up the asphalt road, her heart pounding.

The second she brought the car to a full stop next to the house, the front door opened and Cort walked out. He paused on the porch, as if uncertain for the first time in his life how to proceed.

Todd had no such inhibitions. Without looking at Glynis, he opened the door and scrambled out of the car. But when his feet hit the ground, he stopped and scrutinized the stranger still standing on the porch.

By the time Glynis got out of the car and came around to where her son was standing, the impulse to flee was beating in her veins.

For the longest time, no one spoke. Even Todd seemed to sense the electricity in the air and self-consciously looked toward Glynis.

It was Cort who made the first move. Taking slow, even strides, he walked toward them, his face looking as though it had been chiseled out of granite.

Glynis remained rigid.

He didn't pause until he was within touching distance of them both. Glynis felt the sting of tears behind her eyelids and was doubly thankful for her dark sunglasses as Cort, ignoring her, dropped to one knee in front of Todd.

"Hi," he said, his eyes on the small, thin face in front of him.

"Hi," Todd answered shyly.

"Welcome to the Lazy C Ranch."

Todd eyed him curiously. "Are you my Uncle Cort? My mom said I should call you that."

For the first time, Cort looked at Glynis. Hatred shone in his eyes. Glynis drew in a sharp breath and turned away.

"Er...that's fine," Cort was saying. "I'll answer to anything."

Todd cocked his head sideways. "My friend's dad looks like you."

"Oh, really." Amusement lurked around Cort's mouth now, making him appear younger and more human.

"Yeah, he's..."

"Yes, sir," Glynis interrupted softly.

"Yes, sir, he's tall like you," Todd went on, unruffled, his eyes showing his awe. "And he wears a big cowboy hat, too." He paused thoughtfully for a moment, then added, "I don't have a dad. He died."

"Todd!" Glynis's horrified cry split the air, and for what seemed like an eternity, no one said a word. No one moved.

Finally, when she could bring herself to look at Cort, she wished she hadn't. The hurt mirrored there was so intense, she feared her heart would explode into a million pieces. Her already fragile emotional dam collapsed, and years of heartache and guilt came flooding back to her, threatening to bury her under its impact.

Cort cleared his throat and stood up, resting a hand

on Todd's thin shoulder. "I'm sorry about that... son."

"Me, too, but Mom says he's in heaven."

"I'm sure he is."

"Do you have any horses?" Todd asked then, changing the subject.

"You bet I do," Cort said, once again clearing his throat. "In fact, they're the best."

"Could we go see 'em? Please?"

Cort bestowed on Todd one of his rare smiles. "You bet."

Without so much as another glance in her direction, father and son headed toward the paddock located behind the house.

Glynis stood as if cemented to the spot and watched, tears trickling down her cheeks. Yet she was smiling a wistful smile as she witnessed her son mimicking Cort's long, graceful stride.

Gradually the smile disappeared, and reality set in. She stood there alone. A woman without a shield.

Chapter 5

Cort sipped on his coffee and flipped through a stack of papers on his desk. He was starting to get behind on his paperwork, but then that wasn't anything new. He was usually behind on his paperwork.

Even though his company, McBride Security was the second-largest security firm in the United States and had numerous employees who were more than capable of doing anything he asked of them, he nevertheless believed in a hands-on approach. He wanted to be involved in the day-to-day workings of his empire, was not happy unless he was doing so.

However, continuing to work in the field was not without its price. If it hadn't been for his active involvement, he wouldn't be nursing a bullet wound. But when an old friend had come to him for help, he hadn't been able to turn him down. The "heavies" who were after him obviously meant business.

After coming out of the service, having been skill-fully trained in Army intelligence, Cort had gone into partnership with an Army buddy who thought he wanted to be in the security business. Cort later bought him out and because of his cunning and astute business mind, had become successful far in excess of what he'd ever imagined.

Yet he was not satisfied. His goal was not com-plete. He very much wanted the big, lucrative contract the government was letting out to a private company and was determined to get it. While the bullet wound in his side might have slowed him down, it had not stopped him or dulled his determination.

There were only three things that meant a damn to him in this life: his brother, McBride Security and his ranch. And he'd thought he was content, if not happy with his lot in life. Until yesterday, that is, when it had all changed with a blink of an eye.

A deep sigh escaped Cort's lips as he lumbered to his feet and walked to the window behind his desk, coffee cup in hand. But he didn't drink any coffee. Instead he simply stood and stared outside at the sun and watched it slowly peep over the horizon, hoping the sight would ease the turmoil raging inside him.

It was early, and he knew he was the only one up. It had been an effort in futility to remain in bed a second longer. He'd tossed and turned the entire night as it was, using the mattress and springs as a battle-ground for his frustration and anger.

Unfortunately, he found no solace in the stunning beauty of the rich pastureland where the sun made the dewdrops sparkle like millions of tiny diamonds. Al-ways he could stare at this land he loved and come to grips with whatever was troubling him. Not this morning.

"Damn," he muttered, and at the same time shoved an unsteady hand through his thick crop of hair. Then, turning, he sat his half-empty cup on the desk with a resounding thud and walked to the center of the room, where he eyed with longing a number of dumbbells lining one corner.

When he wasn't working the land or cattle, his favorite pastime was lifting weights; not that he did it to excess, but rather for the pure enjoyment of feeling his anxiety and stress evaporate as if it had never existed. But there would be no weight lifting today or in the near future, unless he wanted to rip out the stitches in his gut.

Still, he yearned for the relief. In his mind's eye he visualized how he'd look pumping iron, how he'd feel in a few weeks after the doctor released him.

Sweat would darken his hair, trickle down his face, roll onto his chest, saturate the forest of coarse hair and finally stop at his waistline and stain the elastic on his briefs.

He'd flex his biceps by doing a series of arm curls before letting the free weight hit the floor. Then he'd grimace from the sheer effort of it all and take deep, slow breaths to control his labored breathing, all the while conscious of the loud music screeching from the stereo.

Once again he thought it was too damn bad he couldn't pick up one of those bells and work the kinks out of both his mind and his body.

Barr and other close friends referred to this sectioned-off part of the house as Cort's sanctuary. And in a sense they were right. Not only had he entertained countless women on the mattress next to the stereo, but he had exorcised the demons inside him.

But not today. There was nothing that could be said or done that could absorb the confusion, the pain and the anger.

Without thinking about it, he walked back to the window and once again stared outside into the sunshine. But there was no sunshine in his thoughts; they were blacker than the depths of hell.

He felt like a loose cannonball, and he knew where to strike.

A son. He had a son. God, he couldn't believe it, didn't want to believe it. But he knew it was the truth. Glynis might be many things, but a liar she was not.

Why? he asked himself again. Why hadn't Glynis contacted him when she found out she was pregnant? She had to have known he'd come back. And how could she have kept Todd from him all these years? Well, there was no use crying over spilled milk, as the old saying went, but one thing was for sure—he would never forgive Glynis for her deception and betrayal.

And to think he had loved her so much, would have given his life for her if he'd had to.

Suddenly, he felt extremely tired. Turning, he made his way toward the mattress and lowered himself down onto it, backed against several pillows and stared into the mirror hanging on the wall in front of him. The grooves around his mouth and eyes stood out like neon signs where a few years ago he'd had to examine his face closely to find them. Scars. His work had put them there. So had Glynis.

When he probed further, he realized he was not so much tired as he was exhausted. He felt like a man who had been to war with himself—and lost.

He thought about home, about his mother who had died when he was a baby, about how his father used to get drunk and beat him, about how poor they were because the old man couldn't hold a steady job.

But most of all he thought about the beautiful blue-eyed boy who was his son. He felt a smile soften his lips as he stared at the patterns created by the sun on the ceiling. But the smile was only fleeting as his thoughts centered on Todd's life-threatening illness. What if he, the father, didn't have what it took to be a donor? What if the doctors couldn't find a suitable donor?

Just when he'd found his son, there was the possibility that... No, he wouldn't think like that. If it took every dime he had, he'd use it to save his son's life. Todd would be cured. Cort couldn't lose him now.

"Damn you, Glynis, damn you!" he spat aloud. "How could you have done this to me?"

Whether she'd believed him or not, he'd planned to come back and marry her. He'd told her that, only she hadn't listened.

He could still remember that fateful day as if it had been yesterday that the bitter words had passed between them. He had been out of the Army only two weeks, and they had spent every waking minute together, much of that making love. He hadn't been able to get enough of her delectable body.

It was after one of those marathon sessions of love-making that he'd told her about his job offer, expecting her to be as excited about it as he was. They had just returned to her aunt's house after spending the afternoon on the lake....

"I have something I want to talk to you about," he'd told her. They had just rid themselves of their picnic gear, plunking it down in the middle of the living room.

Glynis gazed up at him, her golden brown eyes soft and dreamy. "Mmm, and what might that be?"

Grinning broadly, Cort sauntered over and, placing his arms around her, nuzzled her neck, then whispered in her ear, "I got a job."

She pulled back and once again peeked at him from under long lashes. "A job."

"Yes, my darling, a real job."

"Oh, Cort," she cried, "I'm so glad."

He tweaked her nose, a nose that was slightly sunburned. "I knew you would be."

Glynis bit at a finger playfully. "Since I've been assured of a teaching position, and now with your job, we can start to look for a house and…"

"Whoa, wait a minute," Cort said with a laugh, backing up, holding up his hands.

Glynis drew her eyebrows together in a perplexed frown. "You don't want a house?"

"Of course I want a house, darling, only not right now." He smiled again, and his tone was teasing. "Hey, don't you think you're getting ahead of yourself? Don't you think we oughta get married before we start shopping for a place to live?" His smile broadened into a grin. "Why, what would all these old biddies around here think if their children's teacher was living in sin with a man?'' He rolled his eyes. ''Heaven forbid!''

Glynis punched him playfully in the stomach. ''Of course we'll get married first. That goes without saying. In fact, I was thinking this weekend would be as good a time as any.'' There was a teasing note in Glynis's tone as well, but her eyes were serious. ''So tell me about your job.''

''I think we'd better sit down,'' Cort said, looking away.

Her eyebrows arched, as if she sensed something was wrong. ''What's the matter?''

Cort ignored the slight tremor in her voice and instead propelled her toward the couch. Once they were seated and facing each other, he said, ''Nothing's the matter. Or at least I didn't think so until now.''

''Oh, Cort, you're not making any sense.''

''The job I've taken is not here in Lufkin.''

She shrugged. ''That's no big deal as long as it's within driving distance.''

''That's the problem—it's not.''

For a moment there was no sound in the room.

Then Glynis asked, ''What do you mean?''

She was no longer bothering to hide her panic, and Cort felt his heart constrict. This was going to be much more difficult than he'd thought. He'd had no idea she wouldn't understand....

''Just spit it out, Cort,'' she was saying.

He expelled a sigh. ''You remember Hank Chase, that Army buddy from Houston I wrote you about?'' Glynis nodded, and he went on. ''Well, his dad recently died and left Hank his small security company.''

"So?" Glynis interrupted. "What does that have to do with you?"

"It has everything to do with me."

Glynis's eyes widened incredulously. "Surely that's not the job you've taken."

"Dammit, Glynis, don't look at me like that." Cort lunged to his feet, then stared down at her, his mouth stretched in a grim line. "I'm doing it for both of us. For our future." Suddenly he sat back down and grabbed her hands, folding them into his large, callused ones. "It's a chance of a lifetime for me, for us."

Glynis jerked her hands out of captivity, her face filled with uncertainty. "But that means you won't...can't live in Lufkin." Her chin was beginning to wobble.

A furrow appeared between his eyes. "That's right, but—"

"No, that's not right," Glynis contradicted tightly. "For God's sake, Cort, I've just accepted a job, thinking we were finally going to get...get married and...and settle down."

"We are going to get married and settle down," Cort said patiently, "only not right now."

Glynis's sharp intake of breath was the only sound in the room. "What...are you saying, Cort?"

He moved away from the couch and turned his back. Moments later, when he turned back around, she was standing and watching him as if in a daze.

"Not what you want me to, apparently. Glynis, you're blowing this way out of proportion. Look, this job will enable us to have a nice house, money in our pockets, a secure future."

She set her mouth in a firm line. "I don't care about those things."

He felt something jump in his gut. "You don't mean that."

"Oh, yes I do. All I care about is loving you, marrying you." Her proclamation ended on a sob.

"Oh, sweetheart..." Cort pleaded, closing the distance between them.

"Don't," Glynis cried, just as he was about to haul her into his arms. "Don't...don't touch me."

"You're being childish," Cort snapped. Then, realizing his harsh tone was only making matters worse, he tried a different tactic. He tried reasoning. "I thought we felt the same way about things. I thought we were in agreement that we don't want to scrimp and do without like we've always had to all our lives."

"It's you that's always been concerned with money and material things, Cort, not me."

He tensed. "You're damn right. I haven't forgotten what it means to be dirt-poor, to be laughed at because I didn't have enough money in my pocket to buy a penny piece of bubble gum. But apparently you have."

"No, I haven't forgotten what it's like." Her eyes hinted at tears. "Do you think I'll ever forget kids calling me Little Orphan Annie and making fun of my clothes? Of course not. Those memories are branded into my brain and will never disappear. But our past is not the issue here, or rather it's beside the point, because we wouldn't be dirt-poor, as you put it. I'll have a job, and you could go into the logging business with Jay and his father."

Cort's eyes narrowed dangerously. "I've already told you, I have no intention of working for Jay's father."

"Even knowing how I feel, you won't change your mind?" she asked dully.

"No, I won't change my mind, not even for you."

"I see."

"No, you don't!"

"I see more than you think." She paused and gnawed on her lower lip as if sorting through her thoughts. "Security work. What is that, anyway? What would you do?"

"Everything. Install alarms in people's homes, offer protection for one thing or another, track down missing persons."

"A glorified private detective, is that what you're saying?"

His shoulders stiffened. "I guess I am."

"But you aren't qualified for that kind of work."

"I will be once I get my license," he insisted. "Anyway, as you well know, I worked with weapons in the Army. That was my specialty."

Suddenly Glynis placed her hands over her ears and shook her head. "I don't want to hear any more. All this talk of weapons is…crazy. What's happened to you? You're…you're not the same." She shivered. "You've changed."

Cort felt blood rush to his head. "You're wrong about that and you know it. Just because I want us to have a secure future, something better for our children, you accuse me of changing."

She shook her head again. "No, it's more than that. I can't put my finger on it, but it's there."

"Glynis, for God's sake!"

"Are you going ahead with this cockamamy plan?"

He didn't hesitate. "Yes. In fact Hank wants me to go abroad with him on a missing persons case."

Silence filled the room.

"If you go, don't bother to come back." Her words were barely audible.

"You don't mean that," he said roughly, but he knew she did. She had a numbed, desperate look. He longed to hold her close, tell her everything was going to be all right. But he couldn't; he was afraid nothing was ever going to be all right again.

"I mean that with every fiber of my being."

"You mean if I take this job, it's over?"

"That's exactly what I mean."

Cort's anger was barely controllable now. "But why?"

"Because I want a home, children, a husband who comes home to me every night. I want roots. I don't want a man who's more interested in money and adventure than in me."

"Is that your final word?" His gut tightened as if a fist had jabbed him.

"That's my final word."

"Glynis."

"Go away, Cort. Go away and leave me alone."

It was only after he walked out of the house and closed the door behind him that he realized he had tears on his face. But the final blow had come two months later in the form of a letter telling him that she had married Jay Hamilton.

Cort sat upright, and for the longest time he remained perched on the side of the mattress. Then he slowly got to his feet, made his way back to his desk and sat down.

He felt the old, familiar sorrow as he always did when he thought about that terrible time, that terrible year they parted. He'd felt hollow, dead inside, except he'd continued to breathe, to walk, to talk.

It had been only within the past two years that he'd reached a plateau of contentment, if not happiness. And he'd be damned if he was going to let Glynis's unexpected presence change that.

He wouldn't let her get under his skin. Never again would he be vulnerable to a woman. Yet, even as he made this vow, he recalled how it had felt to touch her again, recalled the agony as well as the ecstasy of it. And how she'd looked last night, sitting at the dining-room table after Todd had gone to bed, her features fine in the soft light.

Then later, as she'd left the table and walked toward the door, her fragrance wafted around him and the lure of her perfect body had begun to vibrate inside him.

And he could not remember ever seeing a more beautiful woman.

Suddenly a cry tore through his lips as he pounded the desk with a fist. He knew that in spite of what she'd done to him, he still wanted her.

He didn't realize he was no longer alone until he heard a voice say, ''What the hell's the matter with you?''

Chapter 6

Cort jerked his head up and around. "Dammit, Barr, you got something against knocking?"

At forty-three, Barr McBride, ten years Cort's senior, strode nonchalantly across the threshold. He was munching on a sweet roll and carrying a cup of coffee, his lips curled in a mocking smile.

He was endowed with the same thick brown hair as his brother, only Barr's was devoid of gray and not nearly as neat. It always needed cutting. His eyes were black and unreadable, hiding scars left by his stint in a Vietcong POW camp. Scars that had deepened when he learned upon release that his fiancée had married someone else.

Barr tried to keep the bitterness under a facade of polite indifference, but at times he was unable to pull it off, especially when a woman got too close to him. He immediately turned cold and hostile, thereby driving her away. He, like Cort, was not interested in ties that bind.

Barr made his money in the horse and cattle business. His ranch, adjoining his brother's, was the main interest in his life. He didn't care about the outside world; as far as he was concerned, it didn't exist.

But even though the brothers were different in temperament and outlook, they were close. In fact Barr had been the only stabilizing force in Cort's youth, and for that Cort felt he owed him.

"My, but aren't we full of good cheer this morning," Barr was saying, his eyes slowly raking over his brother's face. He took another healthy bite out of the roll.

"Didn't get much sleep," Cort snapped, pushing himself up from the desk with his forearms.

"That hole in your gut still bothering you?"

"Yeah, but not the way you mean. It makes me madder than hell when there's so much around the ranch I want to do, plus I can't even lift weights. It's damned inconvenient, that's what it is."

Barr snorted. "The way I see it, you oughta be glad you're still breathing. I don't know whether you realize it, but it was touch and go for a while."

"Believe me, I know. Every time I start to do something, I'm reminded once again that I'm not invincible."

Barr's eyes narrowed. "Well, while we're on the subject, are you any closer to finding out who shot you?"

"No, not as far as I know." Cort released a sigh. "Ridley's been on it hot and heavy, but he's turned up nothing so far. I'm expecting a call from him this morning.''

Holding both the roll and the cup in his hand, Barr walked deeper into the room. "So you think it was meant for your client, huh?" He paused, then snapped his free fingers. "What's his name?"

"Boyd Fisher," Cort supplied absently, though his eyes never veered from Barr's. "But you don't."

"Nope, I sure as hell don't," Barr said succinctly. "From what I know of professional killers, they don't make mistakes like that."

Cort's mouth tightened into an exasperated line. "So what are you saying, the bullet was meant for me?"

"It wouldn't be the first time something like that happened."

"I can't argue with that. But in this case you're wrong, big brother, dead wrong." Cort's face was set in hard, impatient lines. "Boyd just got in too deep with his gambling cronies, and someone turned the heavies loose on him, pure and simple."

"Then how do you figure you got the bullet and he didn't?"

"How the hell should I know?" Cort said curtly. "Anyway, that's Ridley's problem. Let him earn that high salary I pay him." He paused and began rubbing the back of his neck with his right hand. "But right now, that's the least of my worries."

Barr was sitting down on the bench next to Cort's desk and had one long leg crossed over the other. Cort came around, hooked a hip on the side of the desk and faced him.

"Kinda figured that," Barr drawled. "Not only do

you look like hell, but you're about as tightly wound as a time bomb ready to go off. Something goin' on I need to know about, little brother?''

Cort focused his eyes on the point beyond Barr's shoulder, realizing that having his brother living so close made privacy almost impossible. Barr knew him so well, instinctively knew when something was bothering him. After all, it had been Barr who had comforted him many a night following his father's drunken beatings.

"Glynis is back."

"You mean in Lufkin?" Barr's tone was incredulous.

"That's exactly what I mean."

"Where? I mean where's she staying?"

"Here."

Barr blinked. "Here?"

Cort nodded grimly.

"Dammit, little brother, have you lost your mind?"

Following Barr's stunned rejoinder, both men were silent for a few moments. Barr chewed on the last of his roll while Cort chewed on something much less edible.

"I have my reasons, Barr," Cort said at last. "Give me credit for having a little sense, anyway."

Barr shook his head, reaching down and brushing off a leaf that was stuck to the hem of his jeans on the right leg. "I do, except when it comes to Glynis."

"What do you mean by that?" Cort's voice was oddly flat.

"Don't be an ass. You know what I mean. She had the power to turn you inside out, and you know it."

Cort lurched off the desk and flashed Barr a hard

look. "Glad you put that in the past tense, because that's exactly how it is now. What we had between us is long dead and buried."

"Yeah, sure. And I'm going to be the next President of the United States."

"Go to hell."

A smile toyed with Barr's lips. "I'll probably do that, too. Ah, come on, if what you're saying is true, then why the hell is she staying here?"

"She's not alone."

Barr sighed deeply, as if his patience was running out. "So, who's with her?"

"Her...son, who's very sick."

"Sick? I don't get it."

"The kid has leukemia."

"Godalmighty, that's too bad. But I still don't get it. I haven't forgotten, even if you have, how cut up you were when she married Jay and later when that kid was born. Why, you nearly went off the deep end—"

"Give it a rest," Cort ordered tersely.

Suddenly Barr slapped his thigh. "Ah, I get it. She's hitting you up for some money for his treatments. I should've known."

Cort sighed. "That's part of it, true."

"Only part."

"Todd's a prime candidate for a bone marrow transplant...." Cort paused, then, before Barr could respond, he went on. "And the right donor is needed."

"So?"

"So hopefully I'm that donor," Cort said flatly.

"Now, why would you qualify to…" Barr broke off and stared at his brother, his mouth gaping open.

"That's right. The kid's not Jay's. He's mine."

Barr sucked in a short, involuntary breath, as if speech was impossible. He shifted his position on the bench. "Well, I'll be damned, little brother."

"Ditto that," Cort said, grim faced.

"And the kid's got leukemia, huh?"

"Has had for the last two years."

Barr ran a hand over his hair. "Suppose you tell me how you found out all this."

Cort told him in detail. When he finished, the room went silent as the two men sized up the situation, figured out what to say, what *not* to say.

"I hope you know what you're doing," Barr said at last.

Cort averted his gaze and stared out the window, deep in thought. "Me, too, but somehow I doubt I do."

"Well, you didn't have to bring them here."

Cort swung around, his feature drawn. "That's where you're wrong, Barr. I want to get to know my son. If only I'd—"

"But you didn't," Barr interrupted. "There wasn't anything you could have done. I told you that then, and I'm telling you again now. The past never leaves us—it's full of things we'd like to change. But you can't, and neither can I. The past is what it is—history, and nobody can rewrite it. It's dead."

"I'm going to remind you of that the next time you get drunk and start resurrecting your past."

Barr almost smiled. "Sounds good anyway."

"Sure as hell does, only we both know it doesn't work. Some memories just won't die."

Barr stood, looking as though he, too, were in a daze. "When do I get to meet the kid?"

Cort's features relaxed. "Maybe I'll bring him over later."

"Good enough," Barr said, grinning. He then turned and walked toward the outside door. Once there he twisted back around, and there was a deadpan expression on his face. "Please, just tell me the kid doesn't look like you."

"Kiss off."

Barr's deep laugh lingered in the room long after the door closed behind him. But there was no laughter inside Cort as he slumped back into the depths of his chair, ran his hands through his disheveled hair and down his unshaven cheeks and chin.

Glynis stood on a portion of the cedar deck that jutted off her bedroom and breathed in the fresh morning air.

She'd taken a hot shower in the adjoining bathroom and then slipped into a slightly oversized gold cotton blouse, jeans and a pair of multicolored sandals.

Thank goodness the hot, stinging water had helped soothe her frayed nerves. However, it was only after she'd finished applying her makeup and running a comb through her thick hair that she felt as though she could face the day. More important, she'd felt able to face Cort.

In the distance, at the edge of the woods, she could see two squirrels chasing each other, their tails flipping faster than she could blink an eye.

As she watched, fascinated by the way the animals scampered from one tree to another, a small smile softened her lips. She wished Todd could see them; he would think they were "neat." Her smile widened to display a set of even white teeth.

Suddenly thinking she heard her son's footsteps, she swung around. "Todd?" she said, craning her neck.

The room behind her was empty. She shrugged, not surprised that she was hearing things. Nor was she surprised that Todd was still asleep. Yesterday had been a long day for him; he'd been exhausted when she'd put him to bed last night long past his bedtime.

But it had been a long day for her as well. That emotional scene when Cort had met his son for the first time had left her totally drained. And the following few hours had brought no relief.

By the time Cort and Todd had returned from taking a quick tour of the barn, she had made her way into the house and straight into the arms of the housekeeper, Maude Springer. Maude had known she and Todd were coming, of course, and had welcomed her enthusiastically, her twinkling gray eyes a suitable backdrop for a naturally sweet grin.

Chatting nonstop, Maude had taken her through a large living room with a stone fireplace and oak floor. Glynis's heels had echoed as she'd walked by the wall of glass that faced the luscious green pastureland and the woods beyond.

When she had finally reached the two guest bedrooms joined by a door, she had realized just how successful Cort had become and just how far removed he was from her.

Later it had taken every ounce of her fortitude to get through the short, tense dinner that followed. Though Todd had been worn out, he'd wanted to eat at the table with them, and she had let him, purely for selfish reasons. She hadn't wanted to be alone with Cort.

But she had worried needlessly. For the most part, Cort had ignored her. Yet she had been aware of him with every beat of her heart, especially when he'd walked into the room, looking and smelling like he'd just stepped out of the shower. His hair had been still damp, and his cologne had sent her pulse racing.

After answering several polite inquiries as to her comfort, Glynis had made it a point not to glance in his direction for fear of seeing nothing but cold hostility mirrored there.

Todd had been a different matter altogether. Cort had many things to say to his son and plenty of smiles. Then, as soon as Maude served the berry pie, Cort had patted Todd on the shoulder and bid him good-night, citing work in his office as his excuse for leaving.

Glynis had been relieved that the ordeal was over, having had no idea what to expect from Cort. And now as she filled her lungs one last time with the intoxicating morning air, she turned and walked back into her room, realizing that she still didn't. All she knew was that she faced the first of many days on Cort's turf with him laying down the rules.

"Mommy, where are you?"

"Right here, darling."

Glynis took another deep breath and pushed a

strand of breeze-tossed hair behind her ear, wondering if the nightmare would ever end.

"Long time no see, Glynis."

At the sound of the deep masculine voice, both Glynis and Todd looked up, startled. They were sitting at the wicker glass-topped table in the breakfast room, watching a black stallion prance around the paddock.

Maude was in the kitchen, busily and happily preparing breakfast. The smell of bacon crackling in the skillet filled the air with a delicious aroma.

"Hello, Barr," Glynis said, standing, a smile lighting her features. Even though he was years older, Barr had always held a special place in her heart, mainly because he'd been so good to Cort.

"Ah, surely you can do better than that." He smiled, a smile she knew did not come easily. "I'll settle for a small hug."

Glynis laughed and dived into Barr's outstretched arms. Following a crushing hug, he pushed her away and peered down at her from his towering six-foot-three height.

"You haven't changed—you're still as beautiful as ever."

"Ha, you haven't changed either. You're still as full of it as ever."

But he had changed. Like Cort, the shadows that lurked around his eyes were more pronounced. But then she had always known that would never go away, that he'd never escape memories of the untold horrors he'd experienced in Nam. And though he'd never had any permanent use for the opposite sex, for her there had always been warm words and hugs. Today was no exception.

Barr laughed, then switched his gaze to Todd, who was staring up at him with his mouth open. "You must be Todd," he said, walking over and holding out his hand.

Todd hesitantly placed his small one in Barr's large one. "Who are you?"

"Why, big fella, I'm your Uncle Barr."

With a puzzled frown on his face, Todd faced Glynis. "You mean he's my uncle, too?"

Glynis nodded. "That's right. He's...Uncle Cort's brother." She couldn't bring herself to look at Barr. "So you'll be seeing quite a lot of him while we're here," she rushed to add.

"That's right," Barr responded. "I own the ranch next to your...Uncle Cort."

Todd's eyes were round. "Do you have horses and cows, too?"

"Bigger and better than the ones here."

Again Todd's eyes sought his mother. "Really, Mom? Does he really?"

Glynis's lips twitched, and she shrugged. "Don't ask me."

"Can I come see 'em?" Todd asked, returning his gaze to Barr.

"Anytime you like."

"Gee, Mom, did you hear that?"

"Yes, son, I heard that."

Suddenly Maude came into the room, carrying a steaming bowl of eggs and a plate of bacon. "Mr. Barr, you want some breakfast?"

"Now, Maude, when have you known me to turn

down anything you cooked?" He massaged his flat stomach and grinned. "Without you, I'd starve to death."

Maude snorted before turning to Glynis. "The biscuits will be out of the oven shortly, Mrs. Hamilton."

"Please, Maude, call me Glynis."

The housekeeper looked momentarily disconcerted, then smiled. "All right, Glynis. How about some more coffee?"

Glynis glanced down at her empty cup and said, "I'd love some."

The minute Maude left, Glynis picked up Todd's plate and began filling it with the food.

"Aw, Mom, do I have to? I'm not hungry."

"Yes, you have to," she said sternly. "If you want to play outside today, you have to eat."

He sighed. "Okay."

"Your mom's right, son. If you plan to keep up with your Uncle Cort and me, you'd best clean your plate."

"Does that mean I can ride a horse?"

"We'll see," Glynis said, reaching for the cup of fresh coffee Maude had left on the table along with the pan of biscuits.

"Well, well, what have we here? Can anyone join the party?"

The low, rough voice came from directly behind Glynis. Her hand stilled, but her head jerked around almost of its own volition.

Cort was standing just inside the doorway.

Chapter 7

Glynis gripped her coffee cup with icy fingers and for a long moment the room was quiet.

She swept her gaze over him, taking in the faded blue cotton shirt unbuttoned to the coolness of the spring morning. Equally worn jeans hugged slim hips and long legs. Only when she reached his boots, dirty and scuffed with use, did she stop.

Cort moved then, drawing her gaze back to his. He completely unnerved her. Half the time she wanted to disappear when he came anywhere near, and half the time she couldn't resist the urge to needle him into noticing her.

He was scowling now, looking as if he'd bitten into something sour. Then he moved forward, the firm cadence of his boots on the tile effectively breaking the silence.

"Where you been, little brother?" Barr's tone was

deep and easy, as if he was oblivious to the tension in the room.

"Working," Cort said gruffly, "the same thing you should've been doing."

Barr raised his eyebrows. "Mmm, I see our disposition hasn't improved."

"My disposition is none of your business."

Both Glynis's and Todd's eyes vacillated between brothers, Todd's wide and confused, Glynis's wide and troubled. For the time being, she knew Cort was taking his anger out on his brother. But she knew that wouldn't last. If Todd hadn't been present, he would more than likely have lashed out at her.

If punishing her was what he wanted, then so be it. She could take whatever he dished out, as long as he helped their son.

"You still want me to come over and look at those cattle?" Cort was saying now, his tone minus the bite of a moment ago.

Barr crossed a booted foot over the opposite leg. "Sure do. In fact I'm counting on it."

While the men continued to exchange words, Glynis lowered her head and forced herself to take several bites of the bacon and eggs she'd put on her plate out of politeness rather than hunger. She hated the reactions Cort stirred in her, loss of appetite being one of them.

Suddenly she felt Cort's gaze swing back to her. At the same time Barr shoved back his chair and got to his feet.

"Glynis, I'd like to take Todd with me," Cort was saying. He twisted his mouth into a cold smile that matched the glacial color of his eyes. "That is, if you don't mind."

A frown crossed her face. "As a matter of fact, I…"

Barr chose that moment to cut in. "Hey, gang, I gotta be going." Then, turning to Todd, he added with an uncharacteristic wink, "I'll see you later, Todd."

"Oh, boy," Todd answered enthusiastically, just after he'd put a large forkful of eggs in his mouth.

"Don't talk with your mouth full," Glynis chastised softly.

"See y'all later," Barr announced, but only after he'd whispered something in Maude's ear that brought the color flooding to her face.

The minute the door shut behind him, Maude, whose color was still high, focused her attention on Cort. "Do you want to eat again? I'll be glad to warm the biscuits and eggs in the microwave."

Cort waved his hand, all the while staring at Glynis. "Thanks, Maude, but no thanks. I'm fine."

"How about you, Glynis? Do you care for anything else?"

Trying her best to ignore Cort's hostile gaze, Glynis smiled. "Heavens no, Maude. It was delicious, but I'm not used to eating much for breakfast. Todd and I both ate more than we're accustomed to."

"And it shows," Cort put in harshly, "especially on you. You never used to be as skinny as you are now."

"I never used to be a lot of things I am now," Glynis countered sharply, feeling the spark of battle ignite inside her. But then, when she saw Todd's reaction to her sharp tone, she forced another smile to hide the antagonism Cort aroused. Her son's face went pale, and he frowned up at her.

"Mom, are you mad at Uncle Cort?"

Glynis felt herself flush and hated it. "No, of course not."

Cort didn't say a word. He simply stood there with a smirk on his lips, as if he enjoyed her agitation and discomfort.

"Todd, honey, if you're through, why don't you run along and brush your teeth and change your shoes. Put on your old dirty ones."

"Then can we go see Uncle Barr?" he asked anxiously, directing his questions to Cort. "He told me his cows and horses were better than yours."

"Oh, he did, did he?" The corners of Cort's lips were twitching. "Well, just so you'll know, Barr likes to tease."

"Oh," was all Todd had to say.

His eyes still on the boy, Cort added, "How 'bout if I show you around the Lazy C, you and your mom? Anyway, I have something I want you to see."

"Neato," Todd gushed, scooting out of his chair and running toward the door that led to the hall.

"Hey, slow down, will you," Glynis called to his retreating back.

When she twisted back around, she sought out Cort's gaze. "Did you mean it when you included me?"

Cort had sat down and was leaning back in the chair, his strong, rugged features fully illuminated by the sun's powerful rays pouring through the blinds.

"What makes you think I didn't mean it?"

The unwavering study of his light-colored eyes and the soft mocking tone in which he spoke made Glynis vividly aware of the primitive charm he used to full advantage. Her heartbeat accelerated briefly, telling her to beware.

Pulling herself together in the nick of time, she dipped her head and took a sip of cold coffee, which nearly gagged her. Then, lifting her head once again, she forced her eyes to meet his.

"Because we both know you don't want me here, that's why," she said, her voice low and oddly breathless. "And why you insisted—"

"You know why I insisted." He ground his teeth together in anger. "You're right, I don't want you here. But I want my son, so…"

"If I'm part of the package deal, you'll just have to find a way to tolerate me, right?"

"Right."

Glynis stood up, her hands clenched by her side, and for another full second, speech was denied her. Finally she managed a jerky laugh. "You've turned into a real bastard," she spat.

"I had a good teacher. I…"

"Mr. Cort," Maude interrupted, standing at his elbow, obviously embarrassed if one was to judge from the heightened color in her round face, "you're wanted on the phone. It's…Mr. Ridley."

"Tell him I'll call him back," Cort replied brusquely, his gaze still holding firm on Glynis.

Maude merely nodded and then shuffled through the archway into the kitchen.

Glynis smiled coldly. "Look, since you have to work, Todd and I'll occupy ourselves."

"No."

Glynis blinked. "No?"

"I don't have to work. We'll take the tour together. Anyway, in light of Todd's reaction to our exchange of words, I think we need to put his mind at ease about…us."

"Does that mean you're willing to call a truce?"

He studied her as the uncomfortable silence stretched out. "Maybe."

Swallowing the angry retort that rose to her lips, Glynis spun around and flung over her shoulder, "As soon as I change shoes, I'll meet you outside."

Cort stood and watched until Glynis was out of sight. With a muttered curse, he strode down the opposite hall and into his office where he shut the door with a resounding thud.

He must have been out of his mind to think he could share the same space with Glynis and not let her get under his skin.

Even the way she dressed rubbed him the wrong way. Or was it because she looked so damn good in what she wore that his blood pressure had risen above the danger level? In that gold blouse the outline of her breasts had been as visible as yesterday when he'd run his palm across a hard, tight nipple. And then, the same as now, every nerve in his body had sizzled to life.

If that weren't enough, she'd looked at him with those big brown eyes filled with a shadowed pain, pain he knew hadn't come merely from her verbal skirmish with him. No, it was the pain of seeing her child suffer with a killing disease. As before, he'd found himself wanting to yank her into his arms, crush her against him and tell her that everything was going to all right.

But he couldn't touch her. Not again. Nor could he let her vulnerability affect his feelings. She had done him a grave injustice, and he must not forget that.

He sighed, recalling how amazed he'd been that a girl of her age could have wielded so much power over him.

Well, all that was in the past. No woman would ever again get her claws into him that deep.

Cort turned his head toward the bar in the far corner of the room and wished it wasn't too early for a stiff drink. A strong shot of Scotch might have soothed his nerves, stamped out that catastrophic desire for revenge that was tearing him apart.

He was so lost in thought that at first he couldn't identify the sound. Then it became glaringly clear. It was the phone, the private line in his office. Knowing that it would be his assistant in Houston, he muttered a sharp curse and reached across the desk for the receiver.

"McBride."

"Got a minute?" Gene Ridley asked.

"Shoot."

"Well, first off, I guess I ought to ask how you're feeling."

"Like hell."

Gene laughed, and Cort pictured his able assistant's face. He was more than likely slumped over the desk, leaning on his elbows, his eyebrows furrowed in concentration.

"I wish I could tell you something to ease your pain," Gene said, breaking into the short silence.

"Nothing yet on who's after Fisher?"

"Oh, I have a hunch, all right, but nothing concrete."

"How's Fisher?"

"A basket case, even though we've got men watching his house twenty-four hours a day."

"Maybe that'll teach him to stay out of the big leagues."

Gene gave an uncharacteristic snort. "I doubt that."

"Me, too," Cort said, grinning into the receiver. "It'll probably take another attempt on his life to make a true believer out of him."

"Oh, I don't know so much about that. He's pretty shook up. He came by the office twice yesterday, determined to talk to you. Said he hired you—" Gene stressed the *you* "—personally and that he wasn't happy that you had pulled a disappearing act."

"Why, that selfish SOB. Here I took the bullet that was meant for him and he's the one doing the bellyaching."

"Hope you don't mind, but I told him as much, and I also told him to back off and let McBride Security do its job."

"That's fine by me. Just go with your hunch. Something's bound to turn up."

"Will do."

"We both know it's a sure thing that whoever's after him will surface again, especially since Fisher can't come up with the money to pay off his debt."

"And next time they won't get the wrong person."

"Well, let's just make sure there's not a next time. I want the bastard who put that bullet in my gut."

"That goes without saying, boss."

They were both quiet for a second, both listening to the static crackling between the lines.

Then, changing the subject, Gene asked, "Has the doctor by any chance told you how much longer you're going to be out of commission?"

"Hell, no."

Gene laughed again. "I bet you could bite a ten-penny nail in two by now."

Cort chose his next words carefully. "You got that right. However, something's come up that's shed a new light on things."

"Personal, I take it."

"Very," Cort said, and then told him about Glynis and Todd.

There was a short silence.

"Damn, Cort. I mean that's heavy stuff. A son. God."

"I know. I'm still finding it hard to believe. All of it."

"Yeah, and the leukemia. That's bad."

Cort winced. "But he's going to make it," he said, a determined ring to his voice. "He'll have the very best money can buy."

"If there's anything I can do, just say the word."

"For now, see that you keep the business running on smooth wheels."

"No problem, there, especially since we've got the inside track on the government contract."

"That's good news. You know I want that contract about as bad as I've ever wanted anything."

"Yeah, it would be a challenge, wouldn't it, boss? Debugging an American embassy in a communist country doesn't come along every day."

"Nor does following it up with a new security system."

Gene's deep sigh filtered through the line. "Sounds awesome when you think about it. But I know the firm can handle it."

"I agree. So now all we have to do is get the bid. And here I am, can't do a damn thing to help. Some days just pushing a pencil tires me out."

"Hey, look on the bright side. A man who wasn't in your physical condition to begin with would probably be dead by now."

"That's comforting to know."

Gene chuckled, picking up immediately on the sarcasm in Cort's voice. "I'll be in touch in a day or so."

"Talk to you later, then."

"Oh, Cort, I…er…think it's great about…your kid. I mean that you have…one."

Cort put down the receiver and faced the back window. He stood watching the leaves sway in the gentle breeze until another vision filled his eyes.

Glynis rounded the corner of the house and was smiling down at her son scampering beside her. The sun bathed them both in its warm glow, casting an almost enchanted spell over mother and son. For a moment he was mesmerized, compassion stirring within him.

"You're a fool, Cort McBride."

Then, pivoting on the heel of his boots, Cort

stamped toward the door, but not before another expletive singed the air.

Glynis saw Cort coming toward her and stopped. His jerky gait alerted her to his mood, and her heart sank. She was hoping they could indeed call a truce for she truly didn't know how much longer she could handle Cort's volatile behavior.

Now, as they had done so often since her arrival at the ranch, his eyes sliced over her as he fell in step beside her, matching his stride to hers.

Glynis tensed, reacting to the gut instinct that warned her to tread lightly.

"Good morning again," she said, forcing an end to the growing silence.

"Is it?" His voice was low and cynical.

A knot twisted in her stomach while her lashes fluttered, forming a dark fringe above deepening brown eyes. "Cort, I...I thought..."

"Hi, Uncle Cort," Todd interrupted, dashing over to Cort's side, bestowing on him his toothless grin.

Cort purposefully slowed even more, matching Todd's grin. "Hi, yourself. Did you sleep okay last night?"

"Guess so."

"Good."

"Did you?" Todd asked with unchildlike candor.

Cort chuckled and simply shook his head. "Smart kid," he said turning to Glynis with the smile still intact.

"He is, isn't he," Glynis agreed weakly, suddenly finding her control being stripped away by his unexpected smile. For an instant the hostility faded. In its place was something more dangerous. Glynis had glimpsed the Cort of old. Suddenly she swallowed and turned away.

"You promised to show me something," Todd was saying to Cort. "'Member?"

"Sure, I remember," Cort said, his voice sounding raw. "In fact we're headed there now."

The barn was directly in front of them. Glynis presumed it was their ultimate destination but she was in no hurry to enter the barn's interior. It was lovely outside in the bright sunshine.

No doubt about it, the Lazy C was a showplace. And in spite of everything, she couldn't help but feel proud of Cort for beating the odds and making good. But she shouldn't have been surprised, she reminded herself; when Cort made up his mind about something, he went after it with a vengeance. That was precisely what scared her. If he ever made up his mind to take Todd...

Her son tugged on her hand. "Mom, we're here. Uncle Cort said the surprise is in there, but he won't tell me what it is."

Glynis touched Todd's cheek briefly with the back of her hand. "Well, if you know in advance, it won't be a surprise, right?"

Todd wrinkled his nose.

"Come on, young fella," Cort urged, pointing Todd toward the entrance.

Inside the barn was cool and much lighter than Glynis had anticipated. She stopped and folded her arms across her chest.

"Cold?"

Unwittingly Glynis encountered Cort's mocking

expression. "No, I just wasn't expecting it to be this cool, that's all," she said defensively, though she ached to slap the smirk off his face.

"Show me! Show me the surprise," Todd called from in front of them.

Cort turned his gaze from Glynis and upped his pace. "Hold your horses. I'm coming."

Determined not to be left out, Glynis quickened her steps behind Cort, only to pull up short. Cort had already come to a halt and was kneeling to her right along with Todd. All eyes were on a cardboard box with what looked like an old feed sack draped over the top.

"What's under there?" Todd asked in a hushed tone.

Without answering, Cort slowly and carefully lifted the covering off the box. A white mother cat was lying prone, and several tiny kittens were suckling at her breasts, kittens that reminded Glynis of tiny rats.

"Wow!" Todd whispered.

Glynis met Cort's eyes over Todd's bent head. And once again an electric current seemed to flow between them. Cort was the first to break the contact with a cough.

"They're something, aren't they?" he said to Todd.

Glynis's lashes dropped in confusion. However, before she could even think about deciphering the strange light she'd seen in Cort's eyes, Todd said, "Mom, are you looking?"

"I'm looking, son, I'm looking."

No one said a word for the longest time, each content to watch.

Finally Glynis forced herself to look at Cort again. "Can I talk to you a minute?"

Though he looked puzzled, he shrugged and got to his feet.

"Todd, honey," Glynis said, "you stay here with the kittens while I talk to Uncle Cort. But just look—don't touch them."

"Okay."

Glynis followed Cort to the end of the barn and into the sunlight. Once there, she came straight to the point.

"Before we came to meet you, I had a call from Dr. Johns."

Cort's eyes darkened. "Todd's doctor," he guessed quietly.

"Yes." She paused and took a deep breath, her face chalk-white.

"So what did he say?" Cort prompted.

"Day after tomorrow you're scheduled to have your bone marrow tested to see if you qualify as a donor."

Chapter 8

Glynis sat with hands clasped tightly together in her lap and stared at Dr. Eric Johns, her eyes so large they seemed to take up her whole face.

She and Cort had only moments before arrived at the Texas Children's Hospital and were now enclosed in the doctor's office along with two other physicians. Hammond Peavy and Burt Dupree were oncologists, the best in their field, or so Dr. Johns had said.

Following introductions, Cort had politely declined to sit and was standing to one side of Glynis, looking like a stranger in gray slacks, navy blazer and light gray ribbed shirt. He had all the markings of a highly successful business executive, Glynis thought, instead of a man who preferred the rugged outdoors.

After leaving an excited Todd in Barr's capable hands a few minutes after seven that morning, they had made the two-hour trip almost in silence. Cort had sat rigidly behind the wheel of his Jaguar and concentrated on the road, while Glynis had stared out the window with little interest in the scenery.

It was bad enough, Glynis had told herself, that they were both nervous about the test results, without having to endure the tension that filled the air.

But there had always been tension between them. The first time she met him, she had felt it and so had he. But it had been years later before Cort had actually put those feelings into words.

"Some relationships are chemical, but ours is electric," he'd said.

And he'd been right. Still, it rankled. She didn't want to feel anything for Cort. All she wanted was for her son to get well. Then she could get on with her life, a life that did not include Cort McBride.

Now, as Dr. Johns's gaze included them both, Glynis tried to pretend that she was in control, that her bloodstream wasn't filled with ice.

"Mr. McBride," Dr. Johns began, "I felt you needed to be brought up to date on exactly what's involved for both you and Todd. And of course to answer any questions you might have before we send you to the lab for the test."

"I assume it's a blood test," Cort said, looking as if he was still sizing up the doctor.

"You assume correctly," the doctor responded. "As soon as we're finished here, someone will accompany you to the lab and they'll take blood from a vein in your arm, providing you followed the instructions I gave Glynis over the phone."

"To the letter. I've had nothing to eat or drink, not even coffee, since before twelve last evening."

"Good. Now that that's settled, we can move on."

"Please," Glynis cut in anxiously, "how...how long will it be before we know the results of the test?" Although she spoke directly to Eric Johns, her eyes encompassed the other two doctors.

It was Johns who answered her, his expression kind and his tone gentle. "Two or three hours at the most. During that time I'm sure Mr. McBride would like something to eat. Maybe by the time he's done, we'll know."

Glynis nodded her thanks, though she wanted to shout her relief that they wouldn't have to wait overnight. Stealing a quick glance in Cort's direction, she noticed that he, too, seemed visibly relieved. His features were no longer quite as taut and forbidding.

"What exactly will the test tell us?" Cort was asking.

"Your blood antigens must match those of your son, Mr. McBride."

"Perfectly?"

Shaking his head, Dr. Peavy spoke for the first time. "No, although it would be great if they did."

"But if they don't?" Cort pressed, focusing his entire attention on the broad-faced doctor with thinning blond hair.

"Then we'll still be able to use you, as long as all your antibodies don't cross with your son's."

Cort shoved a hand into his pocket. "So if it's a go, what exactly will take place?"

Dr. Johns turned to his right. "Why don't you answer that, Dr. Dupree? After all, you'll be doing the transplant."

Burt Dupree had dark hair and dark eyes and was

not more than five-foot-seven in height. But that was hardly noticeable as his muscles were honed to perfection, making him appear much bigger than he actually was. He was young and seemed confident of his ability.

"If you are our donor, Mr. McBride, and we'll keep the faith that you will be," Dr. Dupree said with confidence, stepping from the window to Dr. Johns's desk, where he perched on the edge of it, "you'll be taken to surgery along with your son."

Cort placed his hand on the back of Glynis's chair. "Go on, Doctor."

"We'll be concentrating on the pelvic area, where there is an abundance of bone marrow."

"Will I be under anesthetic?"

"Yes, but not for long." He paused a moment before continuing, as if to let Glynis as well as Cort digest what he was saying. "Then I'll insert needles into that soft area and extract the tissue."

"How...many times will you...stick him?" Glynis asked, a lump forming in her throat.

"Approximately two hundred."

Glynis sucked in her breath.

Cort merely asked in a calm voice, "What else?"

But Glynis sensed he was anything but calm. She could hear his breath rattling in his chest, and a muscle pulsed in his jaw. Suddenly she felt a twinge of sympathy she didn't want to feel.

"That's all." Dr. Dupree inclined his head. "The entire procedure will take approximately two to three hours."

"And Todd?" Glynis asked, feeling Cort's brooding gaze swing to her. She kept her eyes averted.

Dr. Dupree's face filled with regret. "I wish I could tell you the boy will have it as easy, but I'm afraid I cannot."

"You mean he'll be in a lot of pain?" Glynis asked tremulously.

"No, he'll be sick to his stomach, just as he was when he took those massive doses of chemotherapy in the early stages of the disease," Dr. Dupree explained. "A few days before we do the actual transplant, we'll give him higher doses of radiation and chemo in order to wipe out his bone marrow."

"Oh, God," Glynis whispered, turning her tormented face up to Cort, who had moved closer to her. For an instant she thought he was going to touch her.

"Take it easy," he said instead, staring at her intently while he dropped his arm limply back to his side.

Then Cort dragged his eyes away and looked at Dr. Dupree. "Then what?" he asked, not bothering to hide his own pain.

"Well, once he's free of his own marrow, we'll insert yours intravenously into his right arm."

"And pray," Glynis added under her breath.

Dr. Dupree went on as if she hadn't spoken. "He'll have to be isolated, of course."

Cort frowned. "Isolated?"

"Placed in a sterile environment to prevent him from being infected. Do you remember the youngster called 'David the bubble boy' who was quarantined for years in a sterile bubble? Well, that's the same procedure we'll use with Todd."

"How long before we know if my marrow takes?" Cort's mouth was thin.

Dr. Dupree stood. "The white blood cells should start reproducing within a week. As for the red cells, they sometimes take up to a hundred and twenty days. And during that time he might need some transfusions."

"God Almighty," Cort muttered, glancing sideways at Glynis, his features pale and grim.

But Glynis could offer no comfort. She couldn't stand the thought of Todd having to endure any more pain. It just wasn't fair. In his young life he had already endured more than his fair share, more than any human ought to have to withstand during an entire lifetime. The thought of him suffering again from the poisons in the radiation and chemotherapy made her want to run screaming from the room, even if the means justified the end.

As if able to read Glynis's thoughts, Eric Johns made his way to her side and patted her shoulder. "I know how upset you are, my dear, but remember the outcome can buy your son a lifetime of good health. And without the transplant..." He paused and shook his head.

"I know," Glynis said, feeling the sting of hot tears behind her lashes, "the leukemia will return."

Cort let out his pent-up breath. "How can you know that for sure?"

"Nothing is for sure, of course, Mr. McBride," Dupree said. "However, with the type of leukemia your son has, the chance of it recurring if he doesn't have a transplant is in the ninety-percent range. And that's based on statistics."

"What about rejection?" Glynis asked, rising to

her feet, her face a study in misery. "What if he rejects Cort's marrow? Will...will my son die?"

That last question alone was heartbreaking, and for a moment no one said a word.

Then Cort spoke, his voice toneless. "Well, Doctor, aren't you going to answer her question?"

"The possibility of rejection is there," Dr. Dupree said, bypassing the question of death. "We all know that. But there are drugs that we'll give Todd to try to prevent it, and in the past, the drugs have done their job in most cases."

"That's some comfort anyway," Glynis said from her position by the window, her eyes straying to Cort. His lips were set in a taut line, and an artery pulsed in his temple. For a crazy second she longed to go to him and beg him to take her in his arms, hold her, comfort her as he'd done so often in the past. But that was then and this was now. And everything had changed.

"There will be several factors to consider before we can proceed, however," Dr. Dupree was saying, his gaze shifting back and forth between Glynis and Cort. "One in particular."

For an instant Glynis just stared at the ceiling. Then in a voice that was barely discernible, she asked, "What?"

Dupree thrust a hand over his thick hair. "Mr. McBride's physical condition."

The words caught Glynis by surprise, though she should have been prepared. Hadn't Cort warned her?

However, before she could say anything, Cort asked, "You're referring to my gunshot wound?" His words were clipped.

"Yes, I am." The doctor spoke quietly.

"It's going to delay it, isn't it?" Glynis's tone was flat.

"Now, Glynis," Dr. Johns put in calmly, "don't get upset. Dr. Dupree is merely pointing out what could happen. We have to cover all the bases. We'll know more, of course, when we get the result of Mr. McBride's blood test."

"What you're saying, Doctor, is my blood loss could be a factor in how soon the transplant takes place?"

"Yes, for the simple reason that your hemoglobin count could be low. And the blood transfusions you've had could also be a factor. Two or three weeks won't make any difference," he went on to reassure them, "or at least we hope not. But under the circumstances there's nothing we can do about it."

"I don't understand," Glynis cried, struggling in confusion and shock. "Why would Cort having had a transfusion make a difference?"

"Because," Dr. Dupree said with gentle patience, "it goes back to the antibodies I just mentioned. They'll be foreign and therefore subject to rejection by both father and son."

Glynis glared at Cort, her face bloodless, her lips so stiff she could barely speak. "Oh, God," she whimpered. Then, on legs threatening to cave beneath her, she crossed back to her chair and sank down weakly into it, all the while wanting to lash out at Cort. Once again his eagerness for danger and adventure had become a source of heartache. This time he had inadvertently put his son's life in danger. Damn him.

''Let's just get the test over and done with,'' Cort said tightly, completely ignoring Glynis.

Dr. Johns punched a button on his intercom. ''Anne, please show Mr. McBride to the lab.''

Glynis watched Cort as he crossed the room to the door, but when he turned around, she lowered her head. It was only after she heard the door close that she looked up, squeezing her eyelids shut to hold back the tears.

When you wanted time to pass quickly, it never failed to move at a snail's pace, or so Glynis told herself, standing at the window in Dr. Johns's office, her back to Cort. But then, playing the waiting game was never easy.

Cort had gone to the lab and had gotten his test, and as soon as he'd finished, Glynis had met him outside the lab and they had gone to the cafeteria. But neither had eaten much. Although Glynis had chosen chicken salad, which looked palatable enough, and a glass of iced tea, she barely touched it.

Cort, too, had been uninterested in food, taking only several bites of his turkey sandwich, before all but throwing it down on his plate.

After that, they had sat in silence and avoided each other's eyes.

Glynis had known she was being unreasonable to blame Cort, if indeed the transplant had to be postponed. But it was the principle of the matter, she'd told herself. If he'd had a normal job like most men, they wouldn't be in this predicament.

Yet regardless of the unrealistic blame she'd placed squarely on his shoulders and regardless of the contempt she had seen in his eyes, she'd been aware of his menacing strength beside her.

The atmosphere between them had not improved after they had left the cafeteria and trudged heavy-hearted back to the doctor's office, where they were now waiting for the result of the test with mounting impatience.

"Everything's going to work out all right," Cort said suddenly, unexpectedly, having stopped his pacing in the middle of the room. His gaze was fixed on Glynis.

"I wish I could be that sure." Her voice sounded strangled.

"It's a cheap shot to blame me, you know."

She didn't pretend to misunderstand him. "Maybe, but that's the way I feel."

"You're determined to exact your pound of flesh, aren't you?"

There was a moment of charged silence as Glynis fought to control her pounding heart. Then, before she could say anything, the door opened, admitting both doctors.

"Well, Doctor, what's the verdict?" Cort asked, hardly breathing, hardly moving.

The recessed fluorescent tube in the ceiling flickered. No one paid it the slightest attention.

Dr. Johns smiled. "For reasons we explained to you, Mr. McBride, there will definitely be a postponement. But as far as a match is concerned, you are perfect."

Chapter 9

"Where's Todd?"

Glynis was sitting at the kitchen table, coffee cup in hand, staring into space when she heard the low, brusque voice.

Twisting around, she watched as Cort sauntered into the room, his jeans riding low on his hips. She looked up quickly and was shocked at his appearance. Lines of fatigue were etched deeply about the corners of his bloodshot eyes. And he looked as if he hadn't slept in a week.

But then neither had she. After they had returned from Houston and picked up Todd at Barr's, she had been exhausted, as much from the strain of being in such close contact with Cort as from meeting with the doctors.

Once they had arrived at the ranch, Cort had disappeared in his office, leaving her and Todd to their own devices, which had been fine by her.

Maude had prepared their dinner, and after they had eaten and watched an hour of TV, Glynis had put Todd to bed. A short time later she'd crawled between the covers herself. But again sleep had eluded her, her thoughts centered on the many reasons why she should leave the Lazy C.

The situation was impossible, threatening to become more so by the day. For the moment, however, Cort had the upper hand, and she had no choice but to try to make the best of it.

Cort made his way to the coffeepot and began generously filling a cup. Without turning around, he repeated, "Where's Todd?"

"Sleeping," Glynis said to his back, observing the way his shoulder muscles rippled with each move he made. Abruptly she turned away, irritated with herself for noticing anything personal about him.

Cort faced her. "At this hour?"

"It's only eight o'clock, Cort," Glynis said with controlled patience. "Anyway, he's used to sleeping late, especially after he got sick," she added in defense of her son, sensing that Cort was being critical. "When he's well enough to enter school, he'll have to be up before seven. That time will come faster than we think—I hope."

Cort didn't say anything for a moment, merely drained the bottom out of his cup.

"Why?" Glynis finally asked. "Did you want him for something?"

"As a matter of fact I did."

"Oh." She let out a breath slowly and nodded. They were behaving like polite strangers instead of one-time lovers who had reveled in the touch and feel of each other.

"Thought I'd take him with me and Barr to look at some horses."

Glynis frowned, and at the same time ran her hand through her silky mane, all the while feeling Cort's eyes track her every move.

"I don't know," she said, shifting in her chair.

He let out an impatient sigh. "What do you mean you don't know?"

Glynis rolled her tongue across her top lip. "Well, I'd planned to go into town to visit Milly and let Todd play with her twins."

"Spare me the excuses." He batted the air in disgust. "You just can't stand the thought of me being alone with my son, can you?"

Glynis looked at Cort a second longer than necessary and then got up and walked to the coffeepot, careful to avoid contact with him.

"Answer me!" Cort demanded once she'd refilled her cup.

Glynis let out a rush of air. "That's not true," she said.

"Prove it, then." His tone was soft, too soft.

"All right," she snapped, "take him with you."

He uttered a muffled oath and slammed his cup down on the counter. Glynis jumped, and their gazes collided.

"And that's not all," he said.

Her heart lurched. "What do you mean?"

"Later this evening I want to take him to the carnival that's out at the VFW grounds."

Glynis dug her fingernails into her palms. "I don't know..."

"Damn, here we go again." Clearly exasperated, he stared at the ceiling, a vein in his jaw pulsing. "What's wrong with him going to the carnival?"

Outside the birds chirped in the huge oak tree nearest the house, but neither Cort nor Glynis was aware of the uplifting sound.

Glynis thought desperately. "It's just that carnivals scare me. I'm afraid of the rides...." Again she let her voice trail off.

"I expect you to come along, if that's any consolation."

She flushed at the sarcasm in his tone, but hers was as crisp as ever. "My being there still doesn't alleviate the problem of Todd getting on those rides. He's never been to a—"

"You mean you've never taken him to a carnival?" Cort interrupted harshly.

"No," she shot back defensively. "And I just told you why. It...was...it is too dangerous."

His look was savage. "Does that go for everything else that pertains to fun?"

"I don't have to justify my actions to you!"

"That's where you're wrong." He was looming over her now. "The days of you turning him into a mama's boy are over."

"How dare you tell me how to rear my son."

"Oh, I dare all right, and with good reason."

"He still needs mothering, in spite of what you think."

"Mothering maybe, but not smothering. There's a difference."

"You don't know what you're talking about. For the better part of his life, he's been too sick, too weak to do the things other kids were able to do. And now..."

"And now, when he's feeling good, you're still holding him back, not giving him a chance to be a boy."

"That's ridiculous!"

"No, it isn't."

"Well, there are worse things than being a mama's boy. For starters, the subhuman you've become."

Cort grabbed her upper arm and jerked her against him. She landed with a thud against his rock-hard chest. His breath burned her face with each word he spoke. "You don't know what the meaning of subhuman is yet, Mrs. Hamilton. But I promise you, if you keep pushing, you're sure as hell going to find out!"

His eyes continued to drill into her, and she could feel his fury. "We'll forget the day's activity, but this evening we will go to the carnival."

"Why, you..."

"Am I interrupting anything?"

Cort released her abruptly, and Glynis turned horrified eyes on Barr McBride.

For a moment no one said a word.

Then Cort faced Glynis and in a deceptively soft tone said, "Remember what I said."

She didn't say a word. Instead she flashed him a murderous look and walked through the door with her head held high and her shoulders squared.

The silence lasted.

The sun warmed the ground with its golden rays.

The sky was baby blue. The trees were tall and straight and perfectly shaped. The grass was so green it looked artificial.

Cort stood at the window and watched the spectacular show of nature with disinterested eyes. At the same time he ignored his brother.

He had already finished off his second mug of coffee, which had done nothing to cure what ailed him.

"Wanna tell me what that was all about?" Barr asked.

Cort didn't move, listening with half an ear to the scraping sound Barr made when he pulled out a chair and sat down. Then finally, feeling like an idiot, Cort shrugged and turned around. "You want some coffee?"

"Nope. I've already had enough to sink a battleship. Thanks anyway."

"Well, I haven't," Cort responded flatly, stalking to the counter and once again filling his cup to the brim.

"From the looks of things," Barr remarked, not put off in the least by the grim expression on Cort's face, "you screwed up by insisting Glynis stay here."

Cort's scowl deepened. "I had no other choice."

"Sure you did."

"No, I didn't," Cort said with more certainty in his voice than he felt. "It was the only way for me to get acquainted with my son. And even that's turning into a battle royal."

"So that's what the…uh…disagreement was about?"

"She doesn't want me around him." Cort's words

were spoken bitterly. "Actually that's putting it mildly. She loathes the sight of me and cannot bear for me to touch the boy."

Barr sighed and pushed his Stetson farther back on his head. "Maybe if you give her more time."

"Time, hell. She's already robbed me of six years. Isn't that enough?"

"Yes, but..."

Cort glowered at his brother. "Whose side are you on, anyway?"

Barr held up his hands in mock surrender. "Hey, calm down. Truth is I'm not on anybody's side."

When Cort didn't say anything, Barr went on, "Just think about it a minute, use your head, dammit. When it comes to the boy, neither of you should be taking sides. Todd's not a bone to be picked over—he's a sick little boy who needs both his mother and his father."

"That's exactly what I tried to tell Glynis, only she won't listen. Hell, man, Todd's under my roof, but for all the good it's doing me, he may as well be living in South Africa."

"It's only natural that she's protective."

"Yeah, too protective to suit me."

"Well, one thing's for sure, you can't keep on like this. Whether you wanna face it or not, Todd's a long way from being well, and the two of you arguing all the time isn't going to help him or the situation."

A nerve in Cort's jaw twitched. "I know."

"So why don't you kiss and make up?"

Cort didn't crack a smile over Barr's attempted humor. His taciturn face remained unchanged. "Funny."

"Hell, Cort, lighten up or you're going to be in worse shape than you are now."

"And just what's that supposed to mean?"

"I've seen the way you look at her."

Cort's jaw instinctively clenched in anger, and his grinding teeth were visible through slightly parted lips. "I don't know what you're talking about."

But he did know, even though admitting it was like the taste of quinine on his tongue. He was having one helluva time looking and not touching. He wanted to kiss her until she begged for mercy. His idea of heaven was falling asleep with the taste of her on his lips and her body hot and pulsating around him, trapping him as he drove deeply into her.

"Don't pull that dumb act with me," Barr was saying.

Cort expelled a ragged breath and forced his attention back on his brother.

"You know very well what I'm talking about. She's working on you just like she used to."

"That's enough," Cort responded.

If Barr heard the steel in Cort's tone, he ignored it. "The way I see it, you've been without a woman too long, little brother. You're like a big bear with a sore paw."

"You're a fine one to be talking. When's the last time a woman warmed your bed?"

Barr raised a heavy eyebrow. "We're not talking about me. We're talking about you and your relationship with Glynis."

"Past relationship, you mean," Cort muttered, tasting bitterness again.

Barr shrugged. "I hope you mean that. I'd hate to

have to put Humpty Dumpty back together like I did after she married Jay.''

Suddenly Cort felt dead inside. "You won't," he muttered without expression.

"Whatever you say," Barr concluded. "But it all goes back to the fact that if you can't handle the situation, you shouldn't have brought them here."

"What would you have done?" The hard note was back in Cort's voice. "You know the condition Dorothy's house is in. I couldn't let them stay there. Anyway," he added darkly, "I need to be near my son for more reasons than are obvious. She's turning him into a sissy."

"I don't rightly agree with that," Barr drawled, spreading his legs more comfortably under the table. "Under the circumstances, it's only natural that Glynis would tend to be overprotective. At the risk of repeating myself, your son is a very sick little boy."

"Don't you think I know that?"

"Well then, ease up on Glynis."

Cort didn't bother to control his irritation. "Hell, Barr, you make me out to be an insensitive jerk."

A smile flirted with Barr's lips. "Well."

"So I'm an ass."

"You said it. I didn't."

Cort regarded Barr impatiently. "I know the kid's been through hell. Every time I look at him I get sick to my stomach and I want to pound my fist through the first door I come to, because I know his suffering's not over."

Barr nodded with understanding and didn't say anything. There wasn't anything to say.

"That's why I don't want Todd to miss out on being a little boy while he's healthy. Does that make sense?"

"Yeah. Only I'm not the one you need to convince."

"Don't remind me," Cort bit out. "I'd almost rather tangle with a bull."

Barr laughed outright. "Can't say I blame you. She's sure developed one helluva temper. It makes her even more beautiful."

"Knock it off, Barr!" Cort's voice cracked.

"Sorry," Barr said, but he didn't sound sorry, especially as he followed his apology with a broad smile. Then, standing, he reached for the Stetson he'd removed from his head and tossed on the knob of the adjacent chair. Once he'd jammed it back on his head, he added without the smile, "You aren't thinking what I think you're thinking, are you?"

"Depends on what you're thinking."

"You're not by any chance going to try to get custody of Todd, are you?"

"The thought has crossed my mind, yes."

Barr shook his head and let out a sharp breath. "I just hope you know what the hell you're doing."

Cort's face was lined and sober. "So do I, big brother. So do I."

"Mommy, hurry. Uncle Cort's waiting. I know he is."

"I'm hurrying, I'm hurrying," Glynis said from the bathroom. "Believe me, honey, it won't hurt him to wait."

"Will too."

Though Glynis heard the petulant ring in her son's voice, she chose to ignore it this one time, knowing it stemmed more from impatience and excitement. And tiredness, too, she suspected, though he'd just awakened from an hour-long nap. They had spent most of the day at Milly's, and Todd had played nonstop for hours with her boys.

Now, as she pulled on her clothes, Glynis tried not to think of what lay ahead of her.

Following her confrontation with Cort this morning, she had felt restless and uneasy. What did he hope to achieve by harassing her like that, making her play by his rules? And if she didn't, would he really try to take Todd away from her? Or was it another ploy to further punish her, like the times he purposely touched her.

If he knew those unprovoked attacks on her senses had aroused more than disgust inside her, he'd be unbearable. Every time she thought of those moments in his arms, fear swept over her.

"Mom!"

Forcing a lightness into her expression, Glynis glanced in the mirror one last time, giving her loose curls one last pat. "All right, son, all right," she mumbled under her breath, silently cursing the impatience of youth.

Then, closing a fist around the knob, she opened the door, only to come to a sudden standstill.

Cort, freshly showered and shaved, stood just inside the room. Her first thought was how well his ever-present jeans and casual shirt fit his lean body.

His gaze flickered coolly over her apricot jumpsuit,

then his eyes narrowed as they came to rest on the sensuous beauty of her hair.

"Don't ever cut your hair," he said unexpectedly, his tone low and brusque.

Her breathing was uneven. "I...I hadn't planned on it," she murmured inanely.

"Uncle Cort, can we go now?" Todd asked in a small voice.

After another moment's hesitation, Cort lowered his gaze to the child and smiled. "You bet we can."

Todd giggled. "I can't wait. I've never been to a carnival before. My friend Jeremy told me they have lots of scary rides. I want to ride them all." His voice gushed with enthusiasm.

"Now, Todd, you know you can't do all the things Jeremy can."

Todd's lower lip began to tremble. "But, Mommy, I wanna..."

"Don't start whining or we won't go at all." Glynis rarely reprimanded him, especially in front of other people. This time, however, she had no choice, for not only did she have to impress upon him that he must obey her, she had to get the point across to Cort that she was in charge.

Todd lowered his head while his shoulders drooped. Then looking up, he said, "I need to go to the bathroom."

Cort laid a hand on the boy's shoulder. "It's all right. We'll wait."

Once Todd had closed the bathroom door, Cort stepped closer to her, the corners of his mouth turned down. "I warned you not to hover and I meant it."

She glared up at him, her face bloodless, her lips

so stiff she could barely speak. "And I warned you about interfering."

"You'll lose if you try to fight me, so I suggest you don't even try." All was delivered quietly, but with a menace that was unmistakable.

Glynis lifted her arm, but before her hand could make contact with the contours of his cheek, his fingers closed around her wrist like a manacle.

He simply smiled, as though her action had been expected. Shifting his gaze to a point beyond her shoulder, he said, "Ah, Todd, you're ready. Good. Let's go."

How Glynis got her purse and followed them outside to the car, she could never remember. She felt numb, and the evening stretched ahead, long and treacherous. She should never have agreed to this outing, she told herself despairingly when Todd was installed in the back seat and she had joined Cort in the front.

But then she hadn't been given much choice, had she?

Glynis stood alone at the edge of the trees that bordered the carnival grounds, though the sounds of voices and music were close behind her. She had separated herself from Cort and Todd and come to the rest room with the excuse of washing the cotton candy off her hands. In reality she had craved time away from Cort's overpowering presence.

Dusk was fast approaching, bringing a slight chill to the air. However, she knew the bumps that dotted her skin had nothing to do with the weather, though she could safely say the evening had transpired without event.

She had made every step Todd and Cort had made, yet she had felt as though she were on the outside looking in. Despite Cort's threat, he hadn't let Todd on the more sophisticated rides, holding him to the rides geared to his own age, such as the bumper cars and the hobbyhorses.

"See, I'm not the monster you make me out to be," he'd retorted in a mocking tone, which she'd ignored.

But for the most part her aloofness went unnoticed. Todd had eyes only for Cort. Glynis was stunned at the way he chatted with Cort, as if he'd known him always, laughing and joking with him and asking him questions that Glynis herself wouldn't have dared ask. And Cort was equally enthralled with Todd. It made her wonder if indeed there was something special about a blood relationship.

It was a sense of uneasiness that suddenly jolted her back to the moment at hand. She was experiencing the same eerie feeling she'd had when Cort had crept up on her unannounced at her aunt's house.

With her heart palpitating, Glynis swung around, positive she would encounter hostile eyes staring at her. But there was no one lurking in the shadows.

A man's back was visible as he leaned against a hotdog stand, seemingly more interested in wolfing down the hotdog than in her. But long after she'd turned back around, that feeling of unease persisted. She shivered visibly and all but ran headlong into the throng of people with their excited voices and smiling faces.

"Glynis!"

Cort's puzzled exclamation had never been more welcome. He came striding toward her with Todd at his heels. Hardly aware of what she was doing, she ran to him and caught herself just before she would have lunged into his arms.

He grabbed her hands to steady her. "What is it? What the hell happened?"

Chapter 10

"Are you sure that's all?"

Glynis massaged the back of her neck and stared up at Cort. "I'm sure. I just overreacted, that's all."

They were still standing at the edge of the fairgrounds, and as the minutes passed Glynis was feeling more like a fool. What had come over her? What had possessed her to think that someone was watching her with evil intent? She had never lost control like that before over something so insignificant. Her nerves were apparently more frayed than she'd thought. Still, that didn't excuse her weird behavior.

"For it not to have been anything, you're sure pale as hell," Cort was saying. He stood so close she could see his chest heaving.

"Mommy, are you okay?" Todd interjected, his small hand nestled tightly in hers.

Transferring her gaze down to her son, Glynis

squeezed his hand and gave him a reassuring smile, realizing that her fear had communicated itself to Todd as well.

"Mommy's fine, son, really I am."

"Good. Can we go back and play some more?" His blue eyes, so like Cort's, darted back and forth between the two adults. "Can we?"

More embarrassed now by her overactive imagination than anything, Glynis was so eager to put the incident behind her that she would have agreed to anything, even Todd's demands.

But Cort had other ideas.

"No more, Todd," Cort said, shaking his head. "Your mother's had a...slight shock, and you've had enough excitement for one day."

To Glynis's surprise Todd didn't argue, but he did turn with longing back to the rides.

Cort squeezed the shoulder nearest him and smiled. "Maybe we'll get to come back before the carnival leaves."

Todd's eyes lighted. "Can Adam and Kyle come with us?"

"We'll see." Then to Glynis, "You ready to go?"

"If you are," she murmured, avoiding his eyes.

Cort hesitated a second longer, then sighed deeply. "Come on," he said, propelling Todd forward. "Let's go home."

The drive back to the ranch was pleasant. Deliberately keeping the conversation light, Cort was an amusing companion, and Todd appeared delighted that his mother was back to normal and was joining in the nonsensical chatter.

Todd, however, was worn out and soon drifted to

sleep in the back seat. Cort turned to make sure Todd was sleeping soundly. Then, his eyes on the road again, he said, "You're right, this wasn't a very good idea."

Glynis glanced sideways at him. "Considering the way it started off, what did you expect?"

"For which I'm to blame, right?"

Glynis concentrated on picking a string off one leg of her jumpsuit. "I didn't say that."

"You don't have to." His voice was flat.

Glynis shook her head helplessly. "It…doesn't matter about me."

"No, I guess it doesn't," he muttered harshly. "All that really matters is *my* son and the fact that he had a good time."

The way he stressed the word *my* was not lost on Glynis. But once again she schooled her features to show no emotion.

"We can't go on like this, you know," Cort said, following a short silence. "We need to talk."

"Isn't that what we've been doing?" She knew she was being deliberately obtuse, but for the moment that was her only defense against him, against the pull of his powerful masculinity. And it wasn't just that he looked so good and smelled so good. It was more, much more.

She didn't want to talk to him, nor did she want to be confined in the car with him. Her attraction was too strong to deny, and Glynis felt a quiver run through her body as she turned away, feeling a sense of incredulity that she had ever defied him.

"No, we haven't been talking," he said, forcing her thoughts back on track. "We've been arguing."

"Oh, Cort, there's nothing else to say. It's all been said. As soon as the transplant is done and Todd is back on his feet, we'll go on with our lives and you'll go on with yours."

"And never the twain shall meet. Is that what you're saying?"

"No...that's not what I'm saying."

"Well, it sure as hell sounded like that to me."

"Why do you persist in making things so difficult? I intend to...to let you see Todd."

"At your whim?"

"No, at the court's."

"No judge is going to dictate to me."

"You won't have a choice."

"Like hell I won't. For God's sake, Glynis, Todd's my son. My flesh and blood. And I'll be damned if I'm going to cater to you in this."

A quick jolt of fear turned her stomach. Now was no time to go off the deep end, she cautioned herself. She fought her paranoia. He didn't mean it. *He couldn't mean it.* He was merely doing what he did best, which was to torment her, extract his pound of flesh in degrees.

Nonetheless, she noticed that when she tried to speak, her breath was coming in short gasps, and it took several steady gulps of air to steady herself. "Cort, you have your career, your ranch. Those are the only two things you've ever wanted."

"Maybe I've changed."

She chewed painfully on her lower lip. "I doubt that. You're still the most selfish person I know."

She heard his sharp intake of breath, and at the same time she felt his hot glance pierce her. "I'd be careful if I were you, Glynis. I'd be very careful, in fact. Just because I was once crazy enough to bury myself deep inside you…''

A choking sob broke from her lips. "You're despicable!"

"But I made my point, right?" His eyes flickered over her. "I used to let you say and do things to me that no woman has since, but that doesn't mean I'm going to now."

Glynis turned her head and stared blindly out the window. "Oh, you made your point, all right," she said bitterly.

Cort cursed softly, and then controlled himself. "Look, I'm prepared to let bygones be bygones. Would you meet me halfway?"

"There's no halfway mark with us, Cort. What you said just now proved it."

"All it proved is that you're not as indifferent to me as you'd like me to believe."

Glynis was glad for the darkness so he couldn't see the color flood into her cheeks. "You're flattering yourself. Besides, we're not discussing us. We're discussing Todd."

"Need I remind you, Todd is *us*. We made him."

Following that sobering rejoinder, Glynis's stomach did an odd little flip, and for a moment she was at a loss for words. Then, recovering, she whispered, "What…what we shared was a lifetime ago."

"Are you sure?" His voice sounded hoarse.

"Yes, I'm sure."

"When I touched you at Dorothy's house, you weren't exactly repulsed."

Glynis swung around to face him. She could hear

her heart pounding as if she'd been running a marathon. "Just because you caught me off guard doesn't mean I'm dying to jump in bed with you!" she spat. "Though you may find it hard to believe, I don't want you to touch me."

A stifling silence followed before they heard a movement from the back seat. Suddenly Todd's face appeared between the seats; he was rubbing one eye with the back of his hand, his lower lip extended slightly.

"Mommy, I thought you and Uncle Cort liked each other."

"Oh, Todd," Glynis cried.

"You told me you were friends." His lower lip was trembling.

"We are," Cort put in, the tension draining from his features.

"Then why are you fighting?"

Glynis ran a finger down one of his soft cheeks. "I'm sorry if we woke you up. We…didn't mean to."

"But I want you and Uncle Cort to be friends, Mommy," Todd went on with childlike resolve.

"We are, darling, we are."

There was another silence as Todd scrambled over the seat to sit in Glynis's lap. Once he was snuggled against her, she cast a look in Cort's direction. Even though his profile was unclear to her, she sensed his expression was carved in granite. At that moment, he steered the car under a streetlight, and her premonition proved correct. An artery throbbed in his neck, and deep lines pulled at the side of his mouth.

Suddenly she felt her heart constrict. She was crazy to feel sorry for him. He more than deserved her censure after the things he'd said to her, the way he'd treated her. She was a fool to give his feelings a second thought.

"I'm hungry, Mommy," Todd was saying as Cort brought the car to a stop in front of the house.

"Good. When we get inside, I'll fix you something to eat." Even to herself, her voice sounded disjointed, her mind still reeling from her tormenting thoughts.

"Uncle Cort, will you eat with me?"

Glynis and Cort exchanged a brief glance.

"That's up to your mother." His expression seemed to open slightly, revealing a wisp of uncertainty.

A sense of utter futility overwhelmed Glynis. "By all means, eat with him," she said weakly.

By the time they got inside, Todd was scampering ahead, motioning for Cort to follow him. Glynis kept her head lowered, dreading the moment when she would tell Cort her plans, plans that had been on her mind for days, but that had taken on new meaning in light of their verbal skirmish. She knew she could not put it off any longer.

Out of the corner of her eye, Glynis saw that Todd had Cort cornered in the den, showing him some rocks he had collected at Milly's. She, in turn, headed toward the kitchen to see if there were any leftovers in the refrigerator. If not, she would make them all cheese omelets.

But she need not have worried; there was plenty of shaved ham, fresh tomatoes and a pot of Maude's homemade vegetable soup.

In spite of Glynis's trepidation, the meal passed without incident. Glynis concentrated on her food, refusing to dwell on the time when Todd would go to bed and leave her alone with Cort. Sitting at the opposite end of the table, Cort, too, ate with relish, having rolled up the sleeves of his cotton shirt, which exposed his arms, tanned and muscular.

She kept her eyes off him for fear of what she would see reflected in his. However, Cort's attention was focused exclusively on Todd as he encouraged him to eat.

"Mmm, that was delicious," Cort said at last, downing his second cup of coffee, his eyes still on Todd. "How about you and me pitching in and doing the dishes for Mommy?"

Todd frowned. "Aw, gee, Uncle Cort, that's sissy stuff."

"Yeah, Uncle Cort, that's sissy stuff," Glynis chimed in sarcastically.

She knew immediately she had scored with her barb. Color surged into his face, and his mouth flattened into a straight line. "We're talking about apples and oranges, and you know it," he said.

Glynis merely shrugged, while Cort turned back to Todd and forced a smile.

"Who told you boys shouldn't wash dishes?"

"My friend Jeremy."

"Well, your friend Jeremy is wrong." Cort chuckled and tickled him under the chin.

Todd was basking in Cort's undivided attention. "Can I wash 'em?"

"Well, actually I was thinking about putting them in the dishwasher."

Glynis rolled her eyes heavenward, a gesture that was not lost on Cort. He threw her a fulminating glance. She smiled. To her amazement he smiled in return.

And his eyes seemed to search for and hold her own. For a moment they gazed at each other. Glynis's lips parted on a terrified breath; Cort's heart began to pound. She was the first to recover; she averted her eyes and said breathlessly, "It's almost Todd's bedtime."

As if reluctant to do so, Cort shifted his gaze to Todd. "You heard your mother. We'd better get a move on."

Todd giggled. "I'm ready."

Glynis sat anxiously in the den while Cort and Todd were in the kitchen. Todd was obviously enjoying himself, if the splashing of water was any indication. Also, childish laughter rang out in response to Cort's every word. She couldn't help but wonder why Todd had never responded to Jay in that way. She knew the answer. Jay barely acknowledged his existence, much less anything else. Not so with Cort. He seemed to take delight in sharing with his son.

Glynis rose to her feet and paced impatiently around the room. She was overreacting as usual. His interest in Todd was merely a stopgap, a ruse before something else—another big job—diverted his attention. Wasn't that all she had ever been to him?

When they came back into the den a while later, there were circles underneath Todd's eyes.

"It's bedtime for you, young man." Her tone brooked no argument.

"Can Cort read to me in bed?"

Glynis sighed irritably. "No, playtime's over. You're exhausted."

"If Todd…" Cort began, only to have Glynis silence him with an angry look.

"Sleep is the only thing he needs," she muttered tersely, reaching for Todd's hand.

Cort winced, his color rising. "Damn you, Glynis." His tone was low and harsh, meant for her ears only.

During the entire time she supervised Todd's bath, including his brushing his teeth and slipping into his pajamas, Glynis realized she had pushed Cort as far as she dared, that by refusing him the right to get to know his son, she was playing with fire.

So when Todd bounded into the den a short time later and went straight to Cort, she bit her tongue.

"Will you come to my room and tuck me in?" Todd asked, his eyes wide and appealing.

Glynis, watching Cort's face, felt her composure snap and the color seep from her face. She put a hand to her heart and tried to pretend she didn't see the stirring emotions that tightened his face, turned it ashen. Maybe if he'd found a woman…

Suddenly terrified, she balled her hands into tight fists. For all she knew, maybe he'd found that woman. If so, that would certainly strengthen his case against her in the event he chose to fight her for custody. And with his money and influence…

"Can he come to my room, Mommy?" Todd was asking, looking at her with a puzzled frown on his face.

Her lashes veiled her eyes as she gazed downward. "All right," she said tightly.

There was a moment's silence as the child turned

back to Cort. Cort stood and took Todd's hand. "Let's go," he said with a twisted smile that did not reach his dark, unhappy eyes.

Glynis went with them to the bedroom and looked on as Todd climbed into his bed and peered up at Cort with adoring eyes. "Will you kiss me good-night like Mommy does?"

"You betcha," Cort said huskily, and bent down.

It was when Todd's thin arms circled Cort's neck that Glynis left the room, tears trickling down her cheeks. The empty den offered little comfort as she crossed to the window and stared into the inky blackness, a blackness that matched her heart. It was so quiet that she could hear the crickets chirping.

Glynis sensed, rather than heard, Cort come into the room. For a moment she remained still; then, with a visible effort at control, she turned around. He was propped against the mantel with one booted foot on the hearth, a brooding expression on his face.

"We have to talk," she said at last.

"Ah, so now it's you who wants to talk, huh?"

She bit the inside of her lip. "Please, I don't want to argue. I just want to…"

"What? You just want to what?"

"Leave," she said bluntly. "Move out."

His eyes turned to flecks of glittering steel. "We had a deal."

"I know, and I plan to keep my end of the bargain no matter how much I detest it."

"So, I don't get it."

She took a deep breath. "I guess what I'm trying to say is that I intend to remodel Aunt Dorothy's house, and just as soon as it's ready, I'm going to move into it. By then Todd should be over his surgery...."

"Dammit, Glynis, that house is a shambles." He pinched the bridge of his nose. "Why the hell can't you forget about it?"

"I think that's fairly obvious, don't you?" She didn't bother to hide the tremor in her voice. "Anyway, I want a place of my own, a place...to call home."

For a moment she thought she saw his features soften, but then he asked in a hard tone, "Where do you intend to get the money?"

"From the bank." She raised her chin a good inch. "I'm going to apply for a home-improvement loan."

He gave her a long look. "And just how do you intend to pay it back?"

She flushed and looked away. "If Todd's condition permits, I hope to get a job teaching second-term summer school and then apply for a permanent one for the fall."

"Forget it."

"Pardon me?"

"I don't want you to work this summer." He slipped a hand inside his shirt and massaged his throat. "And if you're determined to redo the old house, I'll give you the money."

"No."

His eyes narrowed. "What do you mean no?"

"Oh, Cort!" Glynis was near tears again. "We can't keep on bickering like this. You don't really care about Todd—or me. Why don't you admit it? You have your work and..." Her voice faded.

"Go on," he demanded, inching toward her, his sun-bronzed face grim.

"And...and women...or a woman," she finished rather incoherently, licking her suddenly parched lips.

"And would you care?" His voice had a ragged edge to it. "Would you care if I had a woman?"

Hot, boiling fury gripped her. "Stop it!" she cried. "Stop trying to seduce me with words! It won't work." For a moment her voice broke. "Why won't you believe me when I tell you that *I* don't need anything from you, that I don't want..."

Before she realized his intentions and before she could utter a cry of protest, he clasped her upper arms and backed her into the wall directly behind her. He didn't stop until his body was pinned hard against hers and his mouth was only a hairbreadth from hers.

"No...Cort," she moaned, twisting her head from side to side. He paid no attention to her muted cry. Instead he spanned her cheek with a hand and held her face steady.

"No," she whimpered again, placing her fists against his muscled chest and pushing desperately against him. But he wouldn't budge. Then something in his eyes suddenly brought her struggles to an end, and the resistance seemed to pour out of her.

"Oh, Glynis," she heard him groan with agony as his mouth, savage and tender at once, came down on hers. His tongue was soft and insistent, parting her lips, stroking the inside of her mouth.

Still she squirmed, determined not to give in. But then the weight of his body, the pressure of his mouth, drove all coherent thought from her mind, and she wanted to be closer, to remember, to feel.

She wrapped her arms around his neck, digging her fingers into his hair, and pressed his head closer as she arched against him. The warmth of his body was a powerful aphrodisiac, and the scent of his skin mingled with the scent of passion was equally powerful.

"You're driving me out of my mind!" he muttered feverishly, his mouth seeking hers again. Her legs were giving out under her. Her body was on fire. She was beyond denying that no other man could make love like Cort. And all that mattered was that it should never stop.

Then just as suddenly as the assault had begun, it was over. He had pulled back and was staring down at her, breathing hard.

"Now, by God," he taunted, "tell me you don't want me!"

Chapter 11

Sleep was impossible. The night stretched out long and lonely. Her body ached, and she admitted the reason why. Some wanton part of her cried silently for the fulfillment that only Cort could bring her. Though she tried, she was unable to purge those forbidden thoughts from her mind.

Cheeks flaming, Glynis turned her head into the pillow, but they wouldn't go away. His sweet savage assault on her body had awakened dormant longings within her, bringing to a feverish pitch desires she thought had been stilled with the lapse of time.

She had excused her participation because it had been so long since she'd felt a man's touch, Cort's touch. But that was no excuse, and she knew it. Though she had tried to keep her distance, her body had betrayed her. Her senses had drawn her toward his potent masculinity. She had basked in his scent, the feel of him against her. The feel of his hands kneading her breasts had fanned the fire in the lower regions of her stomach that, even now, threatened to rage out of control.

She hadn't fooled him, either. He'd felt her response. He had relished her surrender for the sole purpose of showing her that he did indeed did have the upper hand.

If only he had wanted to marry her. But a commitment like that was a mirage with a man like Cort McBride. She knew he wanted her. She also knew she could arouse him as easily as he'd aroused her. But a relationship built on physical attraction was not what she wanted. She had loved Cort—loved him with all the tenderness and passion of which she was capable. And he had taken that love and destroyed it.

She closed her eyes against those unpleasant recollections and let her head fall back against the pillow.

In spite of her mental turmoil, she must have slept. The next thing she knew, sunlight was peeping through the blinds and her son was on the side of the bed, leaning over her and running a finger down the side of her cheek.

Suddenly she trapped that finger in her mouth and gave it a gentle bite with her teeth.

"Ouch, Mommy!" Todd cried, drawing his hand back and stumbling to his feet.

She laughed and kicked the covers back. "That didn't hurt and you know it."

"Did, too."

She laughed again, then looked at the clock. Her laughter died. Eight-thirty. Good Lord, she hadn't slept this late in a long time. Her face flamed. What must Cort be thinking?

Then, remembering the horrendous scene between them last night, she didn't give a damn what he thought. After all, *he* was the cause of her exhaustion.

"Mommy, you gonna get up?"

"Right this minute."

"Good."

"Why the hurry?"

"I wanna go back to the barn and look at the kitties."

"Where's your...Uncle?" Knowing her son, she figured he had already asked Cort to take him. And since he hadn't, it was obvious Cort was unavailable. She hoped so, anyway. She wasn't looking forward to crossing paths with him this morning.

"That lady told—"

"Mrs. Springer."

"She told me Uncle Cort was with his foreman, tending to the cows." His lower lip protruded. "Wish I could've went with him."

"Wish you could have *gone* with him," Glynis corrected absently, getting out of the bed and padding into the bathroom.

"Isn't that what I said, Mommy?"

She merely shook her head before bending over the basin and splashing her face with cold water. When she came out of the bathroom minutes later, Todd was eyeing her carefully.

"Can I go to the barn? I've already had my cereal. That lady—I mean Mrs. Springer—fixed it for me a little while ago."

"How about if I promise to take you to see the kittens when we come back?"

He watched her apply her makeup. "Where're we going?"

"To town. I have some business to take care of at the bank. I thought I'd drop you off at Milly's and let you play with the boys."

"Yippee!"

"Have you brushed your teeth?"

"Yes, ma'am."

"Good. As soon as I finish getting dressed, we'll go."

"Okay, but hurry, Mom."

Following that order, Todd dashed out of the room, slamming the door behind him. Glynis sighed and again shook her head, but there was a smile on her face. He was doing so well and felt so good. It was a shame it was soon all going to come to an end. The thought of him going through the transplant seemed to turn the blood in her veins to ice water. If things didn't turn out right... No, she couldn't think like that, she told herself.

"You promised, Mommy."

Todd's light hair fell across his forehead as he turned it up to her, his blue eyes anxious. "I know, son. And I fully intend to keep my promise. Just give me another second to get out of these clothes." She paused and kicked her shoes off. "In the meantime, you go ask Mrs. Springer for some juice and take your medicine."

"Okay," Todd mumbled reluctantly, and headed toward the door.

"And remember to say please."

"Yes, ma'am," he said with resignation.

Once she was alone, Glynis could barely contain her excitement, nor could she stop from patting herself on the back.

As she tossed her skirt on the bed, she laughed out loud, and it felt good. She had gotten the home-improvement loan and she was ecstatic. Although it wasn't for as much as she would have liked, it was nevertheless enough to get started repairing the house.

From the bank, she'd gone to the school district office and applied for jobs. Luck had followed her there as well. While the summer position was doubtful since there was already a waiting list for the job, the fall looked promising, especially as she was certified in special education.

From there, she'd gone to Milly's to pick up Todd. Over a glass of iced tea, she and Milly had toasted her success.

Now, comfortable in a pair of shorts, cotton shirt and Reeboks, Glynis walked out the door. Minutes later there was a spring in her step as she and Todd headed toward the barn.

"Do you think they're still here?" she asked Todd as they entered the quiet coolness of the barn. Todd was tiptoeing to where they had last seen the kittens.

He turned his head. "Of course, Mommy. Uncle Cort said that if we didn't touch them, the mama cat wouldn't move them."

Glynis sighed. "And do you believe everything your...Cort tells you?"

"Course I do, 'cause he knows everything. He's real smart."

"Whatever you say." Glynis tried to ignore the twitch in her heart. How was it going to affect Todd when Cort was no longer a major part of his life? She shuddered just thinking about it.

"See, Mommy, just like Uncle Cort said, they're still here." Todd's voice had dropped to a whisper as he squatted down in front of the box filled to capacity with the cat and her nursing kittens.

"Oh, aren't they sweet," she said, using the same whisperlike tone as her son.

"I'll be glad when I can play with 'em. Uncle Cort said—"

"For heaven's sake, Todd," Glynis cried, lunging to her feet, "must you talk about Cort as if he's some sort of god?" Then, looking down into her son's troubled, upturned face, she regretted her childish outburst.

"I wish you liked him better," he said, his lower lip beginning to quiver ever so slightly.

For a moment Glynis struggled to come up with the right words. "Oh, Todd, honey, there's so much you don't know, can't understand."

"What I really wish is that he was my daddy."

Suddenly Glynis couldn't swallow, couldn't catch her breath. She felt as though she were choking to death.

"Then I wouldn't ever have to leave here," he added, his eyes brightening. "I could live here—"

"Todd!" This time Glynis almost screamed his name, and Todd stared at her, a stubborn expression on his face. "I like it here. Just 'cause you don't—"

"Todd, stop it!" Glynis jammed her hands down into the pockets of her shorts to control their shaking.

Her nerves were stretched to the breaking point. "I don't want to hear any more about you staying here with Cort, do you understand? As soon as we can get Aunt Dorothy's house livable, we'll be moving into it. And then we just might sell it and move back to Houston," she added as an afterthought. "So let's not say any more about living here permanently. Do I make myself clear?"

Todd looked sulky, but he nodded halfheartedly. "Yes, ma'am."

Glynis's breathing eased a bit. "Now, why don't you count the kittens, so you can name them?"

"Can I really name 'em, Mommy?"

They sank to their knees and hovered over the tiny, furry creatures. "I don't see why not," she said, placing an arm around Todd's shoulder and giving it a squeeze.

"I thought I'd find you two here."

For a moment Glynis remained in that same position, as if frozen. Then, along with Todd, she rose to her feet and turned around. Cort filled the narrow doorway.

"Hi, Uncle Cort," Todd said enthusiastically, running toward him, but not before casting a disquieting eye in Glynis's direction.

Dear Lord, Glynis thought, how long had he been standing there? How much of her and Todd's conversation had he heard? She couldn't control her heartbeat as his long stride closed the distance between them.

Their gazes met for a few disturbing moments, then he focused his eyes on Todd, who was now standing in front of him, looking up with a wide grin that emphasized his toothlessness. "Hi yourself, young fellow," Cort said.

Apparently satisfied that he'd gotten Cort's attention, Todd spun around and went back to the kittens, once again kneeling beside the box.

As he turned back to Glynis, Cort's narrowed eyes betrayed nothing, hidden as they were by his thick lashes. But there was a fine line of perspiration dotting his upper lip, and his shoulders were slightly drooped. Both could have been brought on, however, by the fact that he'd been working around the ranch, doing manual labor from the looks of his clothes. His snug-fitting, faded jeans and white shirt were dusty, as were his boots and Stetson. The only thing not dusty were his spurs; their shiny glint was intact.

Glynis cleared her throat, aching to remove her eyes from him, but she simply could not. "Todd was having a fit to see the kittens again," she murmured at last.

A smile relaxed his features. "I'm not surprised."

A long silence followed.

This time it was Cort who cleared his throat. "Did you go into town?"

"How'd you know?" She trailed her tongue nervously over her lower lip. The action focused his attention on her mouth.

He swallowed hard. "Maude told me."

"Oh."

His breathing was labored. "Well, did you get it?"

She blinked. "What?"

"The loan. Did you get the loan?"

A telltale flush reddened her cheeks. She knew she was acting like an imbecile, but all her senses were reacting to his presence with alarming intensity, remembering that moment in his arms. She hated him for putting her on the defensive this way.

"Well?"

She let out an audible sigh. "Yes, I got the loan."

"So you intend to go through with the cockamamy idea of remodeling the house?"

"Yes, and..."

Todd let out a delighted squeal. "Mommy, Uncle Cort, come look. Hurry. The mama kitty's licking the babies."

They looked at each other for a moment longer, then broke eye contact and gave their attention to Todd.

"That's how she cleans them, Todd," Cort said, casually dropping an arm around Todd's shoulders.

"You mean she's giving them a bath?"

"Right."

"Wow, that's really neat."

Cort smiled easily. "Yeah, isn't it?"

"Mommy, you looking?" Todd's upturned gaze was now fixed on Glynis's taut features.

"You like that, huh?" she asked, gazing adoringly at her son, relieved by the interruption.

"When can I pick one up?"

"Soon," Cort said, standing up. Glynis and Todd rose with him.

Without looking at Glynis, Cort asked, his voice low and resonant, "How would you like to go for a ride?"

Todd's eyes rounded, and his lips parted. "Now, with you?"

Cort nodded. "Yeah, on Blackjack, my stallion."

"Cort, I don't think…" Glynis began.

Her quick objection brought a pout. But that didn't stop Todd from pleading. "Oh, please, Mommy, please?"

"He'll be just fine, Glynis," Cort interjected, his tone testy at best. "I give you my word."

"All right," she said, an edge in her voice, "but you better make sure he holds on tight."

"Thanks, Mommy," Todd said, his eyes dancing. "I promise I'll be good." Then, to Cort he said, "I'm ready."

"I'm not. I want to talk to your mother for a minute."

Todd shifted his feet impatiently. "Can I wait for you outside?"

"Yes, but stay away from Blackjack."

"Todd, did you hear what Uncle Cort told you?"

"Yes, ma'am," Todd answered in a low voice, before turning his back and running out of the barn, as if fearing they would both change their minds.

The departure of their son created a stifling silence. Glynis's heart was beating much too wildly, no doubt brought on by the disturbing blue eyes watching her with mocking intensity.

Yet she was the first to speak. "Look, Cort, before you say anything else about the house—"

"Barr and I'll do the work," he interrupted. "Or at least Barr will, as this damned hole in my side rather limits my activities."

Her mouth fell open, and she stared up at him incredulously.

The corners of his lips tilted upward. "Close your mouth."

She gestured impatiently. "What kind of game are you playing now?"

"Believe me, it's no game." What could have been mistaken for a smile suddenly disappeared. "Have you thought about a contractor?"

"No, but—"

"Didn't think you had," he said. "And it's not easy to get one, especially one you can trust."

"Because I'm a woman, is that it?"

"Yes, that's it. But don't take it personally, because that's a fact of life everywhere. Reliable help is hard to come by."

"Well, thanks, but I don't think it's wise for you to tax your strength. I want you to get strong so we can get the transplant over with."

"Glynis."

She ignored him. "I'll get Milly's husband to find me someone."

"No. I told you Barr and I would do it."

"And I said no thank you. I told you I don't want…"

The luster in his eyes turned to metallic steel as he reached out and clamped a hand over her mouth, shutting off the tirade with the swiftness of a falling blade. She pulled at his fingers, but her effort was in vain. He crushed her to his chest.

"I thought we settled this *want* business last night." His breathing was harsh and uneven as he removed his hand. "You can scream all you want. But I wouldn't advise it, unless you want to upset Todd."

"Let me go!" she pleaded breathlessly.

Cort continued to hold her prisoner. Then he lowered his mouth toward her; there was no way she could avoid it. Her whimper went unnoticed as he nudged her lips apart and entered the hot cave of her mouth. By increments he caressed, probed, feasted upon the delights found there, setting her on fire.

His breathing harsh, he lifted his lips from hers and nuzzled the throbbing pulse in her neck. "I can have you any time I want, so remember that."

"No, that's not true."

"You want me to prove it?"

"No!" she cried, using what strength she had to break free of his embrace.

But her freedom was short-lived. He reached for her again.

She stumbled backward and only by sheer force of will did she maintain her footing.

"You'd...you'd have to take me by force," she said, trembling.

"I don't think so." His tone was soft and confidently mocking. "Right now you're as hot as I am, ready to explode."

"No," she whispered just as he grabbed her again and hauled her close to him.

"Yes," he countered, his half-closed eyes glittering as he slowly unbuttoned her shirt, exposing her creamy breasts to his hungry gaze. When his breath caressed a nipple, a small cry tore loose from the back of her throat. To heighten the exquisite torture, he caressed each warm curve with his lips before he lifted his head and reclaimed her mouth.

When a hoarse groan erupted from him, she responded greedily, grasping handfuls of his thick hair. He stroked her back, her hips and inside her thighs, applying pressure between her legs and not stopping until he rocked against her, hot and full.

He groaned raggedly. "Why do I still want you?"

Glynis was aware she should be asking herself that question. She should be the one repulsed. When had her need for him replaced her fear? Why was she aching to hold him instead of shoving him away?

"Cort, please, Cort," she whispered thinly.

"I can't forget how wet and tight you always were," he rasped against her lips, "how you moaned when I slid deep inside you."

The feeling his words aroused in her were primitive, ancient and eternal. She trembled, not with revulsion but with yearning.

"And in spite of what you did to me, God help me, I still want you."

Those last gut-wrenched words seemed to bring him to his senses, because his hold on her relaxed and she broke free.

For the longest moment they were both breathing so hard, speech was impossible.

Then Glynis found her voice. "Getting even. That's what this is all about, isn't it?" she spat, still gasping for breath.

His silence answered her question.

Glynis felt as though a bucket of cold water had been sloshed in her face, but she didn't intend to let him know that. Stiffening her shoulders, she said, "I'll fight you every step of the way."

His gaze slid slowly down her body. He said nothing until his eyes were level with hers again. Then he whispered, "And you'll lose."

Chapter 12

Following the encounter in the barn, the next week passed without further incident, much to Glynis's relief. But then she had made it a point to stay out of Cort's way as much as possible. Her nerves had been raw and close to the surface, and another emotional bout with Cort would have been the final straw.

For the most part Cort remained either in his office tending to business by phone or milling about the ranch with his foreman. It was obvious that Cort wanted to avoid her as well.

There were times when she would stand at her bedroom window, especially early in the morning, and watch him stride out the side door looking tan and fit. She couldn't imagine him dressing in a suit and tie every morning, confined to an office building. Here he seemed to be the consummate rancher, one with the land, the land he loved so much.

When she would see him like that, her senses never failed to stir, bringing back to her mind in full color those moments in his arms, the feel of his lips against hers, the feel of his hands on her bare flesh.

She would quiver with renewed fragments of passion. The only way she had been able to erase those thoughts from her mind was to put on her jogging gear and run until she couldn't run anymore. She would then return to the house, feeling much better, less edgy, more able to cope.

Yet when their paths did cross, that emotional stability would evaporate like a pail of water in the sun. Cort was affected as well. Subsequently, both walked on eggshells, knowing it would take only one wrong word, one accidental touch to send their emotions skyrocketing out of control.

Neither wanted that.

But during those trying days, Glynis made certain Todd did not bear the brunt of her unrest. They spent hours on end together, time they hadn't had since his illness. She treasured those hours and made the most of them. They took long walks through the woods where Todd often played in the creek, and on several occasions were guests at Barr's ranch.

Shamefully she had enjoyed those long, lazy summer days, and consequently she didn't object when Cort asked to take Todd with him. On those days, she'd simply go into town and visit Milly or help Maude with the cooking and household chores.

However, she knew that while things were progressing as well as could be expected under the circumstances, she definitely had to change her plans. Deep down she'd known it all along, known that she wouldn't be able to live in the same town with Cort. It simply would not work, not only because she would never have peace of mind, but Cort would eventually lure her son away, without a lawyer or a court of law.

Now, as she was finishing up one of her early morning jogging stints, that thought was again uppermost in her mind.

In a graceful move, she climbed the stairs onto the deck at the back of the house and sat down on the top step. She pushed tendrils of wet hair off her face. Then, closing her eyes, she took several deep breaths of the fresh morning air, drawing it deep into her lungs.

When she opened her eyes, Cort was rounding the corner of the barn. Her only clue that he'd seen her was the narrowing of his eyes. He began walking toward her, his gait measured.

Her nerves tensed instinctively. After a skipped heartbeat, Glynis stood and waited, her gaze sweeping coolly over his aloof features. And in that moment she found it hard to believe they had ever shared laughter, or passion, or tears, or anything other than the hate and mistrust that now threatened to consume them.

Glynis was the first to speak. "Good morning," she said for lack of anything better to say, never knowing what to expect from him or what his mood would be. Today was no exception.

He stopped a few feet from her and drawled, "Mornin'."

Their gazes locked for a minute, and time seemed to stand still. His southern drawl cut right through her. With an enormous effort, Glynis looked away, but not before she'd seen that glint in his eyes, a glint she recognized only too well, a look that hinted of smoldering passion and unfulfilled desire.

"How was your run?" he asked, drawing her back around to face him, while continuing his slow appraisal of her.

His blue-eyed gaze stripped her as he inspected the way the damp material of her T-shirt clung to the full curves of her breast, blatantly emphasizing her extended nipples.

She found it difficult to speak. "Fine, thank you," she said after a few awkward moments, and wondered if that was really her talking in a tone as formal and unbending as her stance.

He seemed to sense the irony in their conversation, for his mouth eased into a smile. Or was it a smirk? Glynis couldn't be sure.

"You ought to quit running, you know?"

She was taken aback. "Why?"

His eyes were dark and mesmerizing. "You're already thin enough, except for one place, that is."

She spoke before she thought. "And where is that?"

"Your breasts." There was a husky timbre in his voice. "Since you've had Todd, they're fuller, more perfect than…" He broke off, staring hard.

Glynis simply stood there mute and panic-stricken, feeling a tide of hopelessness wash through her.

Finally she was able to drag enough air through her lungs to speak. "Cort, please, you've no right to talk to me like that."

Holding her stare, Cort muttered harshly, "You're right, I don't."

"Can't we forget the past and…and try to be civil to each other? At least until after Todd's surgery?"

Mentioning Todd's name seemed to have a sobering effect on him. His stern expression relented somewhat. But when he spoke, it was in a hoarse whisper. "Do you think that's possible?"

The dryness in her mouth made it difficult to swallow. Her tongue felt swollen. "We…we won't know till we try, will we?"

He looked at her a moment longer with veiled eyes, only to suddenly change the subject.

"I just got back from the doctor."

The blood drained from her face. "And?"

"I'm in good shape."

Glynis's heart lurched. "Good enough to have the surgery?"

"'Fraid not."

She regarded him helplessly. "When, then?"

"Soon. Doc Davis said my blood count is slowly but surely coming back up."

"How soon is soon?" Glynis pressed anxiously.

"Maybe another week. Maybe two at the most."

She fought to hold back her tears. "Well, I guess if that's the best you can do…"

"I didn't deliberately get shot, you know." His eyes weren't kind, but there was no anger, either.

"I know," she said softly, "but surely you can't blame me for being anxious."

He looked away from Glynis and was silent for a moment. "No," he said at last. "I can't blame you."

"Did the doctor warn you about…about taxing your strength?" she asked, striving to keep her voice steady.

"If you're referring to the work on your house, the answer is no."

"I find it hard to believe you're allowed to do exactly as you please."

"Pretty much so."

"Oh."

His lips twitched, but he never actually smiled. "Sorry to disappoint you, but I'm still planning to work on your house, starting this evening."

"This evening?"

"Anything wrong with that?"

"No, it's just that I haven't thought about the materials."

"I took care of that."

"I need to pay you then."

His eyes turned hard. "If you insist."

"I insist."

"Suit yourself," he said, twisting around in the direction of the barn.

"Cort."

He turned back around and waited.

"Do…you think I could help?"

They looked at each other for a long time. Then Cort shoved his Stetson back on his head and said, "I guess it depends on just how good you are with a hammer."

"I'm a fast learner," she said a trifle breathlessly.

He scratched the part of his head that was uncovered and smiled, a smile that went straight to Glynis's heart.

"I guess we'll see, won't we?"

With that he turned and once again sauntered toward the barn.

Unable to stand up on her trembling legs a second longer, Glynis sank back onto the wooden steps, her thoughts more scrambled than ever. He had suddenly become a man of contradictions. She didn't know which Cort was the most dangerous, the moody, unpredictable one, or the sexy, soft-spoken one.

But one thing she did know—both were unhealthy to her peace of mind. As soon as Todd was up and around, they would move back to Houston. For her own good, she had to get away from Cort McBride.

"Mommy, are you having fun?"

Glynis smiled into her son's face as he hunkered down beside her while she was busy ripping a piece of worn linoleum from the floor. "Well, I wouldn't exactly call this fun."

"Why not?" he asked innocently.

"Because it's hard work, that's why." Glynis paused and wiped the sweat from her forehead with the back of her hand.

"It's too bad I can't help you, Mommy."

She smiled. "Why can't you?"

He grinned. "'Cause Uncle Cort's countin' on me to help him. He told me so." His chest swelled proudly. "It's fun, too. Me and Uncle Cort and Uncle Barr are having fun."

With that he stood and scurried out of the room.

"I'm glad someone's having fun," Glynis mumbled to herself, giving another segment of flooring a savage yank. She must have been out of her mind when she'd volunteered to help. But then she hadn't known she was going to be assigned the worst job in the whole house.

From the moment Cort and Todd had piled into Cort's old pickup truck that he kept in the barn, and had subsequently arrived at the farmhouse, Cort had been working nonstop, though doing nothing strenuous as he had promised. The strenuous jobs had fallen on her and Barr, mostly on Barr.

Barr, for the most part, had worked outside, tearing out the rotten windows that were being replaced with new energy-efficient ones. Cort and Todd, working as a team, had started in her old bedroom, pulling off what was left of the tattered wallpaper.

They had been there only an hour when she had slowly risen to her feet to rest her knees. It was then that she heard a squeal of laughter and had tiptoed down the short hall and stood at the door and looked in.

Cort was entertaining his son with a story while they worked, Todd imitating every move Cort made. Once again she'd experienced that sharp pain in her heart. After watching them undetected for a long moment, she'd turned and made her way back to the kitchen. It was only after she'd knelt and begun working that she noticed her eyes were filled with tears.

But the tears had long since dried; she'd taken her frustrations out on the linoleum floor. Now, an hour later, she was making real progress. And so was Barr; she could hear him hammering loudly and steadily.

"Todd said you were having trouble."

As usual when Cort came anywhere near her, every nerve in her body reacted. Scrambling to her feet, she pushed her hair away from her face. "No, really," she responded, "I think I've finally gotten the hang of it."

He was leaning against the kitchen cabinets, looking good enough to eat in worn cutoff jeans and no shirt. His upper body was tanned and lean, and the hairs curling on his chest were damp and glistening with drops of sweat.

She felt her temperature rise as she swallowed hard and added, "But it's...hard work, just the same."

One eyebrow rose. "You didn't expect it to be easy, did you?"

"No, of course not," she said defensively.

As if sensing he'd struck a raw nerve, Cort looked amused. "We're just getting started. Sure you don't want to change your mind?"

"You'd like that, wouldn't you?" she snapped, raising an arm to massage the back of her neck. In doing so, she unconsciously exposed a portion of her bare, upper stomach to Cort's darkening gaze. Like him, she was wearing cutoffs and a cropped top, which just happened to cup her breasts to perfection.

They stared at each other for what seemed like an interminable length of time, then Cort blinked and looked away, a pulse in his neck beating overtime.

"Yes, I would," he finally said in answer to her question, swinging back to face her. "This was a bad idea to begin with. You don't have to live here."

This time it was her temper that rose. "We can't stay with you forever, you know."

"Why not?" His expression was blank.

Hers was disgusted. "You know why not."

"No, not really." His eyes, unblinking and compelling, bored into hers. "It could be an ideal setup. We could share our son, and you wouldn't have to work."

"And just what would you get out of it?" she asked out of curiosity.

"You in my bed every night."

At first she was so stunned, she couldn't speak, then a high-pitched laugh that held no humor pealed from her throat. "Are you suggesting that I become your mistress?"

His face paled. "Only if you choose to look at it in those terms."

She laughed again, her eyes wide. "I don't believe I'm hearing this."

He took a step toward her, his mouth stretched in a thin, straight line. "Why not? It's an established fact that you'd like to crawl in between my sheets just as much as I'd like you to."

"Why, you smug bastard! If you think I'd—"

"Am I interrupting something?" Barr said suddenly, leaning through the kitchen window, his broad shoulders taking up the entire space, a grin on his face. "It seems as if I'm destined to be in the wrong place at the wrong time."

Barr's subtle attempt at humor did little to disperse the growing tension. Glynis and Cort both stared at him, but neither was capable of saying a word.

"Glynis, how 'bout bringing me a glass of that lemonade you brought with you?" Barr drawled when the silence continued. "I'd sure appreciate it. I'll be sitting under that big oak tree out back." After winking at Glynis, he turned and ambled off.

The instant Barr was out of hearing range, Cort faced Glynis. "I'd give my offer some deep thought, if I were you," he said between clenched teeth.

Then he, too, pivoted on his heels and stamped off.

The suffocating tension that had surrounded Glynis seemed to leave the room with him. She hadn't realized just how stiffly she had been holding herself until she drew a free breath.

Yet when she turned and began grabbing glasses out of the cabinet, her hands were shaking uncontrollably. In fact she was shaking all over. How dare he assume she would become his mistress?

With every breath she took, with every move she made, her thoughts churned. *How dare he even ask?*

"You sure you don't want me to go with you?" Barr asked.

"Dammit, do I look like I need a damned keeper?"

"Yeah, as a matter of fact you do."

Cort snorted. "I'm fine."

"Sure."

"Barr, just move your behind."

"I wouldn't turn my back on her if I were you, little brother."

Cort tensed, knowing full well what Barr was getting at, but not liking it just the same.

Barr chuckled. "Yeah, if looks could kill, you'd be deader than a mackerel washed up on the beach."

Cort was gripping the steering wheel so hard, his knuckles were white. "What's the deal, Barr? Do you get off watching Glynis and me fight?"

Barr didn't so much as flinch. "Just curious about what you said that made her so damned mad, that's all."

"Well, for once I'm not going to satisfy your curiosity. You don't find me interfering in your personal business. From now on I'd appreciate it if you returned the favor.'' Heavy sarcasm punctuated every word Cort spoke.

It was lost on Barr. ''See, you're doing it again, gettin' uptight—''

''You're wrong.''

''No, I'm not, not by a long shot. Hey, little brother, it's me you're talking too, remember?'' He paused and, rubbing his day-old beard, leaned further into the open window. ''You're testy as hell. What you need is a good—''

''Give it a rest.'' Cort jammed the Jeep in gear.

''I take that back. What you need is Glynis. She's what you've always needed.''

''What you need is to mind your own damned business and get the hell out of my way!''

Barr sighed. ''All right, Cort, have it your way. But make no mistake, you're a firecracker with a burning fuse. And anytime now you're going to blow sky-high.''

''Stand back,'' Cort bit out furiously. ''I'm going to the cattle auction.''

Four hours later, Cort was on his way back from the auction in Tyler, having made several much-needed purchases. He would have thought that the successful outing would have sweetened his mood, but he was still as uptight as when he'd driven out the gate.

Barr was right, though it galled Cort to admit it. Cort was horny as hell; he wanted, he needed a woman. But not just any woman would do. God help him, he wanted, he *needed* Glynis, only Glynis.

And while rationally he could be appalled at his

raging feeling and his unorthodox behavior, something stronger than his self-respect was prodding him on. Indeed, her nearness was driving him close to the edge, and while love did not enter into the scheme of things, lust did.

In spite of the hell she had put him through, having her close and not being able to touch her was tearing his gut to pieces. And he'd taken enough cold showers lately to last him a lifetime.

Hadn't he known this would happen? Not at first, he hadn't. He had been obsessed with getting to know his son. Thoughts of Glynis were secondary to that urgent need. Anyway, he'd thought he was over her, thought he had gotten her out of his system.

Wrong again. If anything, he wanted her more than he ever had, found her body more desirable. He wanted, ached to touch her. All over. Every inch, as he'd done an eternity ago when he'd felt her grasp him just before he would penetrate her quickly and deeply.

He swore explosively as his hardening flesh pressed against the fly of his jeans. So where did he go from here? Back home? Pretend she wasn't there? Sleep alone? Hardly. Not with this burning pain at the apex of his thighs.

The memory of her sweet, soft lips clinging to his, the ripe fullness of her breasts under his exploring fingers, the scent of her, the enticing sway of her hips tormented him even as the Jeep clicked off the miles.

As he neared a small town, he eased up on the gas pedal. It was only moments later, after he transferred his boot to the brake, that he muttered an expletive.

He had no brakes. Looking up, he saw that the car

in front of him was stopping at the red light. A fine line of sweat popped out above his lips. The choices were slim. He could either crash into the Buick's rear or head for the deep ditch to his right. He chose the latter.

Whipping the steering wheel sharply, he braced himself for the crash.

"Son of a bitch!" he hissed before his head slammed against the steering wheel on impact and a deep blackness pulled him under.

Chapter 13

"Is he dead?"

"I don't know. Do you?"

"No. But I can't find a pulse."

"Here, get out of the way and let me check."

"Did you call the sheriff's office?"

"Yeah, and they're on their way. Told 'em to send an ambulance, too."

"I just hope it ain't too late."

Voices. Cort kept hearing voices, but he couldn't open his eyes and respond, no matter how hard he tried.

"He sure as hell looks dead to me. All that blood sure ain't a good sign, either."

For God's sake, stop talking about me as if I were dead, Cort cried silently. *I'm alive. Can't you see that!*

"Think we oughta try to move him?"

"Hell, no. Here comes the sheriff—he'll know what to do."

I'm alive. Can't you idiots see that? Yet he sure didn't feel alive. The one time he'd tried to move, every muscle, every nerve protested in agony. At least he wasn't paralyzed, not from the waist up, anyway.

Cort identified the sirens. Now if he could just open his eyes, he'd have the battle half won, he told himself. However, that task proved impossible.

It was only after he heard a gruff voice bark "You fellows get the hell out of the way and let us through" that his eyelids fluttered.

The instant he felt a hand on his shoulder, his eyes popped open, and he groaned.

"I'll be damned if it isn't Cort McBride!"

Cort was able to focus his eyes now, and Sheriff Daniel Thompson filled his vision. "Hello, Dan," he rasped.

"Damn, Cort, I thought for a minute that I'd have to call the J.P. to pronounce you dead."

Cort raised his head all the way up and reached a hand to his forehead. When he lowered it, his fingers were coated with blood. "Reach behind the seat, will you, Dan, and hand me a rag?"

The sheriff frowned. "Maybe you oughta keep still until the paramedics get here. They're driving up now."

"No, I'll be all right. Just please get me the rag and then help me out."

"You ain't changed a bit. You're still as hard-headed as a damn mule."

"Yeah, yeah," Cort muttered, dabbing at the blood on his face. Once that was done, he turned his body in the seat, though very gingerly, and with Dan's help managed to get out of the Jeep, which was still nose-down in the ditch.

Two paramedics were standing with a stretcher at the top of the embankment.

''Come on, boys, get down here and load your patient.''

Cort raised his hand, stalling them. ''No, I don't want to be strapped on any stretcher. Just give me a minute, and I'll be fine.''

Dan snorted. ''If you could see yourself, you wouldn't say that.''

Cort winced against a pain that suddenly shot through his side, then cursed. If he'd torn open that wound...

''Cort, don't you dare faint on me now,'' Dan was ordering, ''not after you wouldn't let the paramedics help you.''

Ignoring him, Cort probed his side with unsteady fingers. Sore, but not unbearably so. And there was no blood.

''Come on,'' Dan said, ''let's get you outa this ditch and into my car. At least you'll be sitting down.''

''That sounds good. Give me a hand and let's go.''

Once Cort was seated in the passenger seat of the sheriff's car, he leaned his head back and closed his eyes. Although his head still pounded, his vision was clear, and he no longer had that sick feeling in the pit of his stomach.

Feeling strong enough to finally check the damage to his face, he lowered the visor and stared into the mirror. He grimaced. A large goose egg adorned the center of his forehead, and there was a cut on his right cheekbone. The cut had been the source of all the blood.

He couldn't help but wonder what Barr would say when he saw him. It probably wouldn't be repeatable. And Glynis? Cort's heart skipped a beat. What would she think? Would she be as upset?

He'd lived, and for that he was thankful, given the circumstances of the accident and the fact that it could have been much worse. He could be dead. And this time it wasn't even job-related, he thought with a cynical curve of his lips. Or was it? Suddenly he frowned.

"How you feeling, son?"

Cort angled his head sideways. Dan was peering down at him, the open door bearing the brunt of his weight, which was definitely in excess. But then Cort knew Dan did everything wrong. When Dan was on duty he smoked too much; when off, he drank too much. Still he was a crackerjack law officer, and Cort respected him.

"I'm feeling like warmed-over dishwater, now that you ask."

"Figures. Wish now you'd let those medics haul you to the hospital?"

"Hell, no. I'll be sore for a few days, all right. But then I'll be fine."

Dan didn't look convinced. "If you say so." Then, changing the subject, he asked, "What happened, anyway?"

"That's what I'd like to know."

Dan didn't miss the ugly note in Cort's voice. He straightened up, instantly alert. "Suppose you explain that."

"There's not much to explain. I was coming home from the auction, started to slow down for the light—

there was a car in front of me—and when I put my foot on the brakes—''

"It was like stepping on air," Dan finished for him. "Right."

"Had your brakes been giving you trouble?"

"Hell, Dan, you know better than that. If they had, I'd have fixed them immediately."

"Sorry. In your line of work I guess you can't afford to be careless."

"Right again," Cort said, tight-lipped.

"You thinking what I think you're thinking?"

"Maybe." Cort's tone was cautious.

"Well, I'm thinking they might have been tampered with," Dan drawled.

Cort's face took on a sinister sneer, but he didn't say anything.

Dan scratched his chin. "Well, we'll have the Jeep up momentarily, and then we can take a look."

Both men turned and watched the wrecker, which had appeared on the scene shortly after the sheriff and paramedics, haul the Jeep out of the ditch with one strong tug.

The second it hit level ground, Dan backed away from the car and Cort eased out, though not without a price. His head swam, and his stomach churned. But after he took several gulping breaths, the world righted itself.

By the time they reached it, one of Dan's deputies was on the ground sliding under the right wheel. Cort would have liked to crawl under there himself, but knew that was impossible.

"Findin' anything, Toby?" Dan asked, lifting his hat and wiping the sweat off his forehead. "Damn, it's hot."

Cort made no comment. His gaze was pinned to the deputy, his mouth drawn in a tense line.

"Got it," Toby finally said, scooting from under the Jeep, a hose dangling from his hand.

Cort took it and began examining it immediately.

"Well, what's the verdict?" Dan pressed.

Cort muttered a seething oath. "The damn thing's been tampered with."

"How?" Dan grabbed the hose out of Cort's hand.

"Punctured."

"Ah, punctured so the fluid would drain out slow."

"Exactly." Cort's voice was razor sharp.

Dan thrust a hand through his thatch of graying hair. "Whoever did it had a perfect opportunity while you were inside the auction barn."

"That's my guess."

"Have any idea who wants you gone?"

Cort raised his head sharply, only to then let out a cry of pain.

"You oughta be home in bed," Dan said tersely, "instead of standing out here in this heat. Come on, I'll drive you to the ranch."

"Make that Barr's. I'll get him to drive me home."

Dan nodded.

Cort turned to the driver of the wrecker. "Fred, haul the Jeep out to my place, will ya?"

"Sure thing, Cort."

Once Cort and Dan were in the sheriff's car and turning onto the highway, Cort twisted in the seat and stared out the window, his thoughts in chaos. He didn't want to think he had been so wrong about something he had been so sure of. He didn't want to think that the bullet he'd thought was meant for his client was actually meant for him.

But he was beginning to believe that was the case. Suddenly, his mind conjured up a terrible thought. He flinched. *If* the bullet was indeed meant for him, then Glynis and Todd were in danger.

He muttered to himself, knowing he had a decision to make that had all the earmarks of a double-edged sword. Yet if he sent them to Milly's or Barr's, then they would be out from under his protective eye. He'd be damned if he did and damned if he didn't.

"You're awfully quiet."

Cort sighed heavily. "I'm thinking."

"I'm sure you are. By the way, you never answered my question."

"That's because I don't know the answer," Cort hedged.

Dan threw him a sharp glance. "But you intend to find out, right?"

Cort's eyes were like chips of ice as he narrowed them on the sheriff. "You can rest assured of that, my friend."

Glynis knew she should call it an early night. But why bother, she told herself. She wouldn't sleep. The house was quiet, and she was restless, mainly because Todd was running a slight fever and complaining about a stomachache.

After bathing his face with a cold rag, she'd given him several crackers and part of a Coke, then put him to bed. So far he'd slept peacefully. But if he wasn't considerably better in the morning, she would call the doctor. His ailment could be something more than a virus....

Suddenly furious with herself for borrowing trouble, she lunged off the couch, ignoring the papers that scattered to the floor around her. She'd been going through her files, looking for new ideas for bulletin boards so she'd be prepared when the new school term started.

Now that her concentration was broken, she knew it would be fruitless to try to pick it up again.

She wished Maude hadn't gone to her sister's for a visit. At least she would have been company. Crossing to the window, Glynis toyed with the blinds until she could see outside. The sky was as black as her thoughts, she noted. Not one star was in evidence. Suddenly she saw a streak of lightning followed by a menacing rumble of thunder.

She closed her eyes and leaned her head against the frame, but not before a sigh escaped her. While it was true she was concerned about Todd, she also knew her agitation stemmed from another source as well. Cort.

Since their clash at Dorothy's house last evening, she had not seen him. When she and Todd had gotten up this morning, he'd been gone. And now it was nine o'clock, and he still wasn't home. Which was fine by her, she told herself. In fact, she wished she could take Todd and leave and never see him again.

At first she wasn't sure she'd heard anything. Straightening, Glynis twisted her head to one side and listened. This time she identified the sound. The kitchen door had opened, then closed.

"Cort, is that you?" she asked, her voice sounding hyper even to her own ears.

Silence.

Determined to ignore the way her heart raced, Glynis began walking across the room. Before she got halfway, Cort appeared in the doorway.

She stopped in her tracks, her hand flying to her throat. "Oh, dear Lord!" she cried.

"It's not as bad as it looks. I'm fine, really."

"What on earth…?" Her voice cracked, and for a second she couldn't go on.

"I had an accident."

"You…you didn't injure your side, did you?"

"No, thank God."

"Shouldn't you…be in the hospital?" she stammered, unable to come to terms with this latest turn of events. "You look awful," she added, her stomach feeling as though she were on a roller coaster.

He almost smiled. "That's what Barr said, only worse."

She raised her eyebrows in question. "Barr?"

"Yeah. He brought me home."

"You should be sitting down," she said in a strangled tone, then turned away for fear he would see the tears that were flooding her eyes. To say he looked awful was an understatement. Ghastly was the more appropriate word. The lump on his forehead was a purplish-green color, and the cut above his eye was caked with dried blood and needed attention. Something terrible had happened, and she wasn't sure she wanted to know what it was.

By the time she faced him again, he was sitting down in his chair, his gaze resting broodingly on her.

"You really should be in bed, you know," she said huskily.

"Are you offering to tuck me in?" His voice was low and rough.

For a moment Glynis shut her eyes against the hot tightness that was turning her insides to jelly. Then she stiffened. "You don't give up, do you?" she asked bitterly.

"Glynis, look at me."

She tried to keep her voice natural, but it quivered revealingly. "No. I just want you to tell me what happened."

When he didn't respond, she glanced at him out of the corner of her eye. His eyes were closed, and she saw his jaw turn rigid as a spasm of pain flickered across his face.

Her breath caught sharply. "Do you want me to call the doctor?"

"No," he said, lifting his head. "I'll be fine as soon as I shower and get some sleep."

Glynis dug her teeth into her bottom lip. "I'm...not sure. I think I should call your doctor."

"My Jeep took a nosedive into a ditch on 69."

It took a minute for his unexpected words to sink in. "What did you say?"

With uncharacteristic patience, he repeated himself.

"Did you lose control?"

"Only because someone tampered with my brakes."

She stared at him with disbelief while the color slowly deserted her face.

Cort stood, though not without considerable effort. "I knew you'd react like this. That's why I hesitated to tell you."

"It's job-related, isn't it?" Her voice was toneless.

"Yes."

She shot him a look that was suddenly outraged and cold. "Dammit, Cort, if you let anything happen to you before..." She broke off, horrified at what she was about to say.

"Would it make you feel better if I promise I won't get blown away until after the transplant?" There was an icy edge to his voice. "Would it, huh? Would it?"

Glynis felt terrible. "Cort, I didn't mean—"

"Like hell you didn't," he snapped, his eyes bleak. "Ah, hell, it doesn't matter anyway. I'm going to bed."

With that he turned and strode out of the room, leaving Glynis standing in the middle of the room as if rooted to the spot. She didn't know how long she stood there, too shocked at her own outburst to move.

Dear Lord, she hadn't meant it. No matter what Cort had done to her, the pain he had brought her, she still didn't want anything to happen to him. While she might hate him, she certainly didn't wish him dead.

Suddenly she knew what she had to do.

"Who is it?"

"It's me," Glynis whispered, barely able to hear her own voice over the pounding of her heart.

"Go away."

"Please, Cort, let me come in." She stopped short of pleading.

Silence.

"Cort, I'm not leaving."

"The door's open," he muttered.

With fingers that were far from steady, Glynis turned the knob and walked in. Cort was sitting on the side of the bed, practically naked, dressed only in his briefs.

Paying no heed to her audible gasp, he went on with what he was doing—dabbing at his cut with a cotton ball soaked with antiseptic.

Leaving the door cracked behind her, she ventured deeper into the room while she stared openly at his body, remembering what it was like to run her hands over his hairy chest, down his stomach to the thick muscle between his thighs.... She shut her eyes and groaned deep in her throat, feeling as if something had broken apart inside her. When her eyes fluttered back open, he was looking at her.

"I think you'd better go," he said thickly.

"I'm...sorry," she whispered.

He shrugged. "I told you to forget it."

"It's not that easy."

"Sure it is."

"You're making a mess of that."

He blinked as if the change of subject had thrown him off guard. Then, taking the cotton away from the cut, he shrugged again. "It's not helping, anyway."

Without stopping to think about her actions, Glynis closed the distance between them and sat down on the bed beside him.

"Here, let me do that," she said, and proceeded to take the cotton out of his hand and gently touch the tender area with trembling fingers.

Though she heard his sharp intake of breath, her hand didn't falter. She continued to cleanse the cut.

Then, without warning, he reached up and stilled her hand. Their eyes met and held.

Glynis was so close she could hear the beat of his heart; it was as loud as her own.

"You shouldn't have come," he muttered thickly.

Glynis was trembling all over now. "I had to."

"Oh, Glynis, Glynis." His voice was raw as he slid one hand under the coil of her hair and stroked the sensitive nape of her neck. "What are we going to do?"

She wanted to cry, to weep in shame. But she couldn't. The tears wouldn't come, nor would the words. She simply sat there, trembling, feeling his breath, warm and tantalizing against her lips.

"Why did you do it? Why did you marry Jay? I went through hell. If I'd known you were pregnant as well..." He slid his hand over hers, finding her palm with his thumb. "You remember how it always was with us, and that hasn't changed. God, how I want you, have never stopped wanting you. You're beautiful, do you know that? I've never made love to another woman. Sex, yes—but not love!"

Glynis closed her eyes and swayed, reaching out blindly. He grasped her tightly and clamped his mouth to hers. He probed with his tongue quickly, greedily, and she matched him stroke for stroke. It was an intimacy they both longed for, and it struck them both like lightning. Intense. Beautiful.

She was not fool enough to imagine that the emotions they were deliberately arousing in each other were anything more than an instinctive need for gratification.

Yet she doubted she could have dragged herself away if it hadn't been for the sound behind her. With determination she spun around. Her son was standing inside the door.

"Mommy, I threw up all over the bed."

Chapter 14

"Mrs. Hamilton, the job is yours, if you want it."

"Oh, I want it, Mr. Aimsworth. I want it very badly, only..." Her voice faded, and she looked away from the man who was principal of the Lyndon Baines Johnson Elementary School.

He was tall and thin, almost to the point of gauntness, but he had the gentlest, most caring gray eyes she'd ever seen. She had been looking forward to this visit. But that was before her circumstances had changed, before she'd decided not to remain in East Texas.

Yesterday afternoon she had received a call from Ted Aimsworth asking her to stop by the school at her convenience, saying that he'd looked over her application and would very much like to talk to her. Since she had had to bring Todd in to the doctor, anyway, she'd decided to hear what he had to say.

She was impressed with Mr. Aimsworth and with the job itself, which was going to make turning it down that much harder.

"I'm not pressing you for a decision, Mrs. Hamilton, you understand," Mr. Aimsworth said, bridging the silence that had fallen between them. "There's still plenty of time to let me know." He paused, tipping his head sideways. When he spoke again, his tone was cautious. "I don't mean to pry, but when the district gave me your application, I was under the impression that you were very interested in the job."

They were in his office now, and Glynis was sitting in front of his desk, closely scrutinizing the shelf behind him. It sagged with curriculum guides and other materials pertinent to the profession.

"Oh, I am," Glynis said enthusiastically. "It's just that right now I can't commit to anything. You…see my son is due to have a bone marrow transplant soon, and until that's over…" Again Glynis's voice trailed off.

"I can certainly understand that," Aimsworth said, his features softening sympathetically as he rose behind his desk and extended his hand, indicating the interview was over. "I hope everything goes well. You'll let me know."

"Of course, and thank you very much."

The minute she walked out of the school and into the bright sunlight, Glynis stopped and, balancing her purse on a knee, dug inside for her sunglasses.

Once they were perched on her nose, she strode toward her car, noticing how lovely the morning was. The air smelled clean and fresh, thanks to last night's cleansing rain. She took a deep breath before getting behind the wheel of her car.

A short time later she pulled up in front of Milly's day-care center. Milly's figure appeared in the doorway as soon as Glynis got out of her car.

"Is Todd all right?" she asked anxiously, hurrying up the sidewalk, thinking it odd that Milly was waiting for her.

Milly smiled. "He's fine, going strong in fact."

Glynis's face cleared. "Good. He sure wasn't last night, though. He was one sick little boy."

"That's obvious," Milly quipped.

Glynis stopped abruptly. "Now just exactly what is that supposed to mean?"

Milly laughed, but then it faded almost as quickly. "You look like something the dogs dragged up and the cats wouldn't have."

"Gee, some friend you are, Milly Tatum."

"That's where you're wrong. I am your friend, that's why I said what I did." Milly opened the front door then and with a sweep of her hand indicated that Glynis should precede her inside.

Both women were quiet as they made their way past tables and chairs, chairs filled with boys and girls busily and happily working on various projects.

"Ms. Tatum! Come look," a little blond-headed boy shouted as they passed. He reminded Glynis of Todd.

Milly paused only briefly. "Not now, Albert," she told him with a kind smile. "Hold on to it, and I'll look at it later."

It wasn't until they were in Milly's office behind closed doors, coffee cups in hand, that Glynis spoke.

"Is Todd outside?"

"Yes, but like I told you, he's fine. So stop worrying. I just checked on him before you drove up."

"The doctor said the same thing." Glynis took a sip of her coffee, then frowned. "Heavens, that's hot."

"Blow on it."

Glynis rolled her eyes. "Thanks."

"What exactly did the doctor say?" Milly asked, serious once again.

"A twenty-four-hour bug."

"Just as we'd thought."

"Right, but it sure did me in," Glynis said with a sigh. "Of course I slept with him, afraid he'd get sick again and I wouldn't hear him."

"But that's not the only reason you look like you do."

"Come on, Mil, give me a break. I had a rough night, okay. So let's leave it at that."

As if realizing she'd been overly critical, Milly flushed. "Hey, don't get me wrong," she rushed to say in a conciliatory tone. "You're still beautiful, especially in that outfit."

And she was right. Glynis did look stunning in a bright golden yellow skirt and blouse, necklace and earrings.

"Flattery will get you nowhere, my friend. Anyway, you're just saying that in order to get back on my good side."

Milly shook her head. "No, I'm not. It's just that I'm worried about you. It's your eyes. There's a sadness in them that never seems to fade. And I know it's more than worry over Todd, although that in itself is enough to drive you crazy."

Glynis nodded and ran a finger around the rim of her coffee cup.

When she didn't speak, Milly went on, "Is it the job? Are you afraid you're not going to get it?"

Glynis shifted in her chair and averted her gaze. "The job's mine if I want it."

"What do you mean, if you want it?" Milly frowned. "I thought that was exactly what you wanted."

Glynis focused her attention on the papers strewn across Milly's desk.

"Glynis."

"You're right," Glynis admitted with a sigh. "I did…do want it, but I'm afraid I'm not going to be able to accept it."

"Why not?" Milly was clearly perplexed. "Is it the working conditions?"

"No. In fact, it would be an ideal job. Ted Aimsworth would be great to work for, and aside from that, I'd be in one of the new temporary buildings."

"Then why aren't you going to take it? If you stay here, you have to work—"

"That's just it," Glynis put in quietly. "I'm not going to stay here."

"You're making absolutely no sense," Milly said flatly.

Glynis stood and began pacing the floor. "Don't make it harder than it already is. Do you think I want to go back to Houston, rear Todd there? Well, I don't, but I have no choice. I have to get away from…" She paused and struggled for breath.

"You have to get away from Cort," Milly finished gently.

"That's right." Her voice was no more than a whisper.

Milly threw up her hands. "Stupid me, I should have guessed."

"No reason why you should have," Glynis said wearily, bringing her pacing to a halt in front of the window.

"You still care about him." It wasn't a question.

"Oh, Milly," Glynis cried, gripping the glass rod on the blinds and squeezing it. "I don't know what I think anymore. Sometimes I hate him. Then other times I want him so badly it hurts." *Like last night*, she wanted to add, but didn't. Instead she folded her arms across her chest and rubbed them simultaneously. "But then I hate myself for feeling that way and hate him for making me feel that way. It's a catch-22."

"Is it possible you two might work things out once the surgery is over?" Milly asked hesitantly.

"Absolutely not." She met Milly's gaze unflinchingly.

"Things that bad, huh?"

"He'll never change, Milly. Cort's as involved with his work as he ever was. In fact, he's in so deep, his life's in danger."

"Are you serious?"

Glynis merely looked at her.

"How? I mean where…who?" Milly was spluttering as if she couldn't coordinate her words with her thoughts.

Glynis inhaled. "Someone tampered with his brakes, and his Jeep took a nosedive into a ditch on 69." Just thinking about it, much less talking about it, brought goose bumps to Glynis's skin.

"That's scary."

"So you see, even if we were willing to work

things out, which we're not," Glynis added hurriedly, "it would be impossible. Our goals are still not the same. I want a home with a white picket fence around it and more children, and Cort...well, to tell you the truth, I don't know what he wants. I guess I never did. Only he's changed, Milly—he's hard and cynical and there's no reasoning with him."

"He's threatening to fight you for custody of Todd, isn't he?"

Glynis whipped around. "How did you know?"

"I didn't. I just guessed."

Glynis felt tears filling her eyes, warm and stinging, ready to trickle down her cheeks. She blinked them back and squared her shoulders. "Well, he's not going to take Todd away from me. I told him I'd fight him every step of the way."

"And you'll win, too, honey." Milly sighed and pushed herself up to full height. "But maybe it won't come to that. Maybe after the surgery he'll back off, take another overseas job." She shook her head regretfully. "Only the Lord knows about Cort Mc-Bride."

"Isn't that the truth," Glynis said with a sudden smile, determined to remove that pinched look from Milly's face. She'd put more of a burden on her friend's shoulders than was fair.

"You're feeling better now, aren't you?" Milly asked hopefully.

"Thanks to you." Glynis smiled. "I don't know what I'd do without you."

Milly adeptly switched the subject. "You want to stay and have lunch?"

Glynis glanced down at her watch. "Goodness, no. I didn't realize it was so late. You need to get back to work, and I need to take Todd home. In spite of what he said, I know he's still weak.'' She leaned over and kissed Milly on the cheek. ''You're a doll.''

Milly grinned her thanks. ''I just wish I had the answer to your problems with Cort.''

''You listened, and that's what's important,'' Glynis said, taking one last swig of her now-tepid coffee before making her exit.

Minutes later Glynis settled a tired Todd in the passenger seat, then made her way around the hood of the car. Just as she was about to get behind the wheel, she paused, suddenly nervous. It was there again, that same feeling she'd had that night at the carnival, the feeling that someone was watching her.

Frowning, she slowly turned around and scanned the area. She spotted him immediately. He was leaning against a tree across the street, his features hidden by the bill of a cap.

As her gaze settled on him, he pushed himself away from the tree and ambled down the street, acting as though he didn't have a care in the world.

Glynis stood there a moment longer and stared at the retreating figure.

''Mommy, what's the matter? You look kinda funny.'' Todd had scooted to the driver's side and was peering up at her.

She smiled reassuringly. ''Nothing's wrong, darling. I was just thinking.''

''Can we go now? I'm hungry.''

''Me, too.''

Disgusted with herself for letting herself get so rattled over nothing, Glynis got behind the wheel and promptly dismissed the episode from her mind.

* * *

When she pulled into the driveway at the ranch, there was a vehicle she didn't recognize sitting behind Cort's—a sleek foreign model. A man was in the process of climbing out of it.

"Wow!" Todd exclaimed. "Look at that car, Mommy."

"Mmm, nice, isn't it?" Glynis commented, but her thoughts were on the stranger, not on the car.

She guessed she'd find out who he was soon enough, as Cort and Barr chose that moment to round the corner of the house. By the time she and Todd walked up, they were shaking hands with the man.

Cort was the first to spot them, and his eyes narrowed. Feeling them on her, Glynis deliberately concentrated on the man, who was now propped against the side of his car.

"Glynis Hamilton, Gene Ridley, my right-hand man," Cort said promptly.

"Ms. Hamilton," Gene acknowledged, standing up and accepting her outstretched hand.

He was of average height and build with a receding hairline, which Glynis knew was deceptive. He was much younger than he looked, much younger in fact than his boss. And she was equally certain that his gray eyes, despite the thick glasses, wouldn't miss a thing. She'd bet, too, that he was as loyal to Cort as a lapdog.

"And this is Todd," Cort was saying, his tone abrupt.

"Hi, Todd," Ridley said with a smile.

"Hi," Todd answered shyly.

"Gene's here to discuss some business," Cort said by way of an explanation, his gaze once again fixed on Glynis.

And she knew what that business was: finding a way to keep Cort alive. Without being aware of it, she shivered, then looked up, straight into Barr's eyes. He winked, then grinned. She couldn't help but smile.

Cort cleared his throat. "Barr, why don't you and Gene go to my office? I want to speak to Glynis a minute. I'll be there shortly."

"Can I go with Uncle Barr, Mommy?" Todd chimed in, pulling on her hand. "I'm hungry."

Glynis lifted inquiring eyes to Barr. "Would you mind asking Maude to feed Todd?"

"Consider it done," Barr replied, throwing another grin in Glynis's direction. Then, placing an arm around the boy, he added, "Come on, let's you and me go rustle up some grub."

When the others were out of range, Cort focused on Glynis once more, his expression grim. More than likely his mind was on last night, as was hers, thinking how close they had come to doing something they would both regret.

"Where have you been?"

Glynis was taken aback by his brusqueness. "At Milly's, but I can't see why that's any concern of—"

"Couldn't you just once not make a damn big deal out of everything I say?" Cort thrust a savage hand through his hair and added, "What the hell! I don't know why I even bother to talk to you."

Glynis gasped, but for once, and for reasons she couldn't justify, she curbed her tongue. Maybe it was because he looked ready to fall on his face. His eye was almost swollen shut next to the cut, and the knot on his head had a yellowish tinge to it.

Suddenly an unreasoning fear gripped her. What if the person who wanted to harm him tried again and this time succeeded? The thought of anything happening to him... No, she wouldn't think about that. Not now. After he'd given Todd his bone marrow, then he could go play his dangerous games and get himself killed if he wanted to.

She didn't mean that, she told herself. She hadn't meant it last night and she didn't mean it now. And that, she feared, was the crux of her whole problem.

"Glynis."

She flinched, then looked directly at him.

"What did the doctor say about Todd?"

She relaxed a bit, feeling on safe ground. "He's fine. Just a virus."

"Thank God."

"How about yourself? How do you feel?"

"Do you really care?" he asked in an odd voice.

She swallowed, determined not to let him rattle her again. "Yes, I care," she said softly.

Deep blue eyes looked into her heavy-lidded ones, and for a moment the silence was charged. Then Cort drew in a ragged breath and seemed to regroup.

"How do I look like I feel?"

"Like you've been run over by a Mack truck."

The corners of his mouth curved into a smile. "I couldn't have said it better myself."

They both smiled, and the moment was electric.

Suddenly Cort cleared his throat. "You wanna work on the house this evening?"

Dumbfounded, Glynis lifted her brows. "You're in no condition to work on anything, much less the house."

"I can do a little, which is better than nothing."

"All...right."

His eyes searched hers for another moment before he turned and walked toward the house.

Glynis didn't know how long she stood in the sun, transfixed, wondering if she would ever piece together the puzzle that was Cort McBride.

The minute Cort walked into his office and closed the door, he forced thoughts of Glynis to the back of his mind, though he had a hell of a time doing it. Damn, but she'd looked beautiful standing in the sunlight, the wind molding the material of her blouse to the generous curves of her breasts....

With a muttered curse, he tossed his hat on the desk and turned to Barr. "Did you get Todd squared away?"

"Sure did," Barr drawled, easing back in his chair, spreading his long legs out in front of him. "When I left him with Maude, he was eating like a logroller."

"Good," Cort murmured, the scowl on his face easing somewhat. Then to Gene, "You ready to get down to business?" His tone had turned rough and businesslike.

Before Gene could respond, Barr put in, "You mind if I stick around? I'd kinda like to know who's trying to make you a statistic, little brother."

"That makes two of us."

"Three," Gene interceded quietly, but with the same deadly edge to his voice.

His eyes still on Gene, Cort said, "I guess the first order of the day is to fill you in on what happened."

"That's why I'm here."

Cort told him, and when he finished, the room was quiet.

Gene broke the silence. "Hell, Cort, you're one lucky sonofabitch."

"That's exactly what I told him," Barr added, reaching in his pocket and pulling out a cigarette.

Cort frowned. "I thought you'd quit smoking."

"I only light up when I'm nervous."

Cort snorted, throwing his brother a disgusted look.

"You think you were the target all along, right?" Gene asked, inching forward in his chair.

Cort sat down behind his desk and leaned on his elbows before answering him. "Sure as hell do. The bullet was meant for me, not Boyd Fisher."

Gene loosened the tie around his neck. "And since they didn't get the job done the first time, they tried again." He paused. "And will more than likely try a third time."

"But who?" Cort's tone was low, as if speaking to himself.

"I don't know," Gene said, "but we're going to find out."

"Any ideas?" Barr asked, getting up and stalking to the window.

Cort's stomach twisted into knots. "No, but I know a good place to start."

"Me, too," Gene said. "The prison."

"Right. Check their roster to see if anyone's been released lately who might have a grudge against me."

Gene stood. "I'll get on it now."

"At least stay for lunch," Cort said, standing as well.

Gene grabbed his briefcase. "Thanks, but no thanks. If it's all the same to you, I'll head back to the office and make some phone calls." He paused and turned to Barr. "Nice meeting you."

"Same here."

Gene switched his briefcase to his other hand. "I'll be in touch, Cort."

"Me, too," Barr said, joining Gene at the door. "You watch your step, little brother, you hear?"

"Yeah," Cort muttered tersely, his shoulders slumped in despair. "I hear."

Chapter 15

Glynis cocked her head to one side while she slowly perused the kitchen and the adjoining dining room. Not bad, not bad at all, she thought with a giddy sense of excitement. The renovations on the house were progressing much faster and coming together much better than she'd ever thought possible. And with such quaint charm, too.

She'd chosen an off-white color for the walls, and the floors and counters were bright yellow and orange.

For the past week she, Cort and Barr had outdone themselves, working long hours during the day as well as in the evenings. She found herself doing things that until a few weeks ago were foreign to her—hammering, wallpapering and painting.

Still, the majority of the work had fallen on Barr's shoulders, and she knew she would never be able to repay him for the time and energy he had put into her home.

Cort, for the most part, had continued to supervise, along with Todd. ''Mommy, me and Uncle Cort are the foremen on this job,'' her son had announced one morning. The memory brought a smile to her lips.

She thanked God that Cort had adhered to the doctors' orders and hadn't done anything strenuous. But then she'd suspected he hadn't partly because he hadn't felt like it. The wreck had set him back more than he wanted to admit. She had seen the way he grimaced when he turned a certain way or moved too quickly. Every time that happened, she was reminded of the accident and her stomach would knot.

However, with both Cort's and Gene Ridley's expertise, there was no doubt in Glynis's mind that whoever was responsible for the attempts on Cort's life would be caught and dealt with accordingly. She certainly didn't envy the culprit. When provoked, Cort was without mercy.

After all, wasn't she living testimony to that? Suddenly twisting her lips bitterly, she walked out of the kitchen and into the living room where she sank into one of the lawn chairs that Cort had brought from the ranch.

It wouldn't be long now before she and Todd would be able to move in. The time couldn't come soon enough; she honestly didn't know how much longer she could last under such nerve-racking conditions.

The knowledge that she was tangled in a web she'd never intended to weave was enough to keep her awake most nights and upset most days. It forced her to work that much harder to get the house livable.

This morning saw no change. She'd been out of bed at seven o'clock and at the house by eight. She had been working nonstop ever since.

And if her torrid relationship with Cort wasn't enough, she now had another worry to contend with. A much more serious one: Todd. At the beginning of the week, he had developed a low-grade infection. It had scared her so badly that she and Cort had made a fast trip to Houston. While not serious enough to hospitalize him, it was a cause for concern.

Until the infection cleared, Dr. Johns had told them a date for the transplant could not be discussed, even if Cort received a clean bill of health.

Now, after a week of following the doctor's orders, Todd was better. Not well, but definitely better. If only Cort would get a good report, she thought, peering down at her watch. He was due back from the doctor's office any moment now, and she expected him to stop and give her the verdict before going to the ranch.

The air-conditioning unit suddenly clicked on, claiming her attention. She listened to its steady hum for a minute, as if in a trance.

"Get a move on," she said aloud to her weary limbs. She moved quietly toward the bedroom where Todd lay sleeping on a pallet.

Just as she reached the door, he sat up and began rubbing his right eye with the back of his hand.

"Hi, darling," Glynis said, peering at him closely. Beyond looking a little weak, he seemed his same, endearing self.

"Hi, Mommy," he replied.

Glynis crossed to the pallet and sat down beside

him. Then, pulling him into the crook of her arm, she whispered, "I love you."

"I love you, too, Mommy."

"How do you feel?"

He snuggled close to her breast for a moment and let her hold him. "I feel okay."

"Are you sure?" Glynis laid her hand to his forehead and was visibly relieved when he felt cool to her touch.

"Uh-huh," he muttered. "I'm thirsty, though."

She kissed him on top of the head and gently pushed him away. "Well, Mommy can take care of that problem right now. I brought you some white grape juice in the ice chest."

"After I drink it, can I help you work?"

She smiled at him and pushed a strand of hair out of his eyes. "I'm sure there's something you can do, but remember Dr. Johns doesn't want you to get too tired."

His bottom lip drooped. "I know," he said sadly.

Glynis sympathized, pulling him to her and giving him another quick squeeze before letting him go and getting to her feet. "But it won't be long and you'll be as good as new." She prayed silently that she spoke the truth.

"Mom."

Todd's low-keyed voice stopped her at the door. She swung around and faced him, her brows raised in question. "What, darling?"

He had reached for one of the many comic books scattered around him and was holding it. "Are you and me gonna live here?"

"Yes," she said, though not without a slight hesitation.

He frowned. "What about Uncle Cort?"

Glynis leaned against the door for support. "What...what about him?"

"Won't he be lonesome if we leave him?"

She kept her voice even with effort. "I'm sure he'll miss you...."

"I know he will, too, 'cause he told me."

Glynis's heart sank. "He told you that?"

Todd nodded his head.

"When?"

"Last night, Mommy. Don't you 'member?"

She felt herself shiver. "That's right. He...he brought your medicine to you at bedtime."

"And that's when he said he'd miss me—a whole bunch."

There was such a mixture of turbulent emotions churning within her now, she could barely put her thoughts into coherent words. "He'll come see you."

"But it won't be the same," Todd said petulantly.

"No, it won't be the same," Glynis echoed, massaging the throbbing pulse at her temple.

"Then why do we have to move? Why can't we stay with Uncle Cort?"

She had known the question was coming. Still, it hurt; the pain was like a dull knife in the heart. She struggled to hold her patience and her temper. "We've been over this before, Todd. And my answer is the same. We are not going to stay at the ranch. Mommy wants us to have a place of our own. And as soon as the house is fixed up, we're going to move in."

He didn't say anything; he just looked at her, then turned and flopped onto his stomach, cradling his chin in his hands.

Her lungs ached from the sheer effort of breathing. *I won't let him have you!* her mind screamed. *I'll see him in hell first.* After looking at her son for another long moment, she swung around and headed toward the kitchen, feeling as if her heart were lined with lead.

She had just poured Todd's juice and was on her way back to the bedroom with it, along with his medicine, when a cloud of dust rose outside the living-room window. She paused and stared outside.

A Jeep had just pulled up outside the house.

Cort switched off the ignition and then sat back and watched as the dust settled around the Jeep. Damn, but they needed a rain, he thought idly. It wasn't just the farmers, either. The ranchers, himself included, were beginning to feel the pinch. June had been an unusually dry month, and July had started out the same.

But the weather was not what was dominating his thoughts. It was Glynis. Even though he hated to admit it, he was concerned about her.

Maybe what he was about to tell her would restore some of the color to her face that had been missing since Todd had gotten that infection. She'd been worried sick about him, but then so had he.

When they had walked into Dr. Johns's office, it was as if they were both headed for the guillotine. Even though the news had not been traumatic, as expected, Glynis had taken the setback quite hard.

In addition, their situation wasn't helping any. And he knew who was to blame. If he'd known what he knew now, he would never have insisted she stay at the ranch.

"Damn!" he spat aloud, yanking his hat off and slamming it down on the seat beside him.

The need for Glynis had become an ache deep inside him ever since she'd burst through the door at the farmhouse and he'd seen her anxious eyes and heard her scalding tongue.

Suddenly he looked up and saw Glynis standing at the window, staring at the Jeep, probably wondering why he was still sitting there.

He muttered another nasty expletive, then reached for his hat and after plunking it down on his head, he jerked open the door and got out.

When he walked inside, Glynis was coming out of the small bedroom, pulling the door to behind her, looking good in cutoffs that displayed her long limbs to perfection and a T-shirt that did the same for her upturned breasts.

She paused, and while their eyes met and held, he felt the involuntary response of his body.

Glynis was the first to break the eye contact. She walked toward him, not stopping until she was within touching distance. That was when he noticed her eyelashes were clumped together in tiny wet spikes. He frowned inwardly.

He waited, as did she, the silence seeming to tear at both of them.

Cort finally found his voice. "What's wrong?"

"Nothing," she said quickly.

He knew better. "You've been crying."

She looked away, but not before he saw her lower lip tremble. It took every ounce of willpower he possessed not to grab her and haul her into his arms and tell her that everything was going to be all right. But he couldn't, because he didn't know if anything was ever going to be all right again.

"Glynis, is it Todd?" He heard the panic in his own voice.

She ran a tongue over her upper lip without opening her mouth. "No, actually, he's feeling better. He's clear of fever and beginning to get restless."

"Where is he now?"

"On the pallet in the bedroom, looking at his comic books."

"Then why the tears?" he asked carefully.

She looked up at him, her wide-spaced eyes large and confused, and again he went instantly hard. He coughed and averted his gaze.

"I guess I'm just scared and tired of waiting," she finally said.

While he wasn't satisfied with her answer, he knew it would do no good to press any further, not with her chin jutted obstinately. So he said, "That makes two of us, but as far as I'm concerned, the wait is over."

Her cheeks reddened. "You got a good report?"

"Yeah, how 'bout that? My blood count is back to normal, and everything is functioning properly."

She pressed her hand against her forehead. "Thank God for that. Now as soon as Todd gets over this infection, we can get on with it."

"But in the meantime you need a break."

"What?" Caution had crept into her voice.

"A break," he repeated, "a break in your routine."

She shook her head. "No, that's exactly what I don't need. I want to be settled into this house before Todd has his surgery."

Cort's eyes took on a hard glaze. "There's no need to rush, you know."

"I disagree," she replied firmly.

"All right then, I'll take Todd by myself."

He saw fear spring into her eyes, and he cursed himself silently.

"Where?"

"Fishing."

"Fishing?"

"Yeah, fishing. You know, where you take a minnow and attach it to the end of a pole and put the pole…"

The look she gave him spoke louder than words.

"Just answering your question," he said with mock innocence. "Barr and I have a cabin on Lake Rayburn, and I've been looking forward to taking Todd there."

"Todd's not able to go fishing." Her tone was emphatic.

"Who says?"

"I do."

"So, what if I disagree?" His voice had dropped to a dangerous level.

"It doesn't matter."

He struggled desperately to hold on to his temper. "I thought we had all this settled. All I want to do is take the boy fishing." He stared up at the ceiling. "Surely you can't begrudge me that?"

She seemed to wilt right there on the spot, as if she couldn't bear to see the dull hurt reflected in his eyes. "I won't let him go without me."

"If you'll recall, I invited you, too."

"I'll…we'll go only on one condition."

"And what is that?" The blood vessels on his neck stood out.

"Barr. I want Barr to go, too."

For a moment there was silence. Cort took a step closer, his eyes flashing like glittering steel. "All right," he spat, "I'll agree to that, but hear this...." He paused and loomed closer, watching the color drain from her face. "*If* I wanted to crawl in your bed and take what you so dangerously offered the other night, you, Barr or a whole damned army couldn't stop me."

With that he turned and strode toward the door, only to suddenly stop midway and swing back around. Totally ignoring Glynis's open mouth and chalk-white features, he added, "We're leaving in one hour. Be ready."

Chapter 16

"Oh, Mommy, we're gonna have so much fun. I can't wait."

Glynis forced enthusiasm into her voice. "I'm glad you're looking forward to it."

She and Todd were in the Jeep, buckled in and waiting while Cort was on the phone, having received a call just as they were walking out the door. She suspected it was from his office in Houston or he wouldn't have stalked back inside to take it.

Todd squirmed in the seat. "Uncle Cort said there are big fish in the lake and that I'll be able to catch one—one that big, Mommy." He proceeded to stretch his small arms as wide as they would go.

"Now, darling, not everything Uncle Cort tells you is necessarily true," she cautioned, reaching out to push the hair out of his eyes. Although she smiled, there was a seriousness in her tone that he picked up on.

"Why?" he asked, looking slightly crestfallen.

She searched for the right answer. "Well, for one thing Uncle Cort knows how to catch the big ones and you don't."

"He'll help me," Todd said confidently, his smile wide and innocent. "He promised."

Glynis swallowed a sigh. "I'm sure he will."

Before Todd could reply, Cort opened the door on the driver's side and got in.

No one spoke while he jammed the key in the ignition. Then, turning impersonal eyes on Glynis, he asked, "All set?"

"What about...Barr?"

Though his lips tightened, his voice remained as calm and impersonal as before. "He'll be down later."

Glynis released her breath slowly and stared straight ahead, trying her best to disregard the way the inside of the vehicle seemed to shrink the moment Cort got inside. She was instantly aware of his cologne, the way his hands moved in a caressing motion around the steering wheel, the same way they had once caressed her....

She blinked and turned her head to gaze outside the window, watching as the city limits of Lufkin disappeared and the highway toward Etoile and Lake Sam Rayburn stretched in front of her.

Beside her, Todd was hanging on to Cort's every word, listening to tales of fishing ventures.

It had crossed her mind earlier to tell Cort she'd changed her plans, that she and Todd weren't going after all. But she hadn't been able to do that to Todd. When she'd told him that Cort was taking him fishing, his pale face had brightened, and he'd gotten so excited that she hadn't the heart to disappoint him.

So she had decided to make the best of the outing, thereby conserving her energy and her wits. Though she was loath to admit it, the break would do her good as well.

How long had it been since she'd laughed, really laughed? She didn't know, but it had been a long time. Too long. And maybe, just maybe, she might even catch a fish herself.

Suddenly she felt a hand on her arm. In a jerking motion, she looked down into her son's upturned face.

"Mommy, what's funny?"

"What makes you think something's funny?"

"'Cause you're smiling, that's why."

"Mmm, so I was," Glynis said, venturing a glance in Cort's direction.

As if feeling the pull of her eyes, he turned and looked at her.

"Why, Mommy?" Todd was asking again, jerking on the hem of her shorts.

She turned her gaze from Cort to her son. "I was thinking about the time I caught a big fish."

Todd bounced in the seat. "Wow! Really, Mommy? You caught a fish?"

Over her son's display of excitement, she heard Cort's swift intake of breath. Then he looked at her, and for a brief moment his eyes seemed to absorb every part of her face and body. "So you do remember." His voice was rough.

"I remember," she said huskily.

"'Member what, Mommy?" Todd was looking back and forth from her to Cort.

With her heart thumping, Glynis finally focused on

Todd. "The fish, son. I remember catching a big fish."

"Just one. That's all you ever catched?"

"Caught," she said gently.

Cort was smiling down at Todd. "Your mommy wasn't the best with a fishing pole, that's for sure."

Todd wrinkled his nose. "Most girls aren't. They don't like crawly worms or little fishes they have to put on the hook."

Cort laughed a deep, hearty laugh, one that sent Glynis's pulse skyrocketing. She eased another glance in his direction, but saw that he had eyes only for Todd.

Suddenly Glynis ached for him to look at her like that again—with tenderness and love instead of raw desire—only to then rebuke herself for her maudlin thoughts, knowing there would never be anything but red, hot desire between them.

Glynis was roused out of her thoughts a short time later when Cort stopped the Jeep in front of a small grocery and bait store.

"Why are we stopping?" she muttered inanely.

"Why do you think?" There was a touch of acid in his tone. "For food and bait."

"Oh."

Cort shook his head and beckoned for Todd to come with him.

Glynis scrambled out the door on her side, feeling foolish. "I'll help," she said unsteadily, upping her pace to catch up with them.

Cort stopped and swung around. "You think you can handle rounding up some sandwich stuff—chips, drinks, etcetera?"

She reacted as if stung. "Yes, of course I can."

Once they were back in the Jeep and on their way, Glynis leaned her head back and closed her eyes, wondering how she was going to get through the next two days.

"Mommy, Mommy, we're here!" Todd was saying, once again bouncing up and down in the seat between them.

"Goodness, darling," Glynis said gently but firmly, "you'd best settle down or you'll be worn out before you ever wet a line."

"Are you gonna go out in the boat right now?" Todd demanded of Cort, while Glynis looked around at her surroundings.

"Yep. Just as soon as we get unloaded. Here, give me a hand, will ya?"

"Sure thing," Todd said in his most grown-up voice.

Glynis had her hand on the door handle, but she couldn't move. "You call this a cabin?" she challenged, her gaze swinging to Cort. "Why, it's nicer than most people's houses."

Sitting on top of a hill, the two-story brick was a replica of a Swiss chalet, made even more spectacular by the terraced yard that didn't stop until it reached the lake.

"I take it you like it." His lips curved into what she thought was a smile.

"Like it? It's beautiful."

"Yeah, it is, isn't it." He sighed. "I just wish I could spend more time here."

"You could—you just won't," she responded without thinking.

His expression changed. "You're right, I could.

And I just might remedy that once the transplant is over and Todd gets on his feet.''

His meaning was not lost on her, but before she responded in kind, his booted foot hit the ground and, with Todd in tow, they headed for the cabin.

Glynis had no choice but to follow, though she fumed with every step she took.

The inside was every bit as beautiful as the outside, Glynis noted. The downstairs was composed of the kitchen, dining and living area, the latter dominated by a fireplace and bookshelves. But what made the house special was the view from the ceiling-to-floor windows that flanked an entire wall. The lake twinkled in the distant sunlight like millions of tiny diamonds.

However, she didn't have much time to soak up the primitive beauty. By the time she put the groceries away and tossed their overnight bags in the bedrooms upstairs, Cort had the boat loaded and was ready to go.

"I'm coming," she shouted before taking another second to tie her hair back with a ribbon that matched her green shorts and halter top. Then, bounding down the stairs, she made her way outside and down the slope where the boat was moored, feeling excited in spite of herself.

"You gonna bait your own hook, Mommy?" Todd asked twenty minutes later, after the boat was safely anchored in an alcove that Cort promised was loaded with white perch.

She frowned. "Well..."

"That's okay, Mommy, I'll do it for you."

"Would you?" Her tone oozed relief. "I'd sure like that."

From his place near the back of the boat, Cort snorted.

Glynis flashed him a look. "I can do it, you know."

"Well, then, do it," he said flatly. Then, directing his gaze to Todd, his expression lightened, and he grinned. "Got to learn the rules up front, Todd, my boy. If you fish, you have to bait your own hook."

Todd giggled. "Mommy, Uncle Cort says you have to stick your hand down in that box and get one of those little fishes and stick that hook through his eye—"

"Todd, that's enough!" She shivered.

This time both Cort and Todd threw back their heads and laughed. Glynis merely glared at both of them. But in the end, and much to the delight of her son, she did indeed bait her own hook as she'd been taught by Cort many years before.

Just as she was about to lower the baited hook on the end of a cane pole into the water, Cort came up beside her. Her hand stilled in mid-action.

"Here," he said, handing her a hat with a sun visor, "you'd better wear this in addition to suntan lotion. You have put on the lotion, haven't you?"

After anchoring the pole on the side of the boat, Glynis looked up at him steadily for a long minute, her head tipped back slightly. "No," she murmured, suddenly thrown into confusion by the way his eyes were targeted on her halter top. "I put some on Todd, but...but I didn't use it on myself."

"Well, I suggest you do." His voice sounded rough, like sandpiper. "You know how tender your skin is."

She touched her throat and kept staring at him, the

intensity of the moment as burning as the sun bearing down on them.

At last Cort muttered tautly, "Todd and I'll be fishing in the rear."

Her heart was still beating harder than it was supposed to seconds later when she watched him stop beside Todd, lift his rod and cast it into the water.

She was captivated by the way the muscles pulsed in his shoulders and arms every time he flicked the rod. Having discarded his shirt shortly after they arrived, he was skimpily clad in cutoffs and tennis shoes without socks. With his tanned face and body and his head bent in concentration, he reminded Glynis of a Greek god.

Glynis would have stared at him a second longer, only he chose that instant to swing around, as if feeling her hot gaze.

They stared deep into each other's eyes. The connective force of their gaze was palpable.

"Uncle Cort," Todd said, pointing a finger in the opposite direction. "Look, there comes another boat."

The moment was gone. Cort's expression tightened, and he turned around. Yet Glynis was unable to pull her eyes off the father and son who stood side by side eyeing the boat with the skiers trailing behind.

"Oh, no," she whispered, feeling as if she'd suddenly been punched in the stomach. Why hadn't she noticed before how much they actually favored each other, how wonderful, how right they looked together.

Violent and conflicting emotions suddenly charged through Glynis, and in order to squelch them, she grabbed the pole, only to then yelp with pain.

"Damn, damn, damn," she muttered under her

breath. At the same time she stared down at the end of her middle finger. The hook that should have been in a fish's mouth was now stuck in her.

"What now?" Cort was beside her, his voice harsh and impatient, as though he resented the interruption.

"It's…nothing," she said, clamping her lips together, determined not to bother him.

"Let me see." His voice no longer had that hard edge. His concern seemed genuine. No longer narrowed and filled with hostility, his eyes moved over her searchingly.

Without warning, he reached for her hand. "Don't lie to me," he said between clenched teeth, obviously not wanting to alarm Todd, who was intently watching his rod, unaware that anything out of the ordinary was going on.

A colorful expletive split the air when Cort saw the hook protruding from the end of her finger.

Glynis hadn't wanted to demonstrate any weakness, but she was losing control. Her stomach was beginning to heave sickeningly.

"I…I was going to pull it out, but…"

The rest of the sentence died on her lips as he took the hook out of her flesh and brought her finger to his lips and sucked on it.

Glynis's heart almost died in her chest, and for a moment the wound was of secondary importance. Their eyes met and locked, and even when he turned sideways and spat the blood into the water, they never broke eye contact.

Her breath came in short, gaspy spurts that drew his eyes down to her breasts. Glynis's eyelids fluttered, while she blushed uncontrollably, knowing that he was watching her nipples turn rigid.

He swallowed and looked at her intently. Her eyes were filled with awe that he cared. His burned with desire.

Then, as if angry with her, or with himself, he dropped her hand and drew back. "I've got some turpentine. If you'll soak your finger in it, it won't be sore."

Following that brusque delivery, he made his way back to his tackle box, and after rummaging through it for a second, came back, holding a bottle in one hand and a small cup in the other.

She forced her eyes on the bottle and watched as he poured its contents into the cup. But in reality that was all she was able to do. Her body felt hot and cold by turns, and tremors were shaking her lower body with want.

"Mommy, Mommy, come quick!" Todd laughed out loud, still unaware that anything was amiss. "Come see what I caught."

"I'm coming." Taking a deep breath, Glynis set the cup aside, stood, and without looking at Cort, slowly made her way to where her son was standing.

In spite of the shaky start, Todd's first catch was the beginning of a successful afternoon. After she had soaked her finger, the pain was gone except for a slight tenderness.

In no time the cooler boxes were filled with nice-sized fish, a mixture of bass and white perch, both native to the fresh waters of East Texas. It had been so long since she had tasted either that her mouth watered.

Thinking about dinner made her suddenly glance at her watch. Six o'clock. How the time had flown.

And she suspected Todd was getting tired even though he would never admit it.

"Cort," she called from her seat at the front of the boat, pulling in her pole and shading her eyes, "don't you think it's time we called it quits, got Todd back to the house?"

Cort was busy helping Todd reel in a fish and didn't answer her for a minute. Todd's excited squeal could be heard for miles around.

Once the fish was off the hook and safely in the box, however, Cort turned toward her. "Yeah. It's getting late."

"Aw, Uncle Cort," Todd wailed, "do we have to?"

Cort smiled down at him. "Yes, we have to," he mimicked.

"Can I drive the boat home?" Todd asked eagerly.

Cort swatted him on the rear and grinned. "Thought you'd never ask."

It was only after they had arrived back at the house and put the gear away, and Cort and Todd had cleaned and filleted the fish, that the back door opened.

"Hiya everybody," Barr drawled, breezing in.

Cort paused in his actions and stared at his brother with a smirk on his lips. "I knew you'd show up after all the work was done."

"You mean I missed all the fun?"

Cort snorted. "Yep, you sure did."

Barr ambled deeper into the room and winked at Todd, who rushed up to him. "Meant to get here sooner, but I got busy working on the house and time got away from me."

"Too bad you weren't with us, Uncle Barr," Todd said, grinning broadly. "We catched a lot of fish."

Glynis closed the refrigerator and faced Barr, a frown marring her features. "You mean you worked this afternoon?"

"Yeah. Put the finishing touches on several things. If all goes well, you and Todd should be able to move in next week."

Glynis's eyes brimmed with excitement. "We can? Oh, Barr, that's great."

"Mommy," Todd began, "I told you I don't—"

"Not now, Todd," Glynis cut in quickly. Her tone brooked no argument.

Todd hung his head. "Yes, ma'am."

Cort turned a piercing gaze on Glynis. "Why not let the boy finish?" he said in a soft, dangerous tone.

Glynis raised her chin a notch. But before she could say anything, Barr chimed in, his gaze on Todd.

"Hey, fellow, how 'bout you and me taking a spin in the boat? No fishing, just a ride out on the lake to watch the sun set."

Todd switched his gaze to Glynis. "Mommy, can I?"

Doing her best to regroup, Glynis twisted her head toward her son. "Oh, Todd, honey, I don't think so. You've had a long afternoon...."

"Oh, please, Mom, please. I'm not tired. I cross my heart, I'm not." With childlike movements, he proceeded to do just that, crossing his thin arms over his chest.

Glynis couldn't help but smile, only to have it turn into a quick frown. "He's had a long afternoon, Barr."

"I promise we won't be gone longer than an hour."

Glynis tweaked Todd's ear. "All right, you little con artist. But when you come back, it's dinner and straight to bed."

The second Todd and Barr exited the room, Glynis cut a glance in Cort's direction. He was leaning against the hearth, his arms folded across his chest.

There was a drawn-out silence.

Her skin felt hot under his gaze. Finally, in a halting voice, she said, "I'm…going to take a shower."

"You should listen to Todd, you know." His tone was soft, yet its timbre made it sound thunderous in the quiet room.

She didn't pretend to misunderstand him. "Todd's only a child. He'll make adjustments." Then, without giving him a chance to respond, she wheeled around and dashed up the stairs.

Thirty minutes later she was back downstairs with a new resolve. She would not let Cort rattle her or goad her into arguing with him over her and Todd's imminent departure from the ranch.

She found him on the deck, fiddling with the electric fish fryer, the fish and french fries ready for frying on a nearby table.

It was obvious he'd also showered, as his hair was damp. But he hadn't bothered to shave. There was more than a hint of stubble on his face and chin.

She paused in the doorway and swallowed against the rising heat inside her, trying not to notice how the tight, worn jeans did little to minimize the bulge between his thighs. She forced her eyes away, despising the way her body responded, yet unable to control it.

She felt like a frayed cable that was stretched too tight. She had to get away from him.

Nervously stepping forward, she said with a forced lightness she was far from feeling, "Need any help?"

He spun around, as if unaware she'd been watching him. "No," he said. His eyes raked over her, before coming once again to rest on her breasts.

Glynis averted her gaze toward the sun setting across the water. Her eyes widened.

"It's something, isn't it?" Cort drawled, following her eyes.

"It's absolutely breathtaking. I can understand why you like to come down here."

"Feel free to use it anytime you like," he said unexpectedly.

"Do you mean that?"

His head came up quickly. "I wouldn't have said it if I didn't."

"Well, er, thanks," she said uneasily, still not trusting his motives. Yet she wasn't about to look a gift horse in the mouth. "I've never seen Todd so happy."

Cort actually laughed. "Yeah, he did have a great time. The little bugger is a damned good fisherman."

"Yes, he is, isn't he? Just think, when he gets well, he can fish every day."

"Only he won't be around to fish, will he?"

"What do you mean?" Her mouth was dry.

"You know exactly what I mean. You don't intend to stay in Lufkin, do you?"

"Who told you that?"

He thrust his face close to hers. "You did."

She backed up and stopped only when she plowed

against the brick wall. "You don't know what you're talking about," she hedged.

"Deny it, then."

Her temper flared. "I don't owe you an explanation one way or the other."

"That's where you're wrong. As long as I'm footing Todd's bills, you damn sure do."

"I'll pay back every cent!" Glynis cried, her eyes blazing, her arms outstretched as if to stop him from getting closer.

"I think I'll settle on payment right now."

"Don't." Her voice was little more than a hoarse croak as she struggled to brace herself.

But there was no stopping him. Their lips were only a hairbreadth apart. She shoved at his chest to ward him off.

With little effort, he grasped her arms and pulled her against him.

"Don't fight me," he groaned, burying his mouth in her scented neck. "You want this just as much as I do."

He trailed kisses around her cheek until he reached her lips. He kissed her hard. She tried to wiggle free, still determined not to give in, but he was indisputably in control. He sought entrance into her mouth, and with the tender penetration, he used his mouth as a weapon to skillfully wipe out her resistance. It worked.

Glynis was burning. She had never wanted anything the way she wanted Cort's mouth, his hands, his body. She matched his stroking tongue with hers, tasting him until their lips fused as one breathless, intoxicating unit.

With her hands in his hair, she drank him in, feeling his steely hardness between her legs.

Finally gasping for breath, Cort moved her to arm's length, and for a moment their eyes clung as each remembered how it once had been between them, how it hopefully would be again.

The wind whistled through the trees as the evening's shadow settled around them, creating a cooling balm for their heated skin. But nothing had the power to dissipate their hungry craving for each other.

He lowered his eyes to her breasts, taking in her nipples as they dented her T-shirt. He fingered one, then the other while she touched him, her fingers tracing exquisite patterns.

Cort jerked his head up and groaned as if in mortal pain. Then returning glazed eyes to her, he began tearing at the tiny buttons on her shirt. Finally the last one was undone, and her breasts spilled into his waiting hands.

Groaning again, he dipped his head and took a breast in his mouth; her nipple throbbed, and a long sigh that was his name broke from her at the pleasure his lips were bringing her. He moved to nuzzle her long throat, but her breasts were too close, too tempting, and he bent close to suck them again—first one, then the other, harder.

Still that didn't seem to satisfy him. He nuzzled her neck, massaged his face between her breasts, nipped at her collarbone with his teeth and inhaled the scent of her body like an aphrodisiac.

"Glynis?" he asked softly.

"Yes," she whispered, even as she lowered her hand to caress him.

"Oh, God," he said in a half-strangled cry, before

quickly turning her in his arms and propelling her urgently through the open glass door into the living room. Together they sank as one onto the thick carpet.

"This is for all those times I've dreamed of," he whispered, quickly and adeptly peeling their clothes from their bodies.

With nothing between them but the air they breathed, he bent over her and watched with glowing eyes as he trailed his fingers feverishly, urgently across her breasts, down to her stomach, to the insides of her thighs, where he lingered. And while holding her, sealing his lips to hers, he eased his fingers inside her.

"Oh, Cort!" she cried.

He stopped kissing her to whisper, "Did I hurt you? You were so wet...."

"No!" she cried again, moving her hips rhythmically in response to his fingers, feeling that terminal heat inside her.

"Forgive me," he rasped suddenly, "but I can't wait. It's been so long...."

He entered quickly and deeply then, and she grasped him, her arms and legs locking him to her. She heard a deep cry, but she didn't know if it was her own or his. She could only feel him inside her.

She began to shake. Only then did Cort bury his face in her hair and surrender to an explosion of release so intense, so shattering that he lost himself in her.

Chapter 17

They lay on the couch in the living room, fully clothed now, Cort at one end, Glynis at the other. They both had mugs full of hot coffee, and their bare legs were entwined. It seemed for the moment that the feeling of skin against skin was a sensation they both needed.

At least for Glynis, anyway. From under thick eyelashes, she watched Cort as he sipped from his mug as if he was enjoying it. The lines around his eyes and mouth weren't nearly as deeply embedded, nor was he holding himself with such iron control.

She knew their lovemaking was crazy and would likely lead to more heartbreak, especially for her. But she didn't regret it.

Cort had been right. She had wanted, ached for his touch and she could blame no one but herself when it blew up in her face.

And Cort. Well, she had no idea what was going through his mind, but again she didn't care. At this very moment, he was the same man she had fallen in love with. For now that was enough.

With this thought in mind, Glynis slowly and shyly moved her leg against his in a massaging motion.

"Glynis."

"Mmm?"

"Was Jay good to you...and Todd?"

Her leg fell still. "What do you mean?"

His eyes were so intent, he forced her to look at him. "You know what I mean. Did he ever...hit you?"

"No," she said, her voice trembling. "But he came close to it one time." She turned away.

"When?"

"Shortly...after Todd was born. He never could, never did accept him."

"Is that why you never had any more children?"

"Yes."

"Speaking of children. Are you...using anything?"

Everything inside her seemed to shut down. "Do you mean, am I on the pill?"

"I guess that's what I'm trying to say."

"I'm not," she said, then added when she saw the color recede from his face, "but you don't have to worry, it's not the right time of the month."

Without responding, he changed the subject. "Jay started drinking shortly after Todd was born, right?"

She bit her lip as she let her breath escape in a slow sigh. "How did you know?"

"Oh, I knew, all right." His tone was low and husky. "I made it my business to know."

"Oh, Cort," she whispered, moisture collecting in her eyes, "we made a mess of things, didn't we?"

"Mess. That's hardly the word. I'd say we screwed up royally."

The tears chose that instant to spill from her eyes. Cort scowled. "Come here."

Glynis didn't hesitate. She crawled the length of the couch and snuggled into his outstretched arms.

He cupped a breast in his hand and began tugging on the nipple.

"Having a baby hasn't changed you all that much," he said quietly.

"How…how do you mean?"

His hold on her tightened. "You're still tight inside, hot…"

"Oh, Cort," she groaned, lifting her eyes to his, the sound of his voice, his words, disturbing her almost as much as the glare she saw in his eyes. Her breathing quickened.

"Don't look at me like that," he whispered.

"Like what?"

"Like how good it was when I was inside you—"

"Cort, please," she said, her voice shaking.

"Ah, my darling, my nemesis," he murmured, stroking her as if reveling in the feel of her next to him.

"I didn't mean to be," she said, trying to keep her thoughts on track.

"I know." The thickly spoken words came after he'd set both cups on the coffee table, and after his hard mouth had swooped down on hers, prolonging the embrace until she hung weak and shuddering in his arms.

It was much later when she said his name on a ragged breath. "Cort."

"Uh-huh?"

"Have…have there been lots of…women?"

For a moment he didn't say anything; he just continued to knead her breast. "There have been some."

"Were…any of them important to you? I mean…I thought you would…have married.…" She broke off, feeling like an utter fool. But even if his answer killed her soul, she had to know.

"Well, you thought wrong," he said flatly.

"I didn't mean to pry," she began awkwardly, realizing that she had shattered the fragile moment into a thousand pieces.

He rolled into a sitting position, then stood, offering her his hand. "Come on," he said in a strained voice, "I hear the boat."

"So do I," she whispered, her voice as dry as a rustling leaf.

Though he continued to hold her hand, he looked anywhere but at her. Finally he stared down at her.

Something soft and strange flickered across his face, some emotion she wasn't able to read—maybe pain, maybe something that went beyond pain. "I…" he began at last.

Glynis shook her head. "I know what you were going to say, that this doesn't change things between us.…"

"No, that wasn't what I was going to say."

She felt hot and cold by turns. "What…were you going to say, then?"

Footsteps pounded on the deck. He dropped her hand and stepped back, his face closed, as if a door had slammed shut on it.

Her skin burned where his hand had been.

"Cort?"

His eyes delved into her for a long, static moment. Then he said, "Forget it. It wasn't important anyway."

For the longest moment, Glynis couldn't move, feeling as though she'd been kicked in the stomach.

"Mommy, why do I have to go back to the hospital?"

Todd's face was pale and pinched, and his blue eyes, so like Cort's, locked on Glynis.

"You want to be well, don't you?" she asked softly, patiently.

"But I am well," he countered sullenly.

Glynis's troubled gaze sought Cort, who was standing against the wooden rail of the deck at the ranch, his hands jammed into his pockets. His tightly drawn features told her he was as troubled as she.

They had driven in from Houston only thirty minutes earlier, and after going to their respective rooms to change clothes, had met on the deck, where she and Cort planned to tell Todd about his upcoming surgery and Cort's role as donor.

After examining Todd and finding no traces of infection, Dr. Johns had scheduled the surgery for two weeks from today. It had been Glynis's decision not to tell Todd on the way home, because he had been so hyper after being poked and pulled on for an hour. He had slept in her arms for most of the trip home.

Once they had gathered on the deck, Mrs. Springer brought a tray of cookies and a pitcher of lemonade. And though their plates were piled high with goodies, they had remained untouched.

"Look, Todd," Cort was saying now, having ambled over to where Todd and Glynis sat next to each other, "going into the hospital is never any fun. Your mother and I know that and so do you." Before Todd could answer, Cort sat down in a lounge chair next to them and drew Todd's slight body between his legs.

"Then why do I have to go?" Todd asked again, climbing up on one of Cort's knees.

Without looking at Glynis, Cort went on, "Because like Mommy told you, this time when you get out, you'll be well."

Todd's wide eyes darted to Glynis and then back to Cort. "You mean I won't have to go back ever again?"

Glynis couldn't have answered him if she'd wanted to; there was too big a lump in her throat. All she could do was listen as Cort patiently and tenderly talked to his son.

Already Todd had been to hell, and he was soon to go there again. Sometimes, like now for instance, she didn't think she could stand it. If only she could bear the pain for him.

And she knew Cort was experiencing similar emotions, though he would never allow his emotions to get out of control. Yet a long moment passed before he spoke again.

"Yeah, that's what it means." Cort smiled and goosed him under the chin. "No more of that yucky-tasting mess that you've had to swallow for so long."

Todd angled his head. "Will you be at the hospital with Mommy?"

"You bet."

"Promise."

"I promise."

"Good," Todd said, showing wisdom far beyond his years, "'cause Mommy always cries when they hurt me."

"What if I cry, too?" Cort's voice seemed to come from a long way off.

Suddenly Glynis stood and averted her face, determined they wouldn't see the tears that were coursing down her cheeks. Nonetheless she felt Cort's eyes bore into her for a second, before he turned back to Todd.

Todd was grinning. "You wouldn't do that, Uncle Cort. Only girls cry." Then suddenly the grin disappeared, and his face fell. "But I cry sometimes, too," he admitted, lowering his head, "especially when it hurts."

Cort grabbed Todd then and pulled him close. "That's all right," he muttered roughly. "I know, and I understand. That's why I'm going to give you something from my body that's going to make you well."

Todd squirmed out of his arms and looked at Glynis. "Did you know that, Mommy?"

"Yes, darling."

Todd turned back to Cort. "What are you gonna give me?"

"Maybe we better let your mother explain. She knows more about it than I do."

Glynis did, and when she was through, Todd was quiet for a moment as if deep in thought. Then, wide-eyed, he said to Glynis, "Someday I'll be tall like Uncle Cort, won't I?"

Glynis couldn't bring herself to meet Cort's eyes, even though she felt them on her. "Yes, son," she whispered against the fresh onslaught of tears flooding her eyes. "You'll grow up to be just like...Uncle Cort."

Cort stood and cleared his throat. "Todd, how does a surprise sound to you?"

Glynis smiled at her son. "Mmm, sounds like fun to me."

"Me, too!" Todd gushed.

"You two stay put and I'll be right back."

A few minutes later Cort reappeared with a scruffy puppy in his arms that looked no older than six weeks.

"Wow!" Todd cried, running toward Cort, his arms outstretched.

Excitement replacing the tears in Glynis's eyes, she followed.

"Oh, Todd, isn't he cute?" she said, watching as Cort handed the squirming puppy to Todd.

The puppy began licking Todd's face with its tiny wet tongue. Todd giggled wildly while trying his best to control it. "What's it's name, Uncle Cort?"

Cort laughed. "That's for you to decide. You can name him whatever you want. He's yours."

"Mine," Todd whispered in awe.

"All yours, but you have to take care of him, which means feeding him every day."

With the puppy still wriggling in his arms, Todd shifted his gaze to Glynis. "Can I keep him, Mommy?"

Glynis leaned over and rubbed the top of the puppy's head. "Only if you do what Uncle Cort said."

"Oh, I will, I promise."

"Okay, we'll see," Glynis said somewhat sternly, yet with a bright smile on her face.

Suddenly Todd's face clouded. "But who will take care of him while I go to the hospital?" His chin wobbled slightly.

"Oh, I'm sure Mrs. Springer will be glad to do that for you, or maybe Uncle Barr will." Cort's tone was both gentle and reassuring and seemed to satisfy Todd. His features instantly brightened again.

"Have you thought of a name yet?" Glynis asked, glancing down at her son with adoring eyes.

"Not yet, Mommy. Give me time, will ya?"

Glynis laughed along with Cort. "Sorry, son, didn't mean to rush you," she said.

Todd lowered the puppy to the ground. "I'm going to take him for a walk," he announced proudly.

"All right, but remember to walk slowly."

When Todd scampered off, the puppy followed, its short legs pumping madly to keep up with Todd. Glynis raised her eyes to Cort's, which were already centered on her, and she and Cort both smiled.

"That…was thoughtful of you," she said, her mouth feeling as dry as cotton. "He's…Todd's never had a puppy or any animal of his own."

"Which is a damned shame."

"I know," she whispered, unable to tear her eyes from his.

She knew by the way he watched her mouth when they talked, and by the way his eyes seemed drawn to her body, that he wanted her, had not stopped wanting her since that day at the lake, the day he'd taken her.

And now, she could hear his breathing, could feel condensation forming in the space between them. She reached out to him frantically, only to suddenly stiffen in the arms that were locked around her like a vise.

The sound of an approaching vehicle shattered the moment as swiftly and accurately as an explosion would have done.

Pushing her away, Cort swore loudly and violently. "Who the hell..." he began, only to let his words fade. They both recognized the car that stopped in the drive.

"It's...it's Gene," Glynis said unnecessarily, grappling to regain her composure.

Cort didn't reply.

Nevertheless, his expression wasn't lost on her. "He's here about the...your accident, isn't he?"

"Yeah." Cort's response sounded laconic at best.

"Do you have any leads?" Glynis asked, saying the first thing that came to mind.

Cort kept his eyes on Gene, who was getting out of his car and walking toward them. "I'm about to find out."

"Well, I guess I'll go see how Todd and the puppy are faring," she murmured, feeling as if the ground were still shifting under her feet.

"Yeah, why don't you do that," Cort responded, his tone detached.

Taking him at his word, Glynis turned and headed in Todd's direction, and even though she felt Cort's brooding eyes follow her, she knew his thoughts were not on her.

"Wanna beer, or something?"

Gene Ridley shook his head in response to Cort's offer. "No thanks, not right now."

Cort shrugged. "If you change your mind..."

"I'll holler," Gene said.

They were in Cort's office, and while Gene rummaged through his briefcase, which he'd placed on one edge of Cort's desk, Cort sat in his chair and leaned back, propping his booted feet on the opposite corner.

"What do you have?" Cort asked evenly.

But Gene wasn't fooled. The hard, menacing edge was clearly visible in Cort's tone, and Gene picked up on it instantly.

"Names. I got names."

"Anything else?"

Gene shoved his glasses forward on the bridge of his nose. "Not at the moment."

"Well, the names are a start."

"Oh, before I forget to tell you," Gene said, snapping his briefcase shut, "Boyd Fisher came by this morning. Wanted to know how his case was progressing."

"What did you tell him?"

"I told him that he didn't have a case, that it was you they were after, not him."

Cort threw back his head and laughed. "Bet that rang his bell."

A smile toyed with Gene's rigid mouth. "I don't think he believed me at first, but after I told him about the Jeep, he changed his mind." Gene paused and laid the paper in front of Cort. "Of course, I told him that until we had proof that you are the target and he isn't, we'd still be covering him."

"Good," Cort said, removing his feet from the desk and rolling the chair forward, all in one fluid movement. He then picked up the paper and began scrutinizing it.

After a moment, Cort looked up. "This is the list of recent parolees, right?"

Gene was standing, watching him. He squinted. "Right. Any of those names leap out at you as possible suspects?"

"Yeah, as a matter of fact they do."

"Which ones?"

"John Brodrick, Ames Coleman and Al Sabo."

"As I recall, they each swore to get even with you when they got out of the slammer."

Cort shoved back the chair and stood. "Let's get rolling on this quick. If one of these is our man, I want the son of a bitch stopped. Find where they are and check 'em out."

"It's as good as done."

"Now, about the government contract."

"It's looking good. The papers are underneath the list. Take a good look at them and I'll get back to you in a few days."

"Right."

"By the way, when do you think you'll be back in the office?"

"Not for a while, I'm afraid," Cort answered with a sigh. "Todd's surgery is in a couple of weeks."

Gene gnawed at his lower lip. "I see." Following a moment of silence, Gene added, "You know I hope all goes well."

Cort nodded. "Thanks."

The moment Cort was alone, he sat back down at his desk and picked up the stack of papers, only to suddenly thrust them aside. The day had been long and nerve-racking. He couldn't concentrate on work; it was that simple. He could only think of Glynis and

how good it had felt, *how right,* to make love to her
once again.

Sighing deeply, he leaned back and stretched his
neck from side to side. The muscles in his neck were
so tight, he felt they might snap at any moment. And
well they should, he thought. It would serve him right
for fooling with dynamite on a short fuse.

But now that he'd feasted on the delights of her
body once again...

Suddenly he heard the door creak behind him.
Scowling, he swung around. His scowl deepened.

"Dammit, Barr! That's a good way to get your
head blown off."

"Hello to you, too, little brother."

Cort's face cleared somewhat. "Sorry."

"Apology accepted," Barr said, propping himself
against the door frame. "Maude told me Gene just
left. Did he bring you any names?"

"Yep. Pull up a chair and I'll fill you in."

You can do it, her mind kept telling her. *You can
do it.*

But Glynis wasn't so sure. She had been jogging
forty-five minutes, but her goal was sixty minutes. It
was her only way to combat stress, she kept telling
herself, forcing one leg in front of the other.

Sweat glistened in her hair, rolled down her face.

That passionate interlude with Cort at the lake tore
at her night and day. Making love to him had done
very little to calm the turmoil inside her; it had only
made it worse. She should never have let it happen.
But there was nothing she could do about it now except condemn herself for her weakness.

Their hot coupling had done nothing but fill a temporary need inside her, a need that was threatening to consume her again with each passing day.

And she knew if Cort hadn't regretted that interlude a week ago, heaven help her, but she would have swallowed her pride and gone to him, much as it shamed her to admit it.

If that wasn't enough of a problem, Todd's upcoming surgery had her nerves stretched as tight as they would go.

Suddenly she couldn't make it any farther. Her heart felt as if it were going to burst from her chest.

Taking deep, shuddering breaths, Glynis slowed to a fast walk and turned up the road that led to the ranch. After going straight to her room, she showered, slipped on a blue shirt and jeans and went into the kitchen.

Maude was busy preparing lunch. She stopped what she was doing and stared at Glynis. "My dear, what on earth? You look exhausted."

"I've been running."

"I thought you were supposed to do that either early in the morning or late in the evening."

"You are," Glynis said, crossing to the refrigerator, getting out a jug of juice and pouring herself a full glass. "I pulled a no-no. Ten o'clock is definitely not the best time to run."

Maude sniffed. "If you're not careful, someone will be picking you up off that dirt road one of these days."

Glynis smiled before taking a drink from her glass. "You're probably right, but my nerves needed it."

Maude's look turned sympathetic. "Mr. Cort told me the surgery's soon."

"It is. And speaking of Todd, do you know where he is? He was sleeping when I left."

"He ate breakfast and told me he was going to take Champ for a walk."

"I guess I'd better go find him. I don't want him getting too hot and tired." She paused at the door. "By the way, where is Cort?"

"He's at Barr's, helping him mend a fence."

Fifteen minutes later Glynis still had not found Todd. She had searched the yard and the barn, checking with the ranch hands, who hadn't seen him, either.

Nobody had seen him or the puppy.

By the time she entered the barn farthest from the house, where the horses were stabled, Glynis felt the stirrings of panic. Where was he?

Willis, one of Cort's most trusted hands, was brushing down a horse.

"Have you seen Todd?" she asked without preamble.

The old man raised himself to full height and rubbed his forehead. "No, ma'am, can't say that I have. Why?"

"I can't find him anywhere," Glynis said, hearing her voice crack.

"I'm sure he's around here somewhere, Miss."

"Look, would you please saddle a horse for me?"

"Sure will."

Minutes later Glynis's concern had tripled. She refused to speculate on the many things that might have befallen her son.

By the time she found Cort hunkered over a broken string of fence, fear had gripped her from head to toe.

The pounding of the horse's hooves brought Cort

to his feet. As she jerked the reins to a halt directly in front of him, he frowned.

"What the hell, Glynis?"

"It's...Todd. I...I can't find him anywhere."

Chapter 18

Cort reached Glynis just as she started to get off the horse. Circling her waist with his hands, he lowered her to the ground.

"What do you mean you can't find him?"

Glynis mopped her brow with the back of her hand and looked up into Cort's pale, taut features. "I came back to the house from jogging and began looking for him. Maude told me he ate breakfast and went to play with Champ."

"Did you check the barns?"

"Yes, I've looked everywhere."

"And no one's seen him?"

Glynis shook her head. "No."

Suddenly he felt his heart slam against his rib cage. Had Todd been kidnapped? Had the man after him taken his son?

Fear made him move quickly. With a murderous

glint in his eyes, Cort detached Glynis's clinging
hands from the front of his shirt and put her at arm's
length. Then, twisting his head, he beckoned for Barr,
who was already walking toward them.

"Get the lead out, man!"

"I'm coming, I'm coming," Barr called. "What's
up?"

By the time he reached them, Cort's eyes were
back on Glynis. She looked as though she might faint.
Her face was the color of chalk. He longed to reassure
her that Todd would be found unharmed, but the comforting words wouldn't come. Fear and red-hot anger
threatened to choke him.

"What's going on?" Barr demanded, when both
Glynis and Cort continued to stand mute.

"Glynis can't find Todd," Cort finally said.

If Barr's expression was anything to judge by, Cort
knew his brother was thinking the same thing he was.
"Damn!" Barr muttered. "What next?"

Glynis's gaze swung between the two men. "Is
there something going on I don't know about?" It
was obvious from the way her voice rose several oc-
taves that hysteria was very close to the surface.

Cort's eyes softened as he looked at her, and then,
ignoring her direct question, he said, "Come on, let's
get you back in the saddle. We'll talk later."

Seconds later all three were mounted and ready to
go.

"Where to first, little brother?" Barr asked.

"Let's go back by the house. If he's still not there,
we'll head for the creek."

"The creek!" Glynis moistened her lips. "Oh,
God, I never thought about him striking out there
alone."

"Let's go." Cort gently kicked his stallion in the flanks with his boots. The animal reared on his hind legs, then settled on all fours, pawing the ground.

Glynis bit down hard on her lower lip, but not before a whimper escaped. "Yes, oh, please, let's hurry!"

None of them bothered to say anything as they rode hard, pushing their mounts to the limit. Each was filled with hope that when they pulled up at the house, Todd would be outside waiting for them.

He wasn't.

"Oh, Cort," Glynis cried, looking over at him. "What if…what if he's fallen into the creek?" Her voice broke, and she couldn't go on.

Cort rode up even with her, and she blindly reached out to him. "Cort?" she whispered again.

He pressed her fingers warmly before letting them go. "Let's don't go borrowing trouble," he said in a low tone. "We'll find him, I promise."

Her only answer was to grip the saddle horn so hard that the veins in her hands looked as though they might burst through her skin.

He glanced away, his face savage.

The trek through the forest behind the house was carried out in much the same manner as the ride back to the house—in total silence. Glynis sat tight-lipped and reed-straight in the saddle, her face a study in misery.

Because of her fragile hold on her emotions, Cort was making an effort to keep calm. No way did he want her to know that he feared Todd might have been kidnapped.

After they had covered three-quarters of a mile, Barr broke the silence, turning to look at Cort. "I find it hard to believe he would've wandered this far by himself.''

"Me, too," Cort agreed grimly, "but we have no choice but to check it out."

"Are we...we nearly there?" Glynis's voice sounded raspy, as if her throat were sore.

"Another couple of yards," Cort said, swerving his mount to the right to miss a low-slung branch, then holding it up so Glynis and Barr could pass under it.

Before the creek came into view, it was obvious they had reached it. The rushing water had an eerie sound all its own.

It was hard to say who was first to dismount. It seemed as if all three hit the ground simultaneously, plowed through the underbrush and reached the clearing by the creek with clockwork precision.

Todd, however, was nowhere in sight.

"Barr, let's you and me split up," Cort said. "You go downstream. Glynis can come with me. We'll take upstream."

Barr nodded, as did Glynis, though weakly.

Thank God Glynis hadn't argued with him, Cort thought, taking her hand and pulling her with him. But even if she had, he wouldn't have let her go alone. If Todd *had* fallen into the creek, he didn't want Glynis to find him by herself.

Feeling perspiration oozing out of every pore in his body, Cort walked in front, while Glynis clung to his hand as if it were a lifeline. He dared not look at her for fear of what he would see in her eyes. Somehow he knew he'd be blamed for this, too.

"I'm...so scared, Cort," Glynis sobbed, tears running down her cheeks.

He paused, and turning around, met her eyes. "I know, so am I."

It was in that moment that they heard a loud whistle. Barr's whistle.

Glynis's hand froze in Cort's.

"Come on!" Cort ordered, almost jerking her arm out of its socket.

It took them only minutes to reach Barr. He was leaning against a tree, staring a few feet in front of him.

"Did you find him?" Glynis cried, lifting tortured eyes to Barr, as if unable to look elsewhere.

"He sure as hell did," Cort chimed in, grabbing Glynis by the shoulders and spinning her around.

Both Todd and the puppy lay on the grassy embankment, sleeping peacefully.

Glynis gasped, one hand flying to her chest, the other to her lips.

Suddenly, as if sensing he was no longer alone, Todd opened his eyes, then blinked.

"Hi, Mommy," he said with a grin.

Glynis leaned over the bed and once again caressed her son's cheek with the back of her hand. Even though it had been more than an hour since they had found Todd, Glynis still could not stop touching him, nor could she stop shuddering.

It was a miracle, she knew, that he was unharmed.

"Mommy, you still mad at me?" Todd asked, burying his cheek against her hand.

Glynis felt the prick of tears behind her eyes and she was stunned that she had any tears to shed. "No, son, I'm not," she said, sitting down beside him on the bed. "But I want you to promise me again that you won't wander off like that."

"But Mom, I've already promised three times."

Glynis smiled, but it never reached her eyes. "Promise me anyway."

He sighed. "Okay, I promise."

"Oh, darling, I was so afraid that you'd fallen into the creek and drowned. That's why I fussed at you."

"I already told you I didn't mean to go to sleep, but Champy lay down and wouldn't move. So I sat down, too, and fell asleep."

Those were exactly the words he'd used to Glynis in the woods, with Cort and Barr hovering over both of them. But once he'd been hugged amidst tears and cries of joy, he was severely chastised for his conduct, first by Glynis, then by Cort.

But then Cort had not rebounded. The instant she had put her arms around her son, Glynis had felt the color surge back into her face. Not so with Cort. For the longest time thereafter, he had looked drained.

"Mommy."

The solemn use of her name brought her back to the moment at hand. "What, darling?"

"Do you think Uncle Cort and Uncle Barr are still mad at me?"

"No, of course they're not."

Her words of assurance seemed to pacify him enough that his eyes fluttered shut again. Glynis remained beside him, peering down at him for another long moment, feeling her heart swell anew with gratitude for his safety. Now, if he could just get through the transplant...

After kissing him on the cheek, she stood and said, "I love you."

"I love you, too," Todd whispered without opening his eyes.

When Glynis walked into the den a few minutes later, the tears were no longer in evidence, and her composure was back intact. The men dropped their conversation and gave her their full attention.

"Is he still okay?" Cort asked, concern making his voice low and tense.

Glynis smiled. "He's fine, just tired."

"I guess so," Barr added from his position by the door, his hand on the knob. "He and that puppy took many a step."

"He carried the puppy most of the way because Champ wouldn't walk," Glynis said, her smile easing into a grin.

Barr laughed. "Well, do you blame Champ?"

Cort joined in, and they all laughed, then Cort's expression turned serious and he said, "It's funny now, but it damn sure wasn't a while ago. If that little bugger ever does anything like that again, I'll..."

"Oh, I don't think you have to worry about that," Glynis said with conviction.

"Well, guess I'd better be headin' home," Barr said, focusing his eyes on Cort. "I'm gonna try to finish mending that fence before it gets dark."

Glynis smiled at him. "Thanks again, Barr. Thanks for everything."

"Yeah, thanks, big brother," Cort interjected.

Barr waved their thanks away and turned the knob, only to pause and twist back around. "Oh, by the way, Glynis—in all the excitement, I almost forgot to tell you."

Glynis's head came up quickly. "Tell me what?"

"The house is ready."

"You mean as in ready to move in?"

"That's right."

"Oh, Barr," she exclaimed, "it seems like all I do lately is thank you."

"Think nothing of it," Barr said airily, only to then step hurriedly out the door, as if suspecting he had opened Pandora's box.

The room suddenly filled with a strained silence.

"Did you know the house was finished?" Glynis asked, sliding her hands into the pockets of her walking shorts.

"I knew," he said in a curt voice, his face stony.

He hadn't spoken to her in that harsh and uncompromising tone since they'd made love. She felt heartsick.

"You're moving, right?"

"Oh, Cort, please," she began miserably, "let's not fight about this again. Just accept it as something I have to do."

His eyes turned bleak, and he seemed to be struggling with himself. Then he stared intently at her. "You wouldn't, by any chance, consider letting Todd stay with me until after the surgery?"

Glynis caught her breath, but curiously she didn't feel threatened. Heartsick, but not threatened.

"No," she said quietly and honestly.

He turned away. "I didn't think you would."

Glynis studied his profile, which was cast in relief against the muted sunlight streaming into the room. He was tough, no doubt about it. And opinionated. And brooding. And unforgiving.

But as she continued to scrutinize him, there was more. A fleeting expression? Alerted, she even shifted slightly so that his face was in full view again. Loneliness. Cort was lonely. Even though he had his brother, his business, scads of employees, he held himself aloof. There was a sadness about him as well, a sadness that she hadn't noticed until now. But it was there, lurking in the depths of his blue eyes. Was she responsible for the changes in him?

Before she could sort through her own warring emotions, Cort stared at her with angry eyes. Or were they hungry eyes?

"We'll move your things whenever you're ready."

"You mean you're not going to try to stop me?" Glynis's voice reflected her incredulity. His shifts in attitude kept her continually off balance.

His jaw remained set in a rigid line, but he maintained his composure. "No, in fact I think it will be for the best."

With that he stamped out the door, leaving her standing in the middle of the room with her mouth wide open.

He was actually going to let them go. So where was the elation that should be rushing through her? Hadn't she been praying for this moment, obsessed with getting away from him, away from this house?

Why, then, was the thought of leaving such a bleak one?

"Well, do you like?"

"Of course, I do, silly." Milly grinned. "It's absolutely perfect for you and Todd. It reminds me of a dollhouse."

Glynis and Milly were in the kitchen, drinking iced tea, taking a break from lining cabinets with shelf paper and hanging curtains. They had been working all day and still were not through.

It had been two days since that unsettling conversation with Cort, and today was her first full day of independence. Yet she still hadn't experienced that feeling of joy and well-being she had been sure she'd feel.

Glynis took a quick sip of tea, and as she did, she peered at her watch. She bit her lip in annoyance.

"Buck's going to kill me for keeping you here so long."

Milly shook her dark head vigorously. "No, he won't." She grinned. "But even if he did, I wouldn't care. I'm on vacation this week, and it won't hurt him to feed the twins by himself. In fact, it'll do him a world of good."

Glynis chuckled. "You're probably right."

For a minute they sipped their tea in companionable silence. Then, with a frown marring her petite features, Milly asked, "Do you think it was a good idea to let Todd spend the night with Cort?"

Glynis lowered her eyes and plucked at a string on her shorts. "Probably not," she said with a sigh, "but Todd wanted to, and in a weak moment, I gave in."

"But do you think that was wise?"

Glynis pushed away from the table and crossed her feet at the ankles. "No, but then I'm a pro at doing things that are unwise. We both know that." That was especially true since she refused to muddle through her thoughts, to delve into her feelings. She was too afraid of the answer.

"When the surgery's over, do you think he'll battle you for custody?"

Glynis shifted her attention back to Milly. "He hasn't mentioned it lately, but yes, I suspect he will."

"Then surely I don't have to remind you to beware."

"You don't have to worry about that," Glynis assured her emphatically, "only…"

"Only what?" Milly was watching her closely over the rim of her glass.

"Oh, I don't know." Glynis paused, tilting her head to one side. "It's just that when I told him I was leaving, he seemed relieved, where before he had been adamantly against it."

"And that bothered you?"

Glynis flushed. "Yes, and it still does," she said in a small voice.

"Oh, honey, what a mess…"

Suddenly the sound of wailing sirens claimed their attention.

Milly shivered. "They sound awfully close, don't they?"

Glynis rose and walked to the window and peered into the darkness. "They sure do. I wonder…"

The phone rang.

Their eyes met as neither spoke about their own troubled and vivid thoughts.

"Want me to answer it?" Milly asked.

"No, I will." Glynis crossed to the wall phone and nervously lifted the receiver. She hadn't even said hello before the blood drained from her face.

Milly jumped up and ran toward her. "What's wrong?"

The phone slid out of her hand and bounced on the floor. "Cort…Cort's barn is on fire…and…"

"And what?"

"And…" Glynis's voice was little more than a hoarse whisper. "Todd and Cort are trapped inside."

Chapter 19

The short, hair-raising trip from the house to the ranch passed in virtual silence. Glynis couldn't have uttered a word even if she'd wanted to. Fear held her speechless, fear that was so thick in the car that she could taste it. Milly, too, was at a loss for words.

But the second Milly roared to a stop in the drive and cut the engine, she unbuckled her seat belt and turned to Glynis. "Are you all right?"

"No," Glynis whispered, her lips bloodless. "What...what if they...they didn't get out in time?"

"Don't say it! Don't even think it!"

Nausea welled inside Glynis. "Do you see them anywhere?"

"No, but that doesn't mean anything." Milly paused a split second, then added, "Wait here. I'll go find Barr." Following those clipped words, she jerked open the door and jumped out of the car.

Glynis remained inside, she still couldn't move. It was as if she were frozen. She felt detached, as though the mayhem taking place had nothing to do with her.

Two fire trucks were on the scene, their long hoses spraying the blazing fire with heavy doses of water. Still, flaming tongues of fire licked at the sky.

Everyone—the ranch hands, the firemen, the sheriff and several deputies—was shouting at once. And horses were whinnying loud and long. Glynis shivered.

"Over here!" a fireman shouted.

"No, here! It's outta control over here!"

"No dammit, all of you over here! We've got to get into the barn!"

Barr. That was Barr's voice. Frantically, Glynis's eyes sought the face to match the voice. He was only a few yards in front of her, shouting orders to the foreman.

Suddenly Glynis scrambled madly for the door handle. Once she'd wrenched it open, she stumbled out. But when her feet hit the ground, she almost lost her balance. Her knees knocked together ferociously.

Glynis whimpered as she frantically searched past one face, then another.

There were no signs of Cort or Todd.

"Oh, please, God," she prayed, forcing her legs to move toward Barr.

He turned at that moment and saw her. Meeting her halfway, he reached out and grabbed her arms. His hands and face were grimy with soot, and there was not a dry thread on him.

Glynis clutched at the front of his shirt, her features contorted. "Todd…and Cort… Are they…?"

"Shh, take it easy," Barr ordered softly, trapping her flailing hands against his chest. "They're—"

"They're what?" she panted, unable to let him finish the sentence.

His words were aborted by a loud cry.

"Mommy! Mommy!"

"Todd!" Glynis twisted out of Barr's arms, her eyes searching frantically through the thick smoke for the sight of her son.

"Mommy! Mommy!" Todd cried again, only louder.

"Behind you, Glynis." Barr took her by the shoulders, and treating her as though she were a windup doll, pointed her in the right direction.

"Oh, Todd, my darling boy," Glynis whispered, running to him, arms outstretched, tears streaming down her cheeks. Todd launched against her like a missile.

She bent and hugged him to her, burying his tear-stained face in the crook of her neck.

"Mommy, I…was so scared," he sobbed.

"Shh, it's all right now," Glynis cooed, one hand caressing him, touching him, loving him. "It's all right."

"Me…and Uncle Cort…" he began, only to start crying again.

Cort! Oh, God, where was Cort? Surely if Todd was safe, so was Cort. Biting her lower lip to keep from crying and upsetting Todd any more, she stood and grabbed his hand and walked back to Barr.

He would know if Cort… Oh, God, she mustn't think that way. Of course Cort was all right. He had to be.

Suddenly, a figure loomed large.

She stopped short. "Cort…is that you?"

"Glynis?"

"Oh, thank God." For a moment stinging tears rendered her sightless. She blinked in rapid succession.

Todd raised his head. "Mommy's here, Uncle Cort," he said inanely.

Cort stopped just short of her and gripped her arms, holding her steady. His eyes were like a caress as they roamed over her.

"Are you all right?" he asked huskily.

"I should be the one asking you that question." Glynis didn't even recognize her own voice.

A tiny smile curved his lips. "Why? Do I look like something the dogs dragged up?"

"Worse."

If it hadn't been for Todd in her arms, Glynis was afraid her legs might have caved in under her. Cort's face was smudged with soot as were his hands and arms. He smelled as smoky as the fire itself.

"Are you…hurt?" she stammered breathlessly, fighting off another bout of nausea.

"I'm all right, just madder than hell."

Before she could say anything more, Todd began to swing her hand. "Can I go stand by Uncle Barr and Milly?" he asked. "Over there."

Glynis took her eyes off Cort long enough to follow Todd's pointed finger. The smoke had cleared somewhat, as had the confusion. The blaze, too, seemed to be under control.

Barr, Milly and the sheriff stood deep in conversation, close to the men with the hoses.

Drawing Todd close to her side again, she said, "No, absolutely not. But you can go sit over there against that tree, if you want to, and watch." Though he seemed to have recovered from his scare, Glynis was not prepared to let him out of her sight.

"Okay," he mumbled, and walked off.

Glynis focused her attention back on Cort, who was busy wiping his eyes with a rag. "What happened?"

"Todd and I were in the barn with the vet seeing about one of the horses, when suddenly the whole damn place went up in smoke." He paused, and she saw his eyes glint dangerously. "To save you from the frightening particulars, we had to fight like hell to get out."

Hearing him admit how close they came to being burned alive, hot bile rushed up the back of her throat. "But why?" she whispered in disbelief. "I mean, *who* would do such a thing?"

Cort's eyes narrowed. "The same bastard who put a bullet in my side and tampered with my brakes."

"So you think the fire was set deliberately?"

"No doubt about it. But what I can't figure out is how he did it."

"What…what are you going to do? I mean—this can't keep going on."

"Don't worry, it isn't going to." Cort's voice dripped with determined fury. "I'm going to find the bastard and stop him."

"I hope so, before…before…" She couldn't go on, the thought so horrifying she couldn't put it into words.

Neither said anything for a moment.

Then Cort muttered brusquely, "Why don't you get Milly and go inside and make a pot of coffee."

Glynis nodded. "Todd needs to be in bed, any-how."

"Here."

"Yes."

"What about you?"

"I'd like to stay, too." Her voice faltered. "If it's all right."

Unexpectedly, he reached out and ran the back of his grimy hand down one side of her cheek. "I'd like that. I'd like that very much."

Then, pivoting on his heels, he strode off.

Sweat oozed from Cort's pores like a cleansing rain. He turned toward the mirror while lifting, then lowering, the dumbell in his left hand, watching as the blood vessels pulsed in his upper arm.

It felt good to be back in his routine. He reveled in the free-flowing sweat. Fifty, fifty-one, he counted. He could feel his muscles expand as he pushed them, pushed himself to the limit.

The sweat ran down his face, over his lips, his chest, his stomach. Out of the corner of his eye he could see the raw place on his cheek, remnants of the night's humiliation. He clamped his jaw and held the weight steady, then slowly lowered it to the mat. He was iron-tough. And iron-willed.

If it was the last thing he did, he'd get that bastard....

Shortly, Cort draped a towel around his neck and went to the refrigerator he kept in the corner of the room, took out a jug of Gatorade and downed half of it without pausing. He walked into the adjoining bath, and after stripping off his shorts, stepped into the shower.

Minutes later, still clad only in briefs, Cort stood

at the window staring at the charred remains of what used to be his barn.

He cursed silently, his thoughts splintering into several different directions at once.

He was finding it hard to comprehend that someone had actually broken through security. And he couldn't believe that same someone had guts enough to destroy his property. But both were hard, cold facts. It hadn't taken the fire marshal or the sheriff long to establish that the fire had been deliberately set.

He paused in his thoughts and took in a deep, settling breath, his ear tuned to the sounds of the night. All was quiet, as it should be; it was after midnight. The firemen, sheriff, neighbors, Barr, everyone was gone. And the hands were sleeping, except for those on watch.

Glynis and Todd were both asleep. Before leaving his bedroom and coming to his office, he'd stopped by their rooms to check on them, but hearing no sounds from either, he'd trudged wearily down the hall.

Now, after having worked off some of his frustrations, he should have been too exhausted to do anything other than fall into a deep sleep. He knew better. He still felt useless and more frustrated than ever. His desire for the bastard who had tampered with his brakes and torched his barn was tangible, like lust, and it tingled along his neck and shoulder muscles.

But equally strong was his appetite for Glynis. Forever Glynis.

He bared his teeth, which bore no resemblance to a smile, and stalked to the sofa. Stretching out on it, he tried to forget Glynis, tried not to let her get a stranglehold on him, all the while fighting the impulse to go to her bedroom and lose himself in her body.

No amount of mental flagellation worked. The longer he lay there, the more the turmoil within him grew. The more he mused, the hotter the fires inside.

Suddenly he lunged into a sitting position, and using the excuse that he needed to check on her one more time, he got up and walked out of the room.

He stopped when he reached her door, and after listening a moment, felt certain he heard movement from inside. With his heart pumping overtime, he slowly turned the knob.

Glynis was lying on her side, staring through the window at the moon. She had tried counting sheep, but that hadn't lulled her to sleep. Every time she closed her eyes, the horrors of the last few hours returned like a hideous nightmare.

Flinging the covers off her naked body, she got up and, after slipping into her robe and loosely belting it around her waist, crossed to her purse on the dresser. Maybe a couple of Aspirins would help calm her.

It was when she leaned over and stuck her hand into her purse that she heard the noise. At first she couldn't decide where it had come from, then she turned toward the door.

It was open, and Cort was standing on the threshold. Her hand froze. Adrenaline raced through her.

Moonlight poured into the room, bathing him in its magical glow while they stood mute and looked at each other, wondering what to do, what *not* to say.

"I...heard someone moving around, so I thought..." Cort muttered at last, only to break off and clear his throat roughly. Still his eyes did not waver.

Her gaze tracked his. The top of her robe was gaping, exposing her right breast, full and firm, the nipple and its areola pink and alluring.

Suddenly he drew in his breath. At the same time she saw him go instantly, achingly, erect.

Glynis groaned and snatched the fabric around her, staring at him, stunned. He edged toward her, and she covered her mouth with a trembling hand and watched him approach, unable to move.

She closed her eyes and tried to erase the image of his strong, beautiful body. She shook her head, her shoulders drooping under the heavy weight of her desire.

He gently tilted her chin with his finger.

"Glynis?" he whispered.

The spark in his eyes, the intensity of the heavy brows, formed a silent plea, mesmerizing her. Though her lips parted, no sound escaped.

Her breathing was so quick, so intense, and her heartbeat was so fast, she feared she was having a heart attack. But she couldn't die. Not now. Not with Cort looking at her as if she was his entire world.

"I've never met a woman as beautiful as you," he ground out.

He delved into the velvet brown eyes he had imprisoned, and outlined one side of her cheek with the back of his knuckles, tracing her lips with his thumb. But it was when his fingers touched the fluttering pulse in her neck that she silently pleaded with him.

"Oh, Cort." She struggled for breath, thinking she'd surely lose her mind altogether. He had the power to make her his for the taking.

Abruptly he stopped moving, and his eyes devoured her. "I can't get enough of you."

It was impossible to say who moved first, but it did not matter. What mattered was that they were in each other's arms, where they both longed to be.

Cort covered her mouth with his. She wrapped her arms around his waist. He held her tight until the mounds of her breasts, now completely free of the robe, were like precious gems against his chest.

He thrust his fingers into her hair and gently bit at her neck. She felt her blood race as her heart beat faster beneath his exploring hands and mouth. But then, he knew all her secrets.

"Tell me to leave." He bent his head so that his mouth was nearly upon hers again. "Tell me," he said in a strangled voice.

"No," she breathed, clutching at him. "Don't go...."

He drew her closer into his arms. He stroked her back, then lower. She couldn't get enough air. His kisses smothered her. His tongue invaded her mouth. She pressed her thighs against him and felt his urgent hardness.

"Glynis, you're doing it to me again," he rasped, sliding the robe down her arms, letting it form a puddle at their feet, along with his briefs. He then swung her around and placed her on the bed.

Wordlessly, she reached out and touched his cheek, his neck, his chest with the hot tips of her fingers. Pleased little moans escaped from the back of her throat as she nestled against him, trapping his hard flesh between her legs.

"Ah, Glynis...Glynis...!"

Suddenly he was on top of her, using his mouth,

his hands to render her mindless. It was only after he bent his head and put his mouth on hers and sank his fingers into her again, that she realized she no longer had any control of how much she was willing to give.

Mercifully and finally, clutching her buttocks, he drove deep inside her and spilled into her. And when he sighed and collapsed onto her breasts, she held him, releasing emotions inside her that she had buried so long ago she had forgotten they existed.

When they were through, she lay in his arms, tears running down her cheeks. She could not remember feeling so much physical pleasure laced with so much mental pain.

Chapter 20

She saw him again.

He was standing in the exact same place, across the street from Milly's day-care, slouched against the tree with the same hat casting his face in a shadow.

The hairs on the back of Glynis's neck stood out as she stopped swinging Todd and stared at the stranger.

Who was he? The thought of him watching her son made her blood run cold.

Better still, could he be linked to Cort's trouble? Of course he couldn't, she assured herself, positive her imagination was playing tricks on her again.

"Mommy," Todd whined, twisting around in the swing. "Why'd you stop swinging me?"

For a split second she took her eyes off the man to answer Todd. "Hold on a minute, son."

When she whipped back around, the man was gone.

"Todd, honey," she said, "I'm going to talk to Milly, then we'll be leaving."

Glynis sighed as she made her way across the yard where Milly was playing hopscotch with several children. Stopping by the day-care had been an afterthought on her part when she and Todd had left the doctor's office a little while ago.

Todd had gotten a good report, and she'd decided to share the news with Milly. But they had been there for two hours already, and it was time they headed to the house. Her house.

She sighed again, coming to a standstill. She didn't want to dwell on the traumatic night she had spent at the ranch in Cort's arms, though that was all she had thought about. Giving in to his erotic demands yet again had merely added fuel to an already raging fire, a fire that was destined to burn itself out and her with it.

"Hey, Glynis, you about ready for another glass of iced tea?" Milly was asking.

Glynis smiled weakly. "That sounds good, but it's getting late. We need to be going."

"Sure you won't change your mind?"

"Not this time."

"Come on, then," Milly said, locking arms with Glynis, "I'll walk you to the car."

While Todd ran ahead, the two women walked at a slower pace. Facing Milly, Glynis asked, "Have you noticed a man hanging around the nursery?"

Milly stopped abruptly. "No. Have you?"

"Yes." Glynis's eyes were troubled. "Twice, in fact."

"Where, for God's sake?"

Glynis pointed across the street. ''There, always against that tree.''

''Mmm,'' Milly mused, shaking her head. ''That's strange.'' She paused and peered closely at Glynis. ''Are you trying to tell me you think he's watching you?''

Glynis shrugged. ''I don't know, that's the trouble. Ever since this thing with Cort...'' She let her sentence fade. ''Oh, I don't know. It's just a crazy feeling I have.'' She gestured with a hand. ''Chalk it up to paranoia.''

''Well, in light of what you've been through, I can understand why you'd be paranoid. But I truly don't think there's anything to worry about.''

Glynis was not so sure of that then, nor was she sure now, hours later, after she'd prepared dinner, cleaned up the brand-new kitchen and put Todd to bed. The man was still very much on her mind.

Doing her best to shake off her morbid thoughts, she went back into the kitchen and brewed three cups of coffee. When that was done, she filled a cup and walked back into the living room. The instant she sat down, the doorbell rang. Hurriedly putting down her cup, she went to the door, fearing the noise would awaken Todd.

''Who's there?'' she asked hesitantly, her hand on the night latch.

''Cort.''

''Oh,'' she murmured, her heart pumping wildly.

''Are you going to let me in?''

She slipped the bolt, and without looking directly at Cort, stood aside for him to enter. It had been two days since she'd seen him. However, he'd called both days and talked to Todd on the phone.

Once she'd closed the door behind him, Glynis pressed against it. "Nothing else has happened? I mean…" She faltered, disturbed by the intensity of his eyes as they met hers.

"No, thank God." His face relaxed. "I guess Todd's in bed."

"Yes. He…he was worn out." Cort smelled fresh, of soap and cologne, and she stared unconsciously at his mouth, remembering its exquisite sweetness on her body.

He cleared his throat. "I…er…tried to get here earlier, but I've been working like hell on the barn all day."

"You look like it, too," she commented softly, without rancor.

His dark eyebrows lifted. "And what look is that?" he asked with a faint smile.

"Your usual—tired, exhausted, worn out. Take your pick."

"You wouldn't be offering me any tea and sympathy, now, would you?"

The silence was static.

"Would…you settle for coffee instead?" she asked unevenly.

Something too fleeting to identify flashed in his eyes. But for one electric second they were soft and quiet and excruciatingly gentle. Then the look was gone, and he stared down at his hat. "Sure, especially since beggars can't be choosers."

Not knowing how to respond to that last statement, Glynis let it slide, uneasily making her way into the kitchen where she clumsily poured another cup of coffee. When she got back into the living room, he was standing by the window.

He turned just as she set the cup down. Their eyes locked and held. "Are you making it all right?" he asked.

She could see his labored breathing. His chest rose and fell heavily, as if he were having a hard time getting air in and out his lungs. She was having the same difficulty. He was too close.

"I'm fine. We're...fine."

"Do you need anything?"

"No...no, nothing that I can think of."

"Did Todd not get a good report today?"

"Yes, very good." Her voice was barely audible now.

"Are you sure?"

"Of course, I'm sure. Why do you ask?"

He continued to look at her. "Something's bothering you." It wasn't a question; it was a flat-out statement.

She sucked in her breath. For a moment she'd forgotten how adept he was at reading her, how he seemed to cut through to the bone and blood.

Her gaze fell.

"Glynis, look at me."

She raised her eyes to his, finding shadows, secrets in their depths. Her lips parted on a hopeless sigh as she averted her gaze. "It's nothing."

He moved closer. "Why not let me be the judge of that?"

"It's just my overactive imagination."

"Glynis."

"There...was a man."

He became instantly alert. "A man. Where?"

"At Milly's day-care."

"Go on."

"I've seen him there twice. And...when he'd catch me watching him, he'd just turn and walk off."

Cort's voice was sharp. "Can you describe him?"

Glynis picked up on his concern, his fear. She licked her lips. "No, because he wore a cap that covered his face."

He muttered an explosive expletive and bent over her. "Is there anything you can tell me about him? Anything at all?"

Glynis thought for a moment, then raised large, uneasy eyes to him. "He...he could have had a mustache, but I'm not sure."

"That's something, anyway."

"Cort, you're scaring me. Surely you don't think this is the same man who's...who's after you?"

He pivoted on his heel and rubbed the back of his neck. "I don't know what the hell to think. But at the same time, I...we can't rule out that possibility."

"But why—"

He cut her off. "I want you and Todd to come back to the ranch with me. Now."

"No."

"What do you mean, no?"

"Under the circumstances, I don't think that would be a wise move."

Cort's face grew hard and remote. "What circumstances?"

"You know," she said tautly.

"Damn, woman! My reasons for wanting you back at the ranch have nothing to do with us personally." He paused, his big shoulders rising and falling. "But even if they did, might I remind you that you were just as willing and eager as I was?''

She felt as if he'd socked her in the stomach. ''You always have to bring things down to a baser level, don't you?''

''No, I don't. But you asked for that.''

She lifted her head defiantly. ''Well, Todd and I are not going back to the ranch.''

''Even if the SOB is using you to get to me?''

''You don't know that for sure,'' she argued, knowing that she was being deliberately stubborn, but Cort had no proof to back up his suspicion. And she wasn't going to budge. At this moment facing an unknown enemy was preferable to moving back in with Cort.

His nostrils flared, as if he was reading her mind. ''Is that your final word?''

''Yes.''

''I could take Todd with me.''

Silence.

She didn't flinch. ''But you're not, are you?''

The silence multiplied.

''No, I'm not,'' Cort said tightly.

Glynis released her breath, but was unable to talk.

''Do you still have that gun I gave you years ago?''

The sudden change of subject caught Glynis off guard. She stared at him as if he'd taken leave of his senses. ''What?''

''Do you still have the gun?'' he repeated harshly and impatiently.

''Yes.''

''Then get it and use it if you have to.''

Glynis closed her eyes and reached blindly for the arm of the couch, sinking onto the cushions. It was only after she heard the door close that she realized she was alone.

When she opened her eyes, they landed on the two full cups of coffee that hadn't been touched.

"Betcha you wanted to throttle her, didn't you?"

"That's putting it mildly," Cort muttered tersely. "I believe she's more stubborn than she used to be."

"Seriously, you couldn't make her see reason?"

"Hell, no, she wouldn't listen to a damn thing I said."

Cort and Barr were in Cort's office at noon the following day. They were waiting for Gene Ridley to arrive from Houston.

Rain pelted the window behind Cort's desk. For a minute, both he and Barr stared at it as if they'd never seen it before.

Barr broke the silence by snapping his lighter open and lighting a cigarette.

Cort made a face. "Those damn things are gonna kill you."

"Everybody's gotta die for something."

Cort grimaced. "Your attitude stinks, big brother."

"No more than yours of late, little brother."

Making another disgusted sound, Cort got out of his chair and began pacing the floor behind him.

"You didn't leave her alone, did you?" Barr asked, taking a hefty drag on his cigarette.

Cort stopped his pacing and stared at his brother through a cloud of smoke. "No, of course I didn't. I sent Eddie to stand guard all night."

"I'm sure she'd appreciate that," Barr drawled.

"Yeah."

Barr grinned. "What's with you two anyway?

You're either snapping at each other like dogs over the same bone or you're looking at each other like you're in heat—''

"Go to hell."

The rain slapped against the windowpane, drowning out the growing silence.

Gene Ridley's discreet knock on the door broke it.

"Come in," Cort said from his position by the window. If Ridley felt the tension in the room, he chose to ignore it. After shaking hands with Barr, he gave his full attention to Cort.

"We've hit the jackpot, boss," he said.

"I'm listening."

Ridley swung his briefcase up onto the desk, but didn't bother to unsnap it. "When you called this morning and gave me the description of the man Mrs. Hamilton saw, I knew we were on a roll."

"Which of the three is he?" Cort asked, his mouth stretched into a tense line.

"Al Sabo," Gene announced proudly.

"Who the hell is he?" Barr's tone was gruff.

"Just one of the many scumbags your brother has sent to the joint," Gene said, switching his gaze to Barr.

Cort moved away from the window. "So how do you know Sabo's our man?"

Gene smiled. "I came here via Huntsville. And while I was there I found out the most interesting things about Mr. Al Sabo." His smile broadened into a grin as he focused on Cort. "Yes siree, it seems that our Mr. Sabo had a big mouth, bragged about how when he got out, your *rear*—" he stressed the word "—belonged to him."

Cort's laugh was hollow as he spread both his hands on the top of his desk and leaned heavily on them, his eyes encompassing both men. "So let's find the bastard and see whose rear belongs to whom."

Chapter 21

"Good night, darling. Sleep tight and don't let the bed bugs bite."

Todd giggled. "You're too late, Mommy, they already have."

"I know. That's why I put medicine all over your legs."

"They bit Adam and Kyle, too."

"I'm sure they did. Milly and I shouldn't have let you boys play outside so late."

His eyes lighted. "We had fun. We played robocops and—"

"That's enough," Glynis chided gently. "It's late, past time for you to be asleep."

When she would have switched off the light, Todd spoke again, stopping her.

"Mommy."

"What is it now?"

"When…when can I go back to the ranch to see Uncle Cort?" His face was scrunched into a frown.

The question didn't surprise Glynis. In fact, she had expected it before now. Since the barn fire she hadn't let Todd return to the ranch.

"Soon, I'm sure," she answered evasively.

"When's soon, Mommy?" he pressed.

"Before you go to the hospital. I promise." She smiled at him. "How's that?"

Todd grinned his acquiescence, then closed his eyes.

Once the door was closed behind her, Glynis wandered into the kitchen, where she poured herself a cup of coffee. Noticing that the pot was off, she put the cup in the microwave.

It was ten o'clock, and she knew she should go to bed herself. But since she and Todd had just gotten home from having dinner with Milly and her family, she was too keyed up to sleep.

Todd's transplant surgery was near and very much on her mind. In just a few days he was due to check into the hospital to begin the preliminary work. The thought of what he had to endure before the transplant could even take place was enough to drive her crazy.

With a heavy heart, she trudged into the dimly lit living room, only to stop in her tracks.

A man was standing in the middle of the room, pointing a gun at her head.

She froze, her heart beating in her throat. Horror and disorientation overwhelmed her. He was familiar, yet he wasn't. Then suddenly it hit her. The mustache! He was the man she'd seen around the day care, the one Cort suspected… Oh God!

"What...what...do you want?" she whispered, involuntarily taking a shaky step back.

The short, extremely muscular stranger glared at her, his face pinched and his eyes bright, unusually bright. For an instant the eyes reminded her of someone unbalanced, out of touch with reality. At the same time they gleamed with hatred, instantly filling her with an unknown terror.

"I want a lot, Mrs. Hamilton," he said, his voice low and tense. All the while he waved the gun at her.

Her mouth dried up. Her heart beat so fast, she could feel her muscles jerk with each beat. *Todd! Oh, please don't let him hurt my baby.*

"If...if it's money you...want..." she began, only to find her tongue suddenly thick and her throat dry. But she couldn't lose control. She had to remain calm so as not to disturb Todd. His...both their lives would more than likely depend on it.

He crept forward and laughed a cruel, mirthless laugh. "There isn't enough money in the whole damned world that can give me back what that son of a bitch took from me."

She wet her lips. "Who?" she asked shakily. Didn't the experts say it was best to keep a deranged person talking?

"Cort McBride, that's who," he spat. "And I'm going to make him pay." He paused and edged closer. "With his life, no less. And you're going to help me."

No! This couldn't be happening! Her mind raced, hunting for a solution. *Think, Glynis, think!* But what could she do? She couldn't run, and there was no way to divert his attention.

For the moment she was trapped and at his mercy.

She sank her teeth into her lower lip to keep from crying out her fear.

"You're going to pick up the phone and call lover boy."

She shook her head frantically. "No."

"Yes." He leaned his head to the side. "Or you'll be sorry, or rather your kid in there will be sorry."

Glynis's face turned porcelain-white, and she tried to speak, but nothing came out.

"Ah, that's better. Now that we understand each other, suppose you pick up that phone and make that call."

Still Glynis did not move, could not move. She continued to stand exactly where she was as if she'd been cemented to the spot.

"Move it, damn you!"

She moved; her limbs jumped as though she'd been zapped with a stun gun.

"All right, I'll...do it," she whispered, "but please don't point that gun—"

"Shut up, lady, and just do as I say."

With hands that were oozing sweat, Glynis jerkily crossed to the phone and lifted the receiver. The entire time she punched out Cort's number, the man pointed the gun unsteadily at her temple. He was so close now, she could feel his hot, foul breath on her face. She breathed deeply to keep from fainting.

Then, mercifully, someone lifted the receiver on the other end. "McBride residence."

Her heart lurched. It was Maude Springer. Oh, God, what if Cort wasn't home? What if...

"Quit stalling, lady," the man warned, cocking the hammer inches from her ear.

Sweat popped out above Glynis's upper lip. "Mrs. Springer...it's Glynis. Is...is Cort there?"

"Is something the matter, dear? You sound...oh, I don't know...funny."

Glynis gripped the receiver until she feared her knuckles would crack. "Please, let me speak to... Cort."

Mrs. Springer paused a moment, then said, "All right. Hang on, dear. I think he's in his office."

"Is he there?" the man asked.

Glynis nodded.

"Good. You tell him something's wrong with the kid and for him to get over here quick." His tone was as cold and menacing as the gun. "You got that, lady?"

She nodded again.

"Screw up and you'll be sorry."

"Glynis, is something wrong?"

When the cool, crisp voice sounded in her ear, Glynis's legs almost buckled beneath her.

"Cort...it's..."

"Glynis, for God's sake, speak up. I can't hear you."

Glynis kept her eyes straight ahead. If she dared look at the gun, she feared she wouldn't be able to go on.

"It's...Todd. Come quick."

"I'll be right there."

When the cold dial tone sounded, the phone slid from her fingers, and she faced her tormenter.

"He's...he's coming."

"So far so good, lady. Follow my next instructions and maybe I'll let you and the kid live."

                              * * *

It seemed to Cort as if he stood by the phone forever, his mind in an uproar, when in reality it was
only seconds. Then, with a muttered curse and two
long strides, he was in front of his filing cabinet, jerking it open.

Something was wrong. Something was damned
wrong. And it wasn't just his paranoia, either.
Granted, if something had happened to Todd, it stood
to reason that Glynis would be panic-stricken. But
there was something else as well, something he
couldn't put his finger on, but it was there nevertheless. Terror? Sheer terror? His gut instinct told him
he was right.

After grabbing his shoulder holster containing his
.357 Magnum, he slammed the drawer shut and tore
out of the room. If Al Sabo had gotten to Glynis...
Suddenly a picture filled with sights, sounds and
smells of terror flooded his consciousness, almost
stopping him cold. But no, that couldn't happen.
Eddie was on guard.

Maude was standing in his path in the hallway, her
face wrinkled in concern. "Is...Glynis all right?"

"Call the sheriff and then call Barr," he flung over
his shoulder. "Tell 'em to meet me at her place."

A short time later Cort was on the road that led to
Glynis's house. He brought the Jeep to a sudden halt
and switched off the lights. Total darkness surrounded
him.

He got out and moved quickly but cautiously until
the house came into view. Then he stopped. Lights
blazed from the living room, but from no other room
that he could see.

With exception of his harsh breathing and the occasional sound of a cricket chirping nearby, the night was eerily quiet.

He crept toward the back of the house, trying to reconcile his actions. If Todd had hurt himself or was sick, then caution was not the way to go. On the other hand, if Todd was a ploy to draw him to the house, then he was doing the right thing. Again gut instinct told him the latter was the case.

When he reached the back corner of the house, he flattened himself against the wood and inched his way toward the window. It was then that his foot struck an object. Hoping for the best and fearing the worst, Cort looked down. Sprawled on the ground was a body. Eddie's body. With his heart beating out of sync, Cort knelt and placed two fingers on the pulse in Eddie's neck. The pulse was weak, but steady.

Praying that Eddie would be all right until help came, Cort rose and once again plastered his body against the house. Luck was with him. The blinds were open. Scarcely breathing, he moved closer.

Hesitating only a heartbeat, he then rounded the corner just enough to allow him to see inside the room.

What he saw robbed him of his breath. Glynis was sitting on the edge of the couch. Sabo was standing a few feet from her, a gun aimed at her heart. Todd was nowhere to be seen.

Sweat popped out on Cort's forehead as he withdrew his gun from the holster, contemplating his next move. Sabo was not in control. That in itself was of primary concern. His hand was trembling, which meant the gun could accidentally discharge at any time, whether Sabo wanted it to or not. No doubt about it, Sabo was an extremely dangerous man.

But as long as Sabo kept his back to the door, Cort knew he had a chance, albeit a slim one, but still a chance. Crouching down so that his head was below window level, he ran to the back door. By the time he rose, flush with the house again, his blood was pounding in his skull. If that son of a bitch hurt so much as a hair on Glynis's or Todd's head...

Suddenly the puppy barked.

"Damn!" Cort hissed under his breath. Champ was at the door, barking ferociously and loudly.

"McBride, is that you?" Sabo yelled.

"Yeah, it's me."

"Put your gun down and come inside with your hands raised or I'll waste the little lady."

Cort's eyes glittered dangerously in the dark. "Take it easy, Sabo. This is between you and me. Let her and the boy go. Then we'll talk."

"No!" Sabo shouted. "I'm calling the shots. I give the orders, not you. Understand?"

Cort could hear the tremor in his voice, knew he was hovering on the edge. One wrong word, one wrong move could send him hurtling headlong over that edge.

"All right, Sabo. Take it easy," Cort said again.

"Open the door slowly, McBride, and come in with your hands up. And don't try anything foolish, either."

Cort did as he was told.

The instant he stood on the threshold, his eyes took in the scene in front of him. Sabo had his left arm across Glynis's throat, while his right one held the gun to her temple. Glynis's face was chalk-white, and her lower lip was trembling.

A pulse throbbed in Cort's neck.

"Sabo, let her go," Cort demanded with a calmness he was far from feeling. He felt as if a grenade had been planted in his belly. "This is between you and me."

"That's right, McBride," Sabo cried, wild-eyed. "Only I had to use her to get to you."

"So now you've got me. Let her go."

"No. You're going to pay for what you did to me, for ruining my life, for turning my family against me, for making me a laughingstock in my hometown." He was running his sentences together while saliva gathered at the corners of his mouth. "But...but first I'm going to make those you love pay. Do you hear me, McBride? I'm going to make *her* pay!"

Sabo buried the barrel of the gun deeper into Glynis's temple.

She whimpered, her eyes on Cort.

An alarm went off inside Cort's brain. The silence reached a screaming pitch.

"Mommy!" Todd's unexpected cry split the air like a bullet through a plate-glass window.

Sabo flinched, and when he did, he took his eyes off Cort. That was the break Cort had been waiting for.

"Glynis, hit the floor!" he shouted.

She did, but not before she elbowed Sabo in the gut, causing him to lose control of the gun. It hit the carpet with a thud.

A loud grunt was the only sound out of Sabo as he doubled over like a question mark. Cort moved lightning fast. He grabbed Sabo by his thick hair, jerked his head up and blasted him in the nose with his left fist. It rocked Sabo back, and blood spurted. Sabo shook his head and lunged toward Cort.

"I wouldn't if I were you," Cort warned. He then proceeded to pop Sabo's jaw with the back of his hand. But it was the upper cut to the chin that sent the thug spinning backward onto the couch. His legs spread instantly. His arms sagged. He sat stiff as a corpse, then fell onto his side and was still.

From that moment on, everything seemed to happen at once. Glynis barely had time to answer Cort's tersely muttered, "Are you all right?" before the wail of approaching sirens made further speech impossible.

Instead of waiting to see Al Sabo handcuffed and hauled to the sheriff's car, Glynis had fled down the hall to Todd's room, only to find that he had fallen back to sleep.

She had leaned over and kissed him before dragging herself back into the living room to face what she knew would be a long question-and-answer session.

Now, two hours later, it was all over. She stood by the window and watched as the last of the taillights disappeared down her long drive. It was the ambulance transporting a now conscious Eddie to the hospital.

It was only after Cort came back inside and approached her that she began losing control.

"Glynis," he whispered in a hoarse, uneven voice, lifting his hands as if to hold her, only to let them drop to his side. "It's all over."

Suddenly her shoulders began to shake, and she looked up at him with tear-filled eyes. "Please...hold me."

He didn't have to be asked twice.

* * *

"Are you awake?" Cort asked in a gravelly whisper several hours later, his lean length against her back and buttocks.

"Uh-huh."

"Are you still scared?"

"No," she said quietly.

"It's Todd and the surgery, isn't it?"

She nodded, blinking back tears.

After she'd collapsed in his arms and begged him to hold her, Cort had taken her into her bedroom and laid her tenderly onto the bed. Then he'd lain beside her. But he hadn't made love to her as she had thought—had hoped—he would.

Instead he had undressed her as if she were a baby, and after impatiently discarding his own clothing, had pulled her onto the bed with him. Wordlessly he had caressed her body with an artist's sensitive touch, without so much as a kiss.

He'd held her against him, his lips buried in her sweet-smelling neck, his burgeoning masculinity hard against her buttocks. Then, with a sigh and one hand softly capturing a breast, they had drifted to sleep, but only after their hearts had finally slowed to a normal beat.

Now, several hours later, they were both awake. And he was probing her heart.

"Day after tomorrow is the day," Glynis whispered.

Cort pulled her closer. "I know."

"Are you scared?"

He turned her onto her back and gazed down at her, pain darkening his eyes.

"Yes, I am, believe it or not," he said. "But more for Todd than for me."

He was breaking apart inside, just as she was. It was in that moment she forced herself to face the truth, a truth that had been haunting her since she'd walked back into his life. She still loved him, had never stopped loving him.

But instead of the insight bringing joy, it brought more pain. No matter whether he hurt her or not, she wanted to be a part of him one last time. Moaning, she clutched at him.

"Everything's going to be all right," he whispered, his breath warm on her lips. At the same instant he lifted her on top of him, easing her gently and quivering onto him, rising hot and hard into the core of her body.

With a muted sob, she buried her face into his chest and held on to him as if she'd never let him go.

Chapter 22

The transplant was over. The long wait had ended.

Seated in Dr. Johns's office, Glynis's eyes rested on Cort, who was on the other side of the room, his features tense and unyielding.

Nervously she fidgeted with the ring on her right hand, struggling to maintain her composure.

Dr. Johns was due to walk through the door any moment now and tell them if Todd could go home.

It had been almost four months to the day that Todd had been placed in isolation, his bone marrow flushed from his body and replaced with Cort's.

New white blood cells had been manufactured with no sign of rejection, although anti-rejection drugs had been administered on a daily basis.

New red blood cells had taken much longer to appear, and Todd had had to have several blood transfusions.

During the time he had been in isolation, Glynis had not left the hospital. She had stayed at the Ronald McDonald House and several times a day had entered Todd's isolation chamber dressed in a sterile robe, gloves and mask.

Cort, on the other hand, had continued to stay at the ranch and commuted back and forth. His presence had puzzled her. She'd been certain that once he had fulfilled his obligation to Todd, he would have returned to his condo in Houston.

She had looked forward to Cort's visits to the hospital, though nothing personal was discussed between them. It had seemed as if everything had been put on hold until Todd's ordeal was over. Yet she'd been aware of him with every nerve in her body. She had sensed he felt the same way, even though he had kept his distance.

Still, there had been moments when it was all she could do not to fling her arms around Cort and beg him to hold her, to love her. But she hadn't because she'd known the time had come for her to begin weaning herself away from him.

With that thought uppermost in her mind, Glynis tore her gaze from him and forced herself to check the room for articles she might have forgotten to pack.

"Where the hell is that doctor?" His muttered words split the lengthening silence.

Glynis drew in a jagged breath. "I don't know," she whispered. "Maybe…maybe those last-minute tests they were running on Todd took longer than expected."

"Well, if he doesn't get here soon, I'm afraid I'm going to tear the whole damned hospital apart."

Glynis saw the anguish in his face, heard it in his

voice. Suddenly she knew that no matter what Cort had done to her in the past or regardless of how he felt about her now, she could not deprive him of his son. She had to let Cort be a vital part of Todd's life. Otherwise she would not be able to live with herself.

Dear Lord, she cried silently, how was she going to do it? To see Cort and not be able to hold him or to have him hold her was a fate worse than death.

The sound of the door opening cut into her tormenting thoughts.

Her eyes, along with Cort's, sought out Dr. Johns's as he strode into the room, not pausing until he'd reached his desk.

Glynis couldn't have uttered a word even if she'd wanted to; the lump in her throat was much too large.

Cort cleared *his* throat as if he, too, was having the same difficulty. Still, when he spoke, his voice sounded unlike his own. "Well, Doctor?"

Dr. Johns grinned broadly. "To date there are still no signs of graft-versus-host disease, which in layman's terms means there are no signs of rejection."

"Go on..." Glynis managed stiffly, watching as Cort crossed the room to stand beside her. She was grateful for his presence.

"As far as we're concerned, the transplant is a success."

"Are you...saying he can go home?" Glynis's voice cracked.

Dr. Johns's grin broadened. "That's exactly what I'm saying."

Without realizing what she was doing, Glynis lifted wide, tear-filled eyes to Cort and whispered, "Did you...hear what he said? Our son is going to be all right."

Cort reached out and trapped a tear with a finger. Then he grinned. "Yeah, I heard. Isn't that something?"

This time it was the doctor who coughed, effectively shattering the silence.

"Even though we're dismissing him, Todd will have to be monitored closely," Dr. Johns went on. "You both understand that."

"We understand," Cort responded.

"Before you leave, I'll brief you in detail as to his care."

Glynis frowned. "You mean we can't take him now?"

"When I left him, he was sound asleep. Until he wakes up, I suggest you two grab a bite to eat." He paused with a smile. "Celebrate or something."

"I'm not hungry," Glynis said hastily, "but I do need to go back to my room and pack."

"I'll go with you," Cort put in.

Momentarily disconcerted, Glynis shrugged. "All right."

Dr. Johns came from behind his desk and went to the door. "I'll see you later, then."

On the way back to her small room, they had reviewed every word Dr. Johns had told them, trying to convince themselves it was true.

Now, though, words seemed to have dwindled between them, creating a long and tension-filled silence, a silence that showed no signs of ending. It was as if they both realized the same rules that had governed their lives for months would no longer apply.

Swallowing a deep sigh, Glynis forced herself to fold her things neatly and put them into the suitcase, though her mind was not on the task at hand. Far from it. It was on Cort and the fact that he was standing like a statue by the window, ignoring her.

She squeezed her eyelids shut to hold back the tears, refusing to shed them. After all, this was a moment for joy, not tears. Todd was going to be all right.

Cort was free to return to work, traipse to the far-reaching corners of the globe if he so desired. And she—well, she was free to sell the house and move back to Houston and begin teaching.

Only she wasn't free. Her heart and her soul belonged to Cort, had always belonged to Cort, would always belong to him. Yet he was no closer to belonging to her now than he had been six years ago. He was like the wind, a free spirit, unwilling and incapable of being tied down.

Unable to bear the silence another minute, Glynis snapped the lock on her suitcase and said, "Cort...I'm ready when you are."

Though Cort heard her speak, he pretended not to, stalling for time. There was so much he wanted to say, but the words wouldn't come. Fear held him mute, kept him from saying what was on his heart, his mind.

What drove him now had driven him for years, was his all-consuming desire to get even with Glynis. Only it had backfired. The joke was on him. He had fallen in love with her all over again.

He had to stifle the urge to go to her, to take her in his arms and hold her close and tell her how sorry he was for the pain he'd caused her, that he no longer blamed her for the past because he had been the one at fault. She had pegged him with accuracy. He had been filled with a wanderlust he couldn't conquer, had burned with a need to have material things he had never had.

He hadn't meant to hurt her by his selfishness, but he had. The pain in her eyes broke his heart; he wanted to bring joy and laughter back to them. Was it too late? Was there too much in the way?

He didn't know, he honestly didn't know. His gut was splitting in two.

"Cort, I'm...ready," Glynis repeated haltingly, uncertain of his dark mood, yet wanting desperately to get out of this tiny cramped room that seemed even smaller with him in it.

He turned then and walked toward her, not stopping until he was within touching distance. "Did you mean what you said in Dr. Johns's office?"

Glynis looked confused. "What...what did I say?"

"You referred to Todd as *our* son."

She dragged in a shuddering breath. "Yes, I meant it."

"Does that mean you're going to let me be a part of Todd's life?"

"Yes."

They stared at each other in silence.

A muscle twitched in his jaw. "I would never have tried to take him away from you. You know that, don't you?"

Her chest almost caved in under the emotional pressure. She bowed her head. "I...know."

"Glynis," he said huskily, "look at me."

She bit her lip and looked up. Cort was so close now, she felt herself wanting him, needing him. She remembered well that look in his eyes that warmed her, made her feel secure.

But she knew that was not to be again. Cort wanted Todd, not her.

Hurting inside with all the tears she could not shed, and the emptiness of knowing that she had lost him all over again, she committed everything about him to memory.

"What now?" she whispered, feeling tears burn her eyes in spite of her efforts to keep them at bay.

"What do you mean, what now?" he asked.

"Well, I assumed you'd be off to places unknown, to—" She broke off, her voice fading into thin air.

"Is that what you want?"

I want only you! her heart cried. But she said, "Does it matter what I want?"

"It could, you know."

"What…what are you saying?"

His gaze did not budge. "We…we could get married."

"Yes…we could, but it would be for all the wrong reasons."

"I guess you're right," he said dully. "Anyway, it probably wouldn't work."

Glynis felt her heart crumble into a million pieces. For a moment she had thought, she had hoped…

"Glynis," he said thickly.

She shook her head. "I'm…I'm going to sell the house and move back to Houston," she heard herself say in a small voice.

"No."

Her head jerked up.

"You…you needn't worry. You can see Todd whenever you want."

Suddenly, with a cry straight from the gut, Cort clasped her arms and dragged her against him, roughly aligning their bodies. He was shaking; she could feel it. Something snapped inside her. She went limp, losing all desire to fight him.

"Oh, Glynis," he groaned, "don't do this to me. I don't think I could survive if you walked out on me again."

Glynis twisted out of his embrace and stared at him with disbelief. "Cort, do you know what you're saying?"

"No, but I know what I'm trying to say." His eyes caressed her.

"I'll even let you adopt Todd, if you want to," she said desperately, still certain she was misinterpreting his words.

"You've missed the point," he muttered, grasping her shoulders and pressing her back against him as if he couldn't bear any distance between them. "Sure I'd love to adopt Todd, but only after you marry me."

"Oh, Cort," she cried, nestling against him and feeling his instant response to her closeness. "I... thought it was only Todd you wanted."

"Oh, Glynis, Glynis, I want you both. Surely you know that?"

She started to cry.

"I love you more than it's possible to say."

"And I love you," she whispered.

Groaning, he covered her mouth with his own and didn't pull away until they lay side by side on the narrow bed behind them.

"Oh, Cort," she whispered again.

His kiss cut off her words. Suddenly all the anger

and bitterness and regrets vanished, and they were two people deeply in love in a world all their own.

They made love urgently, hurriedly, as if their time together was still a dream. When he thrust deep within her, she cried out with a sweet pain so intense she thought she'd surely die.

Sated, they remained entwined, their clothes strewn around them.

"I never stopped loving you," Cort said huskily, cradling his head in the palm of one hand and bending over her.

Glynis turned slightly so she could peer up at him. "Nor I you."

"Does that mean you're going to marry me?"

She smiled with lazy happiness. "Just try to stop me."

It was quiet in the room while he kissed her soundly.

"I can't believe all those years we wasted nursing our pride."

Glynis expelled a breath. "Me, neither."

He busily caressed a nipple with the tips of his fingers.

"C...Cort..."

"Mmm?"

"I called you to tell you about the baby."

Cort went completely still. "What?"

"You really didn't know, did you? Your partner back then didn't tell you?"

Cort drew in a harsh breath and let it out slowly, painfully. "No, he didn't tell me."

There was a long moment of silence.

"Can you ever forgive me?" he asked, his features

tormented, "for that and so much more? For being pigheaded…"

She placed a finger across his lips. "There's nothing to forgive, my darling. I was just as stubborn as you. I should have trusted you."

He captured her hand and turned her palm against his lips. That erotic touch set her on fire, driving her closer against him.

"Do you want to live at the ranch?" he asked rather incoherently as she was busy moving her knee up and down his leg.

She frowned and stilled. "I…don't understand. I assumed we'd live in Houston, close to your work."

"You assumed wrong, my darling," he said with an indulgent smile. "I'm going to turn the day-to-day running of the business over to Gene. He's shown me he can handle it. I want to ranch, but more than that I want to be a husband and father."

"Oh, Cort," she said, reaching up and touching his face lovingly. "Are you sure that's what you want? Because it no longer matters to me what you do. I can come to terms with a part-time husband, as long as you're happy."

"Well, I don't want to be a part-time husband or part-time father. I want to be with you and my son."

She smiled. "And speaking of our son, don't you think we'd better go get him?"

"Soon, my love, soon."

"And soon we'll tell him that you're his daddy, the daddy he's always wanted."

Cort's eyes were brilliant. "Have I told you that I love you?"

"Yes, but you can tell me again."

"I love you."

She lifted trembling lips to his. "And I love you."

"Forever this time?"

Her eyes glowed. "Forever."

* * * * *

And now for a special bonus.
Read

MADE TO MEASURE
by Joan Elliott Pickart

First time in print

JOAN ELLIOTT PICKART
is the author of over eighty-five novels. When she isn't writing, she enjoys reading, gardening and attending craft shows on the town square with her young daughter, Autumn. Joan has three all-grown-up daughters and three fantastic grandchildren. Joan and Autumn live in a charming small town in the high pine country of Arizona.

Chapter 1

Murphy flopped down on a small, braided rug, low-ered his chin to his paws and sighed. Mary-Clair pat-ted the old dog on his furry head.

"You're a sweetheart, Murphy," she said, "but Esther said you're to sleep on your rug on the floor next to the bed. Nice try, though."

Murphy thumped his tail on the rug.

Laughing softly, Mary-Clair got into the double bed and pulled up the blankets. She snapped off the lamp on the nightstand, wiggled into a comfortable position, then closed her eyes.

She'd never dog-sat before, was not used to sleep-ing in a strange bed but, she thought, if she relaxed and ignored the creaking noises the house was mak-ing, she would be fine.

Mary-Clair yawned, then gave way to blissful slumber.

Several hours later, she jerked awake and sat bolt upright in the bed, her heart racing.

What had caused her to be snatched from the pleasant dream she had been having? She wondered. Murphy was snoring, the dear old thing. That rumbling noise must be what had wakened her. She'd just have to ignore it and…

"Ohmigod," Mary-Clair whispered, yanking the blankets up to beneath her chin as she sat ramrod stiff on the bed.

She'd heard a thud, then the muffled sound of a man swearing. Oh, dear heaven, she thought frantically, there was someone downstairs.

Was there a telephone in this guest room so she could call the police? She hadn't even looked. Was there an extension in Esther and Bill's room down the hall? She didn't know. There was a robber…or maybe a murderer…tromping around and…

Calm down, she ordered herself, taking a steadying breath. She might not be very big at five-foot-two, but was she a wimp? No, she was not. Was she just going to sit there and wait to be murdered in her bed? No, she was not. She was taking action. Right now. Well, just as soon as she could get her fingers to release their tight hold on the blanket.

A moment later, Mary-Clair slipped off the bed and prodded Murphy with her foot.

"Wake up," she whispered, "and look mean, really vicious." Murphy snored on. "Darn it."

A weapon, she thought, mentally cataloging what she had seen earlier in the now-dark room. Yes, there was a set of golf clubs over in the corner. Perfect.

Tiptoeing around Murphy, then across the room,

her legs trembling with fear, Mary-Clair reached the golf bag, drew out one of the clubs, then made her way toward the bedroom door, her mighty weapon at the ready.

Chapter 2

The light in the kitchen, she realized, was on, casting a dim glow over the living room. Why was the intruder in the kitchen? Was there a big market for stolen microwave ovens?

A chill coursed through Mary-Clair as she made her way across the living room. She stopped at the kitchen doorway and peered around the edge, her trusty golf club held high in the air.

Well, for Pete's sake, she thought, frowning. The crook was making himself a sandwich? He had his back to her but she could see a loaf of bread, a jar of mayonnaise and another of dill pickles on the counter.

Good grief, she thought, swallowing a lump in her throat, he was huge. Her father and her five older brothers were all six-feet tall, but this rotten person who had broken into Esther and Bill's house, was at least six-foot-three!

The bigger they are, the harder they fall, Mary-Clair thought, knowing she was on the edge of hysteria.

She crept forward, the golf club now extended toward the man. Just as he speared a pickle with a fork, she planted the club firmly in the middle of his back.

"Put your hands up," she said, wishing her voice didn't sound like a squeaky mouse. "I mean it. Put them up, or I'll...I'll... Just do what I said, mister."

The man's hands shot up in the air, the fork with the dripping pickle going along for the journey.

"Don't make any funny moves," Mary-Clair said. "I have a vicious attack dog right next to me here just waiting for an excuse to take a bite—" her gaze slid over the man, who was wearing dark slacks and a pale blue knit shirt "—of your gorgeous tush, buster."

"Vicious attack dog?" the man said, with a burst of laughter. "Murphy? I'd bet a buck that he's snoring away on his favorite rug even as we speak."

"Huh?" Mary-Clair said.

The man turned, the fork and pickle in his right hand, and calmly removed the golf club from Mary-Clair's grasp with his left.

"Oh, hey," he said, "look at this. Nice. Uncle Bill said he was shopping for a new set of clubs and he sure went top of the line."

He shifted his gaze to Mary-Clair, who was staring at him with wide eyes.

"By the way," he said, "who are you? And what are you doing in my Aunt Esther and Uncle Bill's house wearing nothing but—" he did a quick head-to-toe perusal of Mary-Clair "—a skimpy nightshirt with a picture of Donald Duck on the front?"

He paused. "Well, you can explain the whole thing while I eat my sandwich. I'm a starving man." He extended the fork toward Mary-Clair. "Want a pickle?"

Chapter 3

The first item to register was the fact, she realized dismally, that she'd just made a complete idiot of herself. This was not a mass-murderer who had decided to make himself a sandwich before killing her deader than a post, he was Esther and Bill's nephew.

The next news that slammed into front row center was that he was the most handsome male specimen she had ever seen.

His features were rugged, as though chiseled from stone, then bronzed by the sun.

His shoulders were wide, the material of the knit shirt stretching across them and the broad chest beneath.

His legs were muscular, his blond hair thick and sun-streaked and just begging to have feminine fingers sifting through it.

His eyes, which had seemed to burn a heated path

over her as he'd scrutinized her, were so blue they would make the most gorgeous summer sky appear anemic.

The last bulletin to reach Mary-Clair caused her cheeks to flush.

She was standing there in all her glory in her Donald Duck nightshirt that fell to midthigh and was made of soft, clinging material, clearly defining, she didn't doubt for a minute, her full breasts.

She had to get out of this kitchen!

"Well," she said brightly, "won't this be a great story to tell Esther and Bill? It's so funny…just… hysterical. I mean, here I thought you were a murderer or…and it turns out… My, my, what a hoot." She yawned and patted her hand against her mouth. "I must get some sleep. Enjoy your pickle. Good night."

Mary-Clair spun around and made it all the way to the doorway before a deep voice boomed and halted her in her tracks.

"Hold it right there."

Mary-Clair sighed and turned to face the man again.

"We've established who I am," he said. He set the fork with the pickle on the counter and leaned the golf club against the lower cupboard. "My name is Connor O'Shea, by the way, but I don't have a clue as to who you are or why you're here. I have a key to the house and I bunk in whenever my company assigns me an advertising contract in Ventura." He swept one arm through the air. "Your turn. For all I know, *you're* a murderer wanted by the FBI."

A flash of fury coursed through Mary-Clair and she planted her hands on her hips. In the next instant she whipped her hands around her elbows as she realized how tightly the material of the nightshirt was being pulled across her breasts. She lifted her chin and narrowed her eyes.

"You have just given a whole new meaning," Connor said, his voice very deep, very rumbly, and very, very male, "to the cliché 'she's beautiful when angry.'"

Chapter 4

"For your information, Mr. O'Shea," she said, lifting her chin even higher, "Esther happens to be my dear friend and secretary...well, mine and my law partner's. Be that as it may, Esther asked me to take care of Murphy because of a family emergency that required Esther and Bill to leave immediately."

Connor frowned. "What family emergency? I just got back from an assignment in Paris and was going to catch up on any messages on my answering machine in my apartment in San Francisco in the morning. What's going on?"

"Oh. Well, Esther and Bill's daughter..."

"My cousin, Betsy," Connor said, nodding.

"Betsy is having some problems with her pregnancy and has been ordered to stay in bed. Your aunt and uncle have gone to Chicago to help tend to the other two children and their son-in-law and... So, here I am. Oh, and I'm Mary-Clair Cavelli."

"Man, that's rough," Connor said, dragging one hand through his hair. "I hope nothing happens to that baby. It's a girl and everyone is so excited because they already have two boys and... Well, it was nice of you to step in and take care of old Murphy."

"Vicious beast that he is," Mary-Clair said, smiling.

Connor stared at Mary-Clair intently. "You have a lovely smile, Ms. Cavelli. It just lights up your face and... Look, I apologize if I frightened you by coming into the house unannounced."

"No harm done," Mary-Clair said, averting her eyes from Connor's. "Since you're here, though, I'll go back to my own place in the morning. Murphy doesn't need two baby-sitters."

"You can't do that," Connor said quickly.

No, no way, he thought. He'd just met this intriguing, beautiful, feisty woman and he wasn't about to let her just disappear, never to be seen again.

"What I mean is," he went on, as Mary-Clair frowned at his sudden outburst, "I'll be putting in very long hours on this assignment and Murphy will think he's all alone and he can't handle that. He'll pine away from loneliness, poor old guy. No, you stay on just as planned. You won't even know I'm around because I'll be working until the wee hours of the night."

Connor smiled and Mary-Clair felt a frisson of heat slither down her back.

"Just don't threaten to golf club me to death the next time I come in late," he said.

"Right," Mary-Clair said weakly, then took a much-needed breath as she realized she'd forgotten to breathe during the unsettling effects of Connor's devastating smile.

"So, we're in agreement?" Connor said. "We'll both stay? Here?" He grinned. "Together?"

Chapter 5

Her name hummed in Connor's mind as he drove through Ventura in the heavy, after-work traffic.

"Mary-Clair Cavelli," he said aloud, making no attempt to curb the smile that formed on his lips.

He could see her so clearly in his mental vision, he realized, it was as though she were sitting right next to him in the car. Her short, curly black hair framed a face with big dark eyes and beautiful, delicate features. She had tawny skin that spoke of her Italian heritage, as did her dynamite temper when she got on a rip. She had a lush figure that her funny nightshirt had been unable to hide.

Mary-Clair Cavelli had caused him to toss and turn through the remaining hours of the previous night because both his body and his mind knew that she was sleeping just down the hall from him in his aunt and uncle's house.

Oh, she was something, Connor mused. He'd had trouble concentrating on the job today, had continually expressed the excuse to those around him that he was suffering from jet lag after flying in from Paris. Ms. Cavelli had had a powerful impact on him, that was for sure...and he liked the feelings she evoked in him, he really did.

He'd been restless and edgy for months, Connor thought, as he maneuvered through the traffic. He was tired of the constant travel his job required, the endless hotel rooms and living out of a suitcase the majority of the time.

And the bottom line that he'd admitted to himself in recent weeks was that he was lonely. He was thirty-six years old and was ready to settle down and get married, have a slew of babies. He wanted a home to come to each night where he would be greeted by the woman he loved and who loved him in kind.

Mary-Clair Cavelli.

Was she the woman he'd been hoping to find? Had fate had a hand in her being in his Aunt Esther and Uncle Bill's house at the exact moment he made one of his unannounced appearances? Was Mary-Clair his soulmate? His destiny? He didn't know.

"But I sure intend to find out," he said aloud, as he turned a corner and left the busy street behind.

He wove his way slowly through the subdivision of large homes with perfectly kept lawns, his heart quickening when he saw a compact car in the driveway of his aunt and uncle's house. He parked at the curb, picked up the bouquet of flowers from the passenger seat, ran his hand down his tie, then got out of the car.

Moments later Connor inserted his key in the door and entered the house, immediately savoring the delicious aroma of mingled spices that wafted through the air. He closed the door quietly behind him, then drew a deep, steadying breath.

"Honey," he called out, "I'm home."

Chapter 6

Honey, I'm home? her mind echoed. Connor was here? Now? But he'd said he'd be working long hours and she'd probably never see him and... Why on earth was she so glad to hear his voice, to know he was just a room away? Why was her heart beating like a bongo drum and a strange heat swirling low within her? She didn't know. She didn't *want* to know.

She'd managed to ignore...sort of...the image of Connor that kept creeping into her mind's eye through the hours of the day. She'd refused to listen...sort of...to the memory of his rich, deep voice that caused shivers to flutter throughout her.

Her reactions to Connor O'Shea were ridiculous and a waste of time because he was in Ventura on a temporary assignment.

Besides that, the man was six-foot-three, for Pete's

sake. She had an ironclad rule about never dating men who were more than five-nine or -ten to give herself at least a fighting chance of being treated as an equal. She was sick to death of being a "cute little thing" and hearing demeaning nonsense like "I want to put you in my pocket and take you home" that had continually been the mantra of taller men.

Honey, I'm home? Mary-Clair thought, setting the spoon on the top of the stove and straightening the edge of her red sweater over her jean-clad hips. Well, she had news for Mr. O'Shea. She was not now, nor would she ever be, his *honey.*

Mary-Clair marched from the kitchen with Murphy lumbering behind her. She reached the center of the living room at the same time Connor did and all rational thought fled her mind as he extended the bouquet of flowers toward her.

"I... Thank you," she said, inhaling the lovely scent of the blossoms. She swept her gaze over Connor, mentally approving of his custom-tailored dark blue suit, pale blue shirt, and dark tie. "You were still asleep when I left this morning, I guess. You look very...yuppyish."

"I had jet lag," Connor said, "so I slept late. What smells so good?"

"Spaghetti sauce," Mary-Clair said, meeting Connor's gaze. "I made it following my mother's recipe. I thought I could freeze some for Esther and... Why are you here so early?"

"Do you want me to say I'm still tired from jet lag?" Connor said. "Or should I tell you the truth?"

"Truth is good," Mary-Clair said, frowning. "I

was raised to believe that truth is a very important thing.''

"Okay," he said, then took a deep breath and exhaled it, puffing out his cheeks. "I'm here, Mary-Clair, because I thought about you all day and I wanted to see you, wanted to ask you to have dinner with me, wanted to spend the evening with you. There. That's the truth.''

Chapter 7

"I'm sorry I got so grumpy," she said. "It's just that I grew up with a father and five brothers who are all six feet tall. Then when I started dating? Grim. Now I *never* go out with a man who is over five-foot-nine or -ten."

A cold fist tightened in Connor's stomach. "I'm six-foot…"

"Three," she finished for him. "I'm a pro at knowing how tall a man is at first glance."

"So you won't go out with me?" he said.

"Nope," she said, poking her nose in the air.

"Would you consider it if I promised to spend the evening walking on my knees?" Connor said.

Mary-Clair laughed. "Oh, good grief."

"I don't get it, Mary-Clair," Connor said. "Why the mind-set against dating tall men? Because you get a stiff neck talking to them or something?"

"There's that," she said, nodding, "but there's even more. Tall men have a tendency to treat me like a child, Connor. They eventually say icky things like I'm so adorable, so cute, or I remind them of a Kewpie doll that should be set on a shelf, taken care of, protected. I'm thirty-one years old, for heaven's sake."

"Mmm," he said, nodding. "Did you notice that as we sit here at the table we're just about the same height?"

"One does not spend one's life on one's bottom, Mr. O'Shea," she said.

"True." Connor pushed back his chair and got to his feet. "Okay, we'll run a test here." He came around the table and extended his hand to Mary-Clair.

Mary-Clair placed her hand in Connor's and stood, looking up at him.

"What kind of a test?" she said.

Connor released her hand, framed her face in both of his, then lowered his head slowly toward Mary-Clair's.

"This one," he said.

Connor leaned down, bent his knees a bit, then his mouth captured Mary-Clair's in a sweet, tender kiss that intensified moments later.

Oh…my…stars, Mary-Clair thought, then quit thinking and simply savored the exquisite, heated sensations that were rocketing throughout her as she returned the kiss in total abandon.

Connor raised his head a fraction of an inch to draw a ragged breath, then slanted his mouth in the opposite direction and claimed Mary-Clair's lips once again.

There had never been, he thought hazily, a kiss like this. He was on fire, had been consumed instantly by passion so hot, so burning, that he was going up in flames.

But it wasn't lust…oh, no…it was desire that was pure, honest, and real. It was the wanting beyond measure of this woman, not just physically but with a need to mesh with her emotionally, as well. He'd never experienced anything like this before in his life. It was rare, wonderful, awesome.

It was Mary-Clair Cavelli.

And she was his.

Chapter 8

When Connor came dangerously close to losing control, he broke the kiss, straightened, and drew a rough breath.

Mary-Clair placed one hand on her racing heart, willing it to return to a normal tempo.

"I..." Connor started, then cleared his throat as he heard the gritty quality of his voice. "I rest my case. Test concluded and passed with flying colors." He paused. "Whew."

"Yes, well," Mary-Clair said, then blinked in an attempt to dispel the sensual mist still swirling around her. "I... My goodness."

"You can say *that* again," Connor said.

"My goodness."

"Let's sit down," Connor said.

They sank back onto their chairs at the table, then their gazes met.

"Mary-Clair," Connor said, "that was no ordinary kiss. Something very special happened between us just now. You won't deny that, will you? Remember that we put major emphasis on truth."

Mary-Clair wrapped her hands around her elbows. "Truth. Yes. Well, no, I can't deny that the kiss was… I've never experienced anything… What I mean is… I have no idea what I mean."

"We desire each other," Connor said, leaning toward her. "It wasn't lust. Desire means that emotions are involved and that was desire, Mary-Clair. Right?"

"Yes, I…but…" Mary-Clair shook her head. "There's no point in having this discussion, Connor."

"Why not?"

"Because it means we're attempting to discover what this is that's happening between us and that's foolish. You're here for a visit and… Besides, you're still six-foot-three."

"Darn it," Connor said, smacking the table with the palm of his hand and causing Mary-Clair to jerk in her chair. "I thought that kiss just proved that it doesn't matter how tall, or short, we are."

"Oh, Connor," Mary-Clair said, "one kiss doesn't erase what I've known for years. It would only be a matter of time before you went into your tall-man mode, with all the bells and whistles."

"No, I wouldn't," he said, none too quietly. "I don't see you as a *short* woman." His voice quieted. "I view you as a woman…period. A woman I desire more than any before. A woman who has knocked me for a loop. A woman who has become very important to me very, very quickly. Don't shut me out, please. Give us a chance to find out what this is."

Before Mary-Clair could reply, the doorbell rang.

"Saved by the bell?" she said, attempting to produce a smile that failed to appear.

"We're not finished talking about this," Connor said, getting to his feet. "I'll go see what kind of salesperson is at the door."

"I'll come with you," Mary-Clair said.

Anything would be better than being left at that table with her own thoughts, she decided, following Connor out of the kitchen. She was so muddled, so terribly confused, so aware of the heat of desire still glowing within her. Oh, dear heaven, what was Connor O'Shea doing to her?

Chapter 9

Connor opened the front door to find a tall, well-built man standing on the porch holding a foil-covered something. "Who are you?" Connor and the man said in unison.

Mary-Clair stepped forward and planted her hands on her hips.

"Dominick Cavelli," she said, "what are you doing here?"

"Hello, Mary-Clair," Dominick said gruffly, his gaze riveted on Connor. "I was visiting our folks and Mom wanted you to have this cake."

"Which you were only too happy to deliver," Mary-Clair said. "You're checking up on me for the family because I'm in this house alone without the benefit of the security guard at my apartment building."

"In this house alone?" Dominick said, narrowing

his eyes. "This guy doesn't look like a dog named Murphy. What's going on here?"

"Come in before you put on a show for the whole neighborhood," Mary-Clair said.

Dominick stepped into the house, pushed the cake at Mary-Clair, then turned to glare at Connor, who matched his stormy expression.

"Connor O'Shea," Mary-Clair said, her voice ringing with fury, "meet my brother Dominick, who is a fine example of some of the bells and whistles I spoke of."

"The what?" Dominick said, glancing at his sister.

"Forget it," she said, placing the dessert on a side table. "Goodbye, Dom."

"Not so fast," he said. "What am I supposed to tell our parents, Mary-Clair? That you're not in any danger over here because there's a big dude living in the house with you and the dog?"

"Oh, now, hey, wait a minute," Connor said.

It was too much, it really was. Dom's sudden arrival, complete with angry accusations, was more than she could deal with, Mary-Clair realized instantly. She was over the top emotionally, due to the unsettling kiss shared with Connor. She had no place to put this.

"Well?" Dom said, staring at his sister. "What do you have to say for yourself, Mary-Clair Cavelli?"

"You've discovered my secret, Dom," Mary-Clair said, slipping one arm through one of Connor's, who stared down at her with wide eyes. "It's time…no, it's long overdue…that the family acknowledge that I'm all grown up and in charge of my own decisions. My darling Connor and I…are…" She waved one hand breezily in the air. "I'd rather not divulge the *intimate* details so…good night, Dom. Tell Mom I said thanks for the cake."

"Mary-Clair," Dom said, "you have five minutes to pack your suitcase and…"

Connor slipped his arm free of Mary-Clair's, gripped the edge of the door and began to move it slowly toward Dominick.

"Nice meeting you, Dom," Connor said, as Mary-Clair's brother found himself back on the porch. "But Mary-Clair and I prefer to be alone. Bye."

Connor closed the door, locked it, then heavy footsteps could be heard stomping away.

"Oh, my stars," Mary-Clair said, pressing her hands to her cheeks. "What have I done?"

Chapter 10

Connor sat on the sofa, his head swiveling back and forth as he watched Mary-Clair pace.

"I can't believe I did that," Mary-Clair said, as she continued her trek. "What could I have been thinking? I *wasn't* thinking...not rationally. I was so jangled from that kiss we shared and...I actually told Dominick that you and I..." She glanced at her watch. "Oh-h-h, Dom will be at my parents' house any minute now with his announcement that you and I... The phone is going to ring. My mother is going to call here and... Oh-h-h."

She kept up her nonstop chatter and as each minute ticked by, Connor O'Shea fell a little more in love with Mary-Clair Cavelli.

Man, Connor thought, unable to keep from smiling, he was on top of the world, felt fantastic. He was honest-to-goodness in love for the first time in his life.

And there she was, the woman who had captured his heart so fast it was unbelievable. There she was. Mary-Clair.

Connor frowned. There she was…coming unglued and he was sitting here grinning like an idiot instead of trying to comfort her.

"Mary-Clair," he said, "I want to help. You said your mother is going to call. And say what? That your five big brothers are being dispatched posthaste to beat me to a pulp?"

Mary-Clair stopped in front of Connor and met his gaze.

"I wish it was that simple," she said, throwing out her arms.

"Oh, thanks a bunch," he said, laughing. "How long does a person have to stay in a body cast?"

"Don't be silly, Connor," she said. "The Cavellis are not a violent family." She paused. "Well, there was the time when I was ten and a boy cut off one of my braids and my brothers… Forget it. That's ancient news."

"Fast forward to the present," Connor said. "What is your mother going to say?" He patted the cushion next to him. "Come here."

Mary-Clair collapsed next to Connor and allowed him to draw her near. She rested her head on his shoulder and sighed.

"My mother," she said, then drew a wobbly little breath, "will invite us to dinner."

Connor waited…fifteen seconds, twenty, thirty.

"That's it?" he said finally. "You're all shook-up because we'll be asked to eat Italian meat loaf, or something?"

Mary-Clair sat up and turned to look at Connor, her face only inches from his.

"You don't understand," she said. "My family won't rant and rave about what I told Dom, about what they believe you and I are... Oh, no, they'll simply march right on to the next step."

"Guess who's coming to dinner?" Connor said, raising his eyebrows.

"You bet," she said, nodding. "They'll put you through the inquisition...big-time. They will do that, you see, because they'll be taking the very firm stand that we are...are getting married, Connor."

Chapter 11

Three cheers for the Cavelli clan! Connor mentally yelled, while maintaining a serious expression.

"I see," he said slowly. "That's certainly an old-fashioned stand, isn't it?"

"This is terrible, just terrible," Mary-Clair said, plunking her head back onto Connor's shoulder. A second later she popped up again. "I'll straighten this out, Connor. I'll tell my mother that I had a hard day, was tired, just lost my temper when Dom..."

"No, now wait a minute," Connor said. "If you do that you'll be viewed as a cute little girl who threw a tantrum because she needed a nap."

"Oh, *blak.*"

"Indeed," Connor said, gripping Mary-Clair's shoulders. "Listen to me. You've taken a decisive step toward your independence, made it clear that you're a mature woman who is capable of making her own decisions. You don't want to lose all the ground you've gained, do you?''

"Of course, not, but…'' Mary-Clair started.

"So, don't,'' Connor said. "We'll accept the invitation to dinner. I can handle the bare lightbulb bit.''

"What's the point?'' Mary-Clair said. "We are *not* getting married, Connor.''

Don't bet the farm on that one, sweet Mary-Clair, Connor thought, his heart soaring at the mere idea of Mary-Clair becoming his wife, his life's partner.

"You're buying time, don't you see?'' he said, tightening his hold slightly on Mary-Clair's shoulders. "This will give your family an opportunity to get used to the idea that you're all grown-up, that you don't need your brothers hovering over you. They'll realize that you're a woman, not a child.''

"But…''

The telephone shrilled in the distance.

"Oh-h-h,'' Mary-Clair said, flinging her arms around Connor's neck. "There's my mother in her stubborn Italian mind-set, determined to find out who this man is who should make an honest woman of her baby girl.''

"Go answer the phone,'' Connor said, as it continued to ring. "Go on. Be brave, courageous, and bold. You can do it.''

Mary-Clair got to her feet. "Are you certain this is a good plan?''

"Positive,'' he said, nodding.

"Why are you putting yourself through this, Connor? It's a lovely thing to do…helping me prove my independence and maturity to my family. It's going to be a grim evening, believe me. So, why are you doing this?''

Because I love you, Mary-Clair Cavelli, Connor thought, and I intend to tell you that just as soon as I think you're ready to hear it.

''I'm a nice guy?'' he said, smiling up at her.

''You're a wonderful guy,'' Mary-Clair said, smiling at him warmly. She pressed her hands flat on her stomach and drew a steadying breath. ''Here I go. Answering the phone. Next week.''

''Mary-Clair!''

''Okay!''

She hurried across the living room and into the kitchen. A few minutes later she returned, sank back onto the sofa next to Connor, and sighed.

''Tomorrow night,'' she said dismally. ''Dinner at the Cavelli homestead. Seven o'clock.''

Chapter 12

Laughter erupted in the dining room at the Cavelli home as Connor related a tale of accidentally presenting an advertising campaign for baby diapers to the directors of a beer company.

Mary-Clair looked at her smiling family, then shifted her gaze to Connor, her heart racing as she drank in the sight of him.

Her family, she knew, was captivated by Connor. And so was she. Time and again during the day she'd thought about how determined Connor had been to help her cement her independence. That was what a special friend would do, and she'd heard so often that the person someone loved should also be her best friend.

Mary-Clair, stop, she told herself. She was not in love with Connor O'Shea. Granted, she melted at his touch, and dissolved when he kissed her. He occupied her mind during the day and caused her to wake in the night suffused with heated desire. She'd found herself counting the hours until she would see him again and…

No. Nothing could erase the fact that Connor was six feet three inches tall. There had not been even a hint that he would treat her like a child, but it was just a matter of time before he began to view her as a cute little thing who needed to be protected from the big, bad world.

There were also the data, Mary-Clair mused on— that Connor resided in…

"You live in San Francisco?" Nick Cavelli said.

Bingo, Mary-Clair thought dismally. And it was miles and miles away.

"Yes, I do," Connor said, looking at Mary-Clair's brother, whom he recalled was a year older than Dominick. "For now."

"Oh?" Rome said.

Huh? Mary-Clair thought, staring at Connor.

Rome, Connor thought quickly. He had been named in honor of the Pope. It was a good thing the two married brothers couldn't make it tonight, or he'd never be able to keep them all straight.

"My company has been considering opening a branch in Ventura," Connor said. "I spoke with the CEO today and said I would be happy to head up an office here. An hour later I got a call saying it was a done deal. I'm going to start scouting locations."

"Isn't that nice?" Marcella said, beaming at her husband, Clemento.

"Sounds good," Mary-Clair's father said. "Then

you'll be a citizen of Ventura, just like our Mary-Clair.''

''Yes, sir,'' Connor said.

No, sir, Mary-Clair thought. Connor was laying it on too thick in his quest to buy her time to establish her womanly identity. Well, she supposed this had merit. When Connor resumed his traveling it would be a ready excuse as to why their relationship didn't work out. Score another point for O'Shea.

But he *would* be leaving.

And the very thought of that, she realized instantly, was causing a chill to sweep through her as she envisioned saying that last goodbye to Connor.

Chapter 13

"*Arriverdeci* gelato," Connor boomed, as he drove through the heavy traffic. "Hey, Mary-Claire, am I good at this Italian stuff, or what?"

"You just said," Mary-Clair said, laughing, "goodbye to ice cream."

"Whatever," Connor said, glancing over at her with a grin. "You are *molto bellino*. That means very pretty, you know."

"*Grazie,*" Mary-Clair said, dipping her head slightly. "Yep, you're a pro at speaking Italian after just one evening at the Cavellis."

"Awesome, isn't it?" he said, chuckling. "Are your other two brothers as good-looking as the three that were there tonight? You Cavellis are certainly attractive people. You could be models."

Mary-Clair frowned. "I'm a tad short to be a model."

"Oops. I didn't mean to hit on *that* subject," Connor said. "Let's talk about food. Your mother is a great cook and that was a delicious dinner. What can I say? I enjoyed myself. You have a fantastic family."

"I love them very much," Mary-Clair said quietly, "even when they're making me crazy." She paused. "You actually had a pleasant evening? Despite the fact you were being given the third degree?"

"Yep," Connor said, nodding. "I just kept reminding myself that your clan believes we're living together…in every sense of the word. If you look at it like that, the drilling they gave me was perfectly understandable. If the smiles, handshakes, plus the hug from your mother mean anything, I didn't score too badly."

"You were wonderful," Mary-Clair said, "considering you were winging it, making stuff up as you went along."

"What do you mean?" Connor said, frowning.

"You know, the bit about moving here to Ventura to open a branch office."

"Oh, *that*," he said. "Hey, we're home. I bet Murphy will be glad to see us, providing he realized we left."

"I guess it will work out all right," Mary-Clair said, as Connor pulled into the driveway. "I'll tell my family you changed your mind about living here, decided you liked traveling after all, and our relationship went south, or some such thing."

"Mmm," Connor said, then got out of the vehicle.

Murphy was snoring when Mary-Clair and Connor entered the house. Mary-Clair went into the kitchen to tend to the bag of leftovers that her mother had insisted she take home, as usual. When she returned to the living room she discovered that Connor had turned on one lamp, casting a soft glow over the area. He was sitting on the sofa, his arms spread across the top.

"Come sit by me, Mary-Clair," he said. "Please?"

Mary-Clair walked slowly forward. "Don't you think that sounds reasonable, Connor? You left to resume your jet-set existence and we fizzled out?" She sat down next to him and looked at him questioningly.

"It would, except…" Connor said, then dropped a quick kiss on Mary-Clair's lips. "Mary-Clair, everything I said tonight was true."

Chapter 14

"What?" Mary-Clair said, her eyes widening.

"I *am* going to head up a new branch office here," Connor said, wrapping one arm around Mary-Clair's shoulders. "I *am* tired of traveling all the time. I *am* going to live in Ventura…permanently."

"Oh," Mary-Clair said, her mind racing.

Connor wasn't going to leave? she thought incredulously. He wasn't going to disappear from her life as quickly as he'd come into it? This was wonderful! No, it was terrible, just awful. He'd be living in Ventura, would be as tempting as a box of delicious chocolates that were taboo on her constant diet and… Dear heaven, now she was even more muddled and unsettled than she'd been since the moment she'd met him.

"You don't look too thrilled with this bulletin," Connor said, frowning.

"I'm—I'm just surprised, that's all," she said. "I

thought you told my family that you were moving here so that our—our relationship wouldn't appear so temporary and tacky and… You're staying?"

"I am," he said, nodding decisively. "I'll finish this job I'm on, find an apartment, go back to San Francisco, and ship my belongings down here. In the meantime, I'll look for a good location for the branch when I have spare time. I'm going to settle in and settle down, Mary-Clair."

"Oh," she said again weakly. "That's—that's… interesting. I'm sure your aunt Esther and uncle Bill and Murphy will be thrilled to have you living in Ventura."

"And you?" he said. "How do you feel about it?"

"Could I get back to you on that question?" she said. "I need time to process this information."

"In that case," Connor said, "you should have all the data so you can do a proper job of processing."

"I'm missing something?" Mary-Clair said, raising her eyebrows.

"Oh, yes, ma'am, you most certainly are." Connor took a deep breath and let it out slowly. "Mary-Clair Cavelli, I, Connor O'Shea, am deeply and forever in love with you. You knocked me over, captured my heart, and I don't want it back. You're my soulmate, Mary-Clair, the woman I was beginning to believe that I would never find. I want to marry you, make beautiful babies with you, spend the remainder of my life with you. Ah, Mary-Clair, I love you so very, very much."

Mary-Clair jumped to her feet, the color draining from her face as tears filled her eyes.

"No, don't say that," she said, her voice trembling

as she wrapped her hands around her elbows. "Don't tell me that you want to marry me, have beautiful babies and… Don't declare your love for me, Connor, because then I won't be able to keep from listening to my heart to discover how I feel about you. I might be in love with you right now, but I don't want to know. I don't. No, no, no." Two tears slid down her pale cheeks, followed by two more. "No."

Chapter 15

Connor got to his feet and gripped Mary-Clair's shoulders.

"Mary-Clair," he said, "talk to me. I don't understand why you're so upset. I have a right to know why you're rejecting me, don't you think? Sit back down. Please?"

Mary-Clair nodded, dashed the tears from her cheeks, then settled next to Connor again on the sofa.

"Oh, Connor," she said, her voice trembling, "I hated the thought of never seeing you again. Then when you said you really planned to live here, I was so happy."

"Go on," he said.

"You're everything I ever hoped to find in a man." Fresh tears filled Mary-Clair's eyes. "Oh, there's nowhere to hide from the truth. I've fallen deeply in love with you, Connor."

"That's fantastic," he said, smiling.

"No," she said, "it's not. I want, *I need* to be an equal partner in a relationship, a marriage, not someone who is protected and fussed over."

"But I've never…" Connor started.

"I know," she interrupted, waving one hand in the air. "You've never done anything to diminish my womanliness, have never treated me like a child because I'm short, small. You even went to my parents' house to help me establish my status as a woman capable of making her own decisions."

"Right," Connor said.

"But it's just a matter of time, Connor," Mary-Clair said. "It will happen. You'll hover, start saying I shouldn't do this, or that, because I'm so tiny and helpless and you'll step in and take care of it."

"No, I…"

"Painful experience has proven to me that what I'm saying is true. The difference in our heights is an insurmountable obstacle that would take a terrible toll on our marriage, no matter how much we might love each other. Some things…some things in life, even those we wish for with all our hearts, our very souls, are not meant to be. I can't marry you, Connor. I'd rather keep the precious memories of our time together than be a party to everything we have being crumbled into dust, destroyed."

"I see," Connor said quietly, his mind racing.

Easy, O'Shea, he told himself. Mary-Clair was at the edge emotionally. He'd defeat his own purpose if he pleaded his case, or argued about what she was saying. Better to keep still for now and savor the knowledge that she loved him, just as he loved her. Oh, man, Mary-Clair Cavelli was in love with him!

"Well," he said, framing her face in his hands, "I'll have to…to deal with what you've said, won't I? But now? Let's create another precious memory. I want to make love with you more than I can even begin to tell you. Will you make love with me, Mary-Clair?"

A jumble of voices seemed to shout in Mary-Clair's mind and she hushed them, listening only to her heart.

"Yes," she whispered. "Oh, yes, Connor, I want to make love with you. Right now."

Chapter 16

A week later Mary-Clair sat at the desk in her office, staring into space.

Glorious, she thought dreamily. That was only one of the adjectives she could use to describe the past seven days, and ecstasy-filled nights of lovemaking shared with Connor.

Mary-Clair sighed and frowned.

And with each tick of the clock, she thought, she fell more deeply in love with Connor O'Shea. Oh, how foolish she was being by existing in a world of fantasy, living out a fairy tale that was *not* going to have a happy ending.

She could not, would not, agree to marry Connor, couldn't face a future of waiting for the inevitable when he would begin to shift, change, start to treat her like a helpless child. And it would happen. That was a given.

Connor, she mused on, had apparently accepted her refusal to marry him and had no intention of attempting to change her mind. He'd declared his love for her endlessly through the past week, but had stopped short of speaking of their having a future together.

Connor knew, as she did, that they were living on borrowed time, creating memories to keep until they had to say their final goodbyes. A farewell that would mean she would cry in the darkness in the lonely nights that followed.

Mary-Clair sniffled.

She was thoroughly depressing herself, she thought, getting to her feet. Enough of this. The workday was at an end. It was time to go home. To Connor.

Mary-Clair took her purse from the bottom drawer of the desk just as her law partner, Jessica, appeared in the doorway.

"I'm off," she said. "Are you and Connor doing anything special tonight?"

"We're going to watch *Casablanca* on television," Mary-Clair said, smiling. "Connor will laugh himself silly when I weep at the icky ending." She paused. "Maybe I shouldn't watch that movie. It will only remind me that *I'm* going to cry buckets when *my* romantic interlude is over."

"Mary-Clair..."

"Jessica, don't start," she said, crossing the room. "There's nothing anyone can say to change my stand. I will *not* marry a man who is six-foot-three. It's a disaster waiting to happen and...I refuse to discuss this again. Good night."

Jessica threw up her hands in defeat. "Good night, Mary-Clair."

When Mary-Clair parked behind Connor's car in the driveway, her heart began to race in anticipation. She hurried across the lawn and went into the house to find Connor standing in the middle of the living room, a serious expression on his face. She went to where he stood, looking up at him questioningly.

"Connor?" she said. "What's wrong? You look as though you just lost your best friend."

"Well put," he said quietly, drawing his thumb over one of Mary-Clair's cheeks. "Mary-Clair, my aunt Esther just telephoned. My cousin is doing fine now. Aunt Esther and Uncle Bill will be returning home tomorrow."

Chapter 17

Mary-Clair felt as though the world had suddenly tilted on its axis. She reached out a shaking hand to grip the arm of an easy chair, then moved on trembling legs to sink onto it.

"Tomorrow?" she said, her voice seeming to come from far, far away. "Esther and Bill will be here... tomorrow?"

Connor pulled a matching chair in front of Mary-Clair and sat down, resting his elbows on his knees, then taking her hands in his.

"Mary-Clair," he said, looking directly into her eyes, "we knew this was going to happen...my aunt and uncle returning home. I'm grateful that my cousin and the baby are all right, but I wish we... Listen to me. This week, this incredibly fantastic week we've shared, must have shown you that we are compatible beyond measure. We're so connected, so in tune, so… We're in love with each other. We're soulmates who are meant to be together forever.''

''Connor, I…''

''Haven't I proven to you that I'd never do anything to diminish your worth as a woman?'' Connor went on, a slightly frantic edge to his voice. ''Don't I treat you as an equal partner in our relationship? Can't you see that what we have together is far more important than how tall, or how short, we might be? Ah, Mary-Clair, please. Say you'll marry me, be my wife and the mother of the miracles that will be the children we'll create. I love you so much. Please, Mary-Clair.''

Her heart, Mary-Clair thought, as a sob caught in her throat, was shattering into a million pieces. She was so cold, chilled to the very core of her being because…because it was over. The fantasy had ended. The last frame of the romantic movie had played and now the screen was dark, so very dark.

''Mary-Clair?'' Connor said, his voice husky with emotion as he tightened his hold on her hands. ''Please?''

As though watching from outside her own body, Mary-Clair saw herself pull her hands free from Connor's, push back the chair, and get to her feet, tears spilling onto her pale cheeks.

''No. No, I can't marry you, Connor,'' she said, then took a sob-filled breath. ''I can't bear the thought of waiting, waiting, waiting for you to begin to change, start treating me like a…'' She shook her head as tears closed her throat.

Connor lunged to his feet and gripped her shoulders. ''Don't throw us away, Mary-Clair. Trust me, believe in me and my love for you. I'm begging you. Don't do this.''

"I have to," she said, sobbing openly as she twisted out of his grasp. "I have no choice because I know, *I know* what will eventually happen and… No, Connor, I love you so much but I can't, I won't marry you. I'm going to pack and go to my apartment now, tonight. I'm going home, Connor, where I belong. Alone.''

Chapter 18

The following week was a study in misery for Mary-Clair and she was, she knew, performing as an attorney practically by rote.

Late in the afternoon of the eighth day since her heart, she was convinced, had crumbled into dust, Mary-Clair sat at her desk in the office. She leaned her head back against the top of the chair and closed her eyes, willing threatening tears to not spill over…again.

Dear heaven, she thought, she missed Connor so much. Ached for him. Wanted to see his smile, feel his touch, inhale his aroma. How long would this pain last? How long would she weep for all that might have been, but would never be? Oh, Connor.

"Mary-Clair," Esther said, appearing in the doorway, "there's a delivery here that you have to sign for, dear."

Mary-Clair raised her head. "Delivery? I didn't order anything, Esther. There must be some mistake."

Esther shrugged. "Well, you best talk to this man who wants your signature and explain that he has the wrong Mary-Clair Cavelli."

"Who is at this address, according to the delivery slip," Jessica said, peering over Esther's shoulder.

"I don't need this hassle," Mary-Clair said, getting to her feet.

She stomped around her desk, and Esther and Jessica stepped quickly out of her determined-to-end-this-nonsense way. The moment that Mary-Clair entered the small reception area she stopped so fast she teetered. The space was filled with seven boxes of various sizes.

"Mary-Clair Cavelli?" a man in a brown uniform said. "Sign here, please, ma'am."

"What is all this?" she said, sweeping one arm through the air. "I didn't order seven…whatever they are. Take them back with you."

"Sorry, ma'am," the man said, "but I can't do that. If there's a problem, you'll have to fix it with whoever sent the stuff."

Mumbling under her breath, Mary-Clair scribbled her name on the paper attached to a clipboard, then the man beat a hasty retreat. Jessica and Esther came to stand on either side of a frowning Mary-Clair, who leaned over and looked at one of the shipping labels.

"The Everything Store," she read. "I've never even heard of it, let alone ordered seven…somethings from there. Now what do I do?"

"Open them," Esther said. "That will give you

more data when you call the store to explain there was an error.''

''Good idea,'' Jessica said. ''Go for it, Mary-Clair.''

Mary-Clair sighed wearily, then tugged at the edge of the flap on the top of the tallest carton. Ten minutes later she planted her hands on her hips and swept her gaze over the bounty.

''Strange,'' she said. ''Seven step stools painted bright, primary colors, each a different height. Seven.''

''Wrong, Mary-Clair,'' Connor said, as he entered the office. He was carrying a yellow stool with three steps and set it on the floor directly in front of him. ''There are eight.''

Chapter 19

Mary-Clair's eyes widened and her heart began to beat in a wild tempo as she drank in the sight of Connor O'Shea.

"Connor?" she said, not totally convinced he was actually standing there.

"Yes, Mary-Clair," he said, no readable expression on his face. "It's me. It has taken me this long to have all these stools custom-made to my specifications after I carefully measured distances from your height to the top cupboard in a kitchen, a closet shelf, the overhead storage compartment in an airplane, and on the list goes."

Jessica and Esther eased into Jessica's office and closed the door…almost…leaving a two-inch gap.

"But why?" Mary-Clair said, sweeping her confused gaze over the stools.

"Just to make things easier for you if you want to

use them,'' he said. "It doesn't diminish who you are as a woman, it's simply a thoughtful gesture on my part. And this stool?'' He gestured to the bright yellow one at his feet. "It will bring you eye-level with me, make you my equal physically as you already are emotionally and intellectually. This stool is for when you want to kiss me, Mary-Clair. You can use it at the altar when we get married if you choose to.''

"I…'' Mary-Clair started.

"Oh, Mary-Clair,'' Connor said, his voice husky, "don't you see? I love and respect you. You. The woman. My love for you has nothing to do with how tall, or short, you might be. Please marry me, be my wife and the mother of our children. Don't allow the pain you suffered in the past because of insensitive men rob us of our happiness now, of our future together.''

Mary-Clair drew a shuddering breath, her mind whirling.

"Listen to me,'' Connor went on. "I shot up to six-foot-three when I was only fourteen years old. From then on everyone expected more from me than I was capable of giving. They thought I should be more mature, more intelligent, more proficient at sports, just because I was tall.

"I would have given anything back then to be the same size as my friends. I understand what you've been saying, believe me, I do. We've walked the same path in the past, which gives us an edge as we travel into the future…together.''

"Connor, I…''

"Ah, Mary-Clair,'' he said, a catch in his voice,

"please. Marry me." He extended his arms toward her. *"Ti voglio bene."*

"Oh, Connor," Mary-Clair said, smiling through her tears, "I love you, too, and…and yes, yes, yes, I'll marry you."

Mary-Clair ran across the room, up the steps of the pretty yellow stool and flung herself into Connor's embrace.

Just as Jessica and Esther peeked out the doorway of Jessica's office, then exchanged satisfied smiles, Connor captured Mary-Clair's lips in a kiss of commitment, a kiss that spoke of their future together, of love that would last…forever.

Indulge in summer savings!

Enjoy the lazy days of summer with a brand-new *sizzling* Silhouette Desire or Harlequin Temptation book.

SAVE $1.00 off your purchase of any Silhouette Desire® or Harlequin Temptation® title

5 65373 00076 2   (8100)0 11057

Indulge in summer savings!

Enjoy the lazy days of summer with a brand-new *sizzling* Silhouette Desire or Harlequin Temptation book.

Silhouette

Desire

❖ HARLEQUIN®

Temptation.

SAVE $1.00 off your purchase of any Silhouette Desire® or Harlequin Temptation® title

52605228

Treat yourself to the ultimate summer delight and save $10.00!

Indulge in your own custom-flavored ice cream creations at home with the

BLACK & DECKER.

Arctic Twister™

It's easy to use!

Just layer store-bought ice cream or frozen yogurt with your favorite candy, nuts, fruit, cookies or cereal for a delicious, one-of-a-kind snack!

It's easy to clean up!

Removable parts are dishwasher safe.

It's delicious fun that will delight all of your friends and family!

Perfect for parties, snacks, gift-giving and escaping the summer heat!

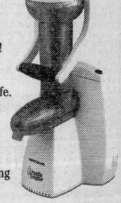

Turn the page to SAVE $10.00 off your own Black and Decker® Arctic Twister™ Ice Cream Mixer!

Indulge yourself with special summer savings—

Log on to our special promotional site at

www.Summersaving.com

You'll get

$10.00 OFF

your online order for the
Black and Decker®
Arctic Twister™ Ice Cream Mixer

as well as

**Special Savings on
other select Black and Decker®
household products, such as fans,
blenders, irons and toaster ovens.**

Log on to make your summer a breeze!

Take a break from life this summer with Treasures...

one of Nestlé® Signatures™ luscious little chocolates.

Nestlé Signatures. A sweet break from life.

Visit us at nestlesignatures.com

There is no easier way for you to own a cellular phone.

TracFone is simple and convenient wireless. You pay as you go. With TracFone you buy the phone and prepay for your minutes as you need them by purchasing TracFone Prepaid Wireless Airtime cards available at over 60,000 retailers nationwide. Your TracFone tracks how much airtime you use and how much is left by displaying the exact airtime balance on the phone, so you control your costs. No more monthly surprises. There are no phone bills!

Every TracFone contains the Airtime Balance Display that shows you how much airtime you use and how much is left.

 minutes never expire with active service

 largest digital coverage area in the U.S.

$30 Mail-In Rebate

Name _____

Address _____

City _____

State _____ Zip Code _____

Day phone (____) _____

E-mail _____

Phone Serial Number (ESN#) _____

$30 rebate or $39.99 (150 unit) prepaid wireless airtime card on the purchase of any digital TracFone wireless phone.
Please select one category ___ $30.00 Rebate or ___ $39.99 Wireless Airtime Card (150 units)
Mail your original dated cash register receipt, the UPC label off the TracFone package along with this completed original form to:
TracFone $30 Rebate Offer
Dept OTCF00032/33 • P.O. Box 8016
Walled Lake, MI 48391-8016

To obtain the ESN# remove battery from the cellular phone and locate the number on the back of the phone.

ADDITIONAL TERMS:
1) 90 days of uninterrupted service is required for qualification plus allow 3 to 6 weeks for processing. 2) Offer limited to U.S.A. ONLY, except where prohibited, taxed or licensed. 3)Valid for new activations only. 4) Limit one Rebate per phone. 5) Duplicate requests will not be acknowledged. 6) Not valid in conjunction with any other coupon, promotion or offer. 7) Not responsible for lost, stolen or illegible submissions. 8) Republication of this offer violates copyright statutes. 9) Photocopies of proof of purchase will not be accepted. 10) Void where prohibited. 11) If no selection is made, you will receive OUR BEST VALUE, the $39.99 airtime card. 12) Offer valid only for TracFones purchased between March and December 2003.
Must be postmarked by March 31st, 2004.

reflect
TRUE CUSTOM BEAUTY

Indulge in a Custom Lipstick at a special price!

Try yours for only $10 ($17 value)

Your lips have never been so kissable. Create your ultimate lipstick with a formula and shade perfect for you— because you help create it!

To redeem this offer, simply:

1. Visit www.reflect.com.
2. **Create a custom LIPSTICK** and add it to your shopping bag.
3. **Enter the following code** in the promotion/gift certificate box during checkout: **KISSMYLIPS**

The discount will automatically be applied.

All of our products are unconditionally guaranteed. Simply contact our customer service representatives. Experience the difference of custom beauty—beauty products made for you.

Offer may be used only once per customer and may not be combined with any other offer. Offer good only for the product indicated. Offer carries no cash value. Offer expires 07/31/04.